'There is a kind of absurd humour particularly in the characterisation of the dogs that I found almost unbearably moving. It's the sort of book that really does create a new imaginary space – one that I was reluctant to leave. Above all it is very *readable* – that very rare thing: a good story, well told'
Lesley Glaister

'The hot fiction debut of the season . . . she shows us animals endowed with consciousness – and makes our familiar condition seem strange, scary and wonderful'
Bazaar

'In an impressive feat of the imagination, Kirsten Bakis makes her bizarre story not only plausible on its own terms but fair ripalong as well'
Q Magazine

'One of the most unique and unusual works of fiction to come along in many years. Like *Frankenstein* before it, *Monster Dogs* is a fabulous fable well told'
USA Today

'On one level it might be compared to "The Island of Dr Moreau" and the dangers of what happens when a mad scientist begins messing about, trying to "improve" upon nature. But this novel is too good to be a mere catalogue of ideas. The characters are too wonderful . . . I admired it greatly'
Washington Post

Kirsten Bakis

Kirsten Bakis was born in Switzerland to parents of Estonian origin and grew up outside New York where she now lives. After graduating from New York University, she attended the Iowa University Writer's Workshop. She works part time as a secretary in a small church in Manhattan. *Lives of the Monster Dogs* is her first novel.

SCEPTRE

Lives of the

Monster Dogs

Kirsten Bakis

Interior art, *Zooks*, by Greg Goebal
Designed by Abby Kagan

First published by Farrar Straus Giroux in 1997
First published in the UK in 1997 by Hodder and Stoughton
A division of Hodder Headline PLC
A Sceptre Paperback

10 9 8 7 6 5 4 3 2 1

A CIP catalogue record for this book is available
from the British Library

ISBN 0 340 71558 8

Typeset by Palimpsest Book Production Limited,
Polmont, Stirlingshire
Printed and bound in Great Britain by
Clays Ltd, St Ives PLC, Bungay, Suffolk

Hodder and Stoughton
A division of Hodder Headline PLC
338 Euston Road
London NW1 3BH

Acknowledgments

Many thanks to my family, and to Caroline Huey, Soyung Pak, Charlie Buck, Deborah Eisenberg, Alex Chee, David Van Fossen, and Elaine Chubb.

A very special thanks to Maida Barbour for brilliant assistance every step of the way.

Sincere thanks, also, to the Michener/Copernicus Society of America.

In length and breadth how doth my poodle grow!
    —*Goethe*, Faust

Preface

In the years since the monster dogs were here with us, in New York, I've often been asked to write something about the time I spent with them. It's also been suggested that I edit the unfinished manuscript left behind by their historian, Ludwig von Sacher, partly because I wrote a lot of articles about the dogs when they were here, and partly because I was Ludwig's friend.

I wanted to do both of these things immediately, but I also wanted to do them slowly, and well. I guess I was waiting for something—for Ludwig's papers to reveal some hidden meaning, for the events I remembered to sift themselves into an identifiable pattern—and it always seemed on the verge of happening.

Now it's been over six years since they were here, and I'm beginning to think that's how it will always be, that I will always be just on the verge of being able to recall and understand everything in the right way. It's as if all the things we see and remember are parts of a long equation that always adds up to a seamless, irrefutable proof of the present—but that's the problem: the present changes from one moment to the next. We never arrive; there isn't any place to arrive.

So I've put Ludwig's papers together in order, including some of his journal entries along with the unfinished manuscript, and I've described as best I could what happened in the years he was writing them, which was when I knew him.

I'd like to thank Lydia Petze, who was also Ludwig's friend, for her help, and most of all for the sustaining friendship she's extended to me and, more recently, to my husband, Jim Holbrook, and our daughter, Eleanor, the first child in the world (I proudly believe) to be blessed with having a Samoyed for a godmother.

When Ludwig began his manuscript it was called *The History of the Monster Dogs,* but later he changed the title to *Lives of the Monster Dogs.* I think (though this is just a guess) that he might have had a plan to add biographies of the living dogs and to have those form the main part of his book, although at the time he stopped writing he hadn't even begun to do that. Whatever the reason, "Lives of the Monster Dogs" is written on the top sheet of his manuscript, which has been sitting on my desk for the better part of the past six years. The book you're holding now isn't exactly the one for which the title was intended, but I felt, somehow, that I couldn't call it anything else.

Even now, we're still inundated with books, movies, and documentaries about the monster dogs. Mine is not the first or the last version of their story. But I knew the monster dogs and I loved them, and I hope that, in my own way, I have done a good job of telling their story. I meant to.

Cleo Pira
New York City
October 2017

Lives of the
Monster Dogs

Prologue

FROM THE DIARY OF LUDWIG VON SACHER
NEW YORK, NOVEMBER 16, 2009

The past is obscure. It is blurred by dust and scratch marks, hidden by wide pieces of brown tape, soot, and mold stains. I am sifting through old documents that are oxidizing and crumbling as I touch them; things that have been burning, slowly, for a hundred years, throwing clouds of tiny particles into the air. Particles that once carried information—a bit of ink in the downstroke of a "d," an infinitesimal part of a space between words—now fly out, disorganized and meaningless, into the world.

I don't know if I will ever finish my research, and I want to leave some record of my endeavors: if not the finished paper, then at least a description of my attempt to write it. I've recently developed an illness, or psychological disorder, which comes on periodically and may soon prevent me from working. I must record what I know while I can still think clearly.

I am searching through these documents for the history of

my race, hoping to organize the information before it disinte-
grates into a chaos of dust. We are a race of monsters, recently
created, so our history is short. I am reading the writings of
our founder, a Prussian scientist who drew up the plans for us
in 1882, but our race did not come into being until nearly a
century later.

The name of the scientist was Augustus Rank, and he conceived the idea of a race of super-intelligent dogs, with artificial
hands and voice boxes, to be used for military purposes, and
devoted his life to creating them. He was fascinated by prosthetic devices—the possibilities. Many hideous animals were
made before we were perfected.

What do you have to say, Augustus? I have here on my
desk a pile of manuscripts and a pile of photocopies, taken from
a microfilm, which are barely legible. He kept a diary. Some
of the entries are short, some hard to make sense of.

*Nearly ran out of cocaine today, but faithful M. came after
dinner, just in time.*

That one is easy: he was a driven man; I can imagine him
in his laboratory, late at night, eyes wide, working fast, thinking
fast.

Disposed of R.S. today: had been complaining.

That one is more difficult. I suppose R.S. was a person who
worked for him; I'm sure Rank drove him hard. But Rank
didn't fire R.S. or let him go. He had a small colony of followers
and assistants from whom he demanded obedience, devotion,
and secrecy. He could not let a dissenter escape into the world.

*When I am done I won't need the people anymore. The dogs
will be my people, perfect extensions of my will. I, who am now
one man, will become an army—an army of dogs. They will be
absolutely obedient to me. Their minds will be my mind, their hearts*

will be mine, their teeth will be my teeth, their hands will be my hands . . .

He was a man who wanted to control things, to extend himself beyond the boundaries of his body. He demanded obedience from his human followers, but it could never be perfect—there would always be dissenters, people who questioned him. Humans could not be perfect extensions of his will. But we could. No human loyalty can equal the fanatic devotion of a dog.

I am trying to imagine Augustus Rank as I read his diary. There are pictures of him. He looks the part of a mad scientist: stiff collar and wild hair, dark staring eyes. The photographs, like the documents, have not been well preserved. Because of the blotches and stains, the dust on the microfilms and the crumbling edges of the papers, I seem to hear his voice through a heavy static, coming from far away.

I can't imagine him clearly, because he has no real smell. His scent is not human—it's the smell of oxidizing paper, dried ink, old photographic chemicals, brown tape used to hold the documents together. I can smell the history of the papers: human hands that have touched them, and the gloved prosthetic hands of dogs, the years spent in cold vaults underground, in the library, the hours inside my briefcase. Everything has left a residue, but there is no trace of Rank anymore. It was too long ago.

Do I think that being able to smell him would help me to understand the history of my race? What is it that I am trying to find out?

At this point I take off my pince-nez and wipe the lenses on the fur of my thigh. Without my spectacles I cannot see very well. I look around my room. I can make out, blurrily, the

gleam of brass and lacquered wood, mirrors and polished mahogany. I occupy a ground-floor apartment in the West Village.
Most of the other dogs live uptown in palatial homes, and seek
out publicity and one another's company, but I enjoy being
away from them. I see my kinship with them, and our shared
culture, as a weakness, not something to be preserved. Our
culture is outdated; it has nothing to do with the world we live
in now. It was forged in the secret city in the Canadian wilderness built by Rank and his followers at the turn of the century, and it has not changed in a hundred years.

Ten years ago, we rebelled against the people of Rankstadt.
These were the descendants of Rank's followers who for four
generations had lived in the hidden city. Because of their utter
isolation from the rest of the world, they had retained the styles
and culture of the town's nineteenth-century Prussian founders.
They had perfected us a few decades before and we lived as
slaves to them in that insular town, although we were stronger
and smarter than they. Of course we rebelled.

We looted the city and took their gold and possessions. But
we knew nothing of what lay beyond the borders of Rankstadt.
Neither humans nor dogs had crossed them during our lifetime,
and so we not only were strangers to the rest of the world, but
had not even heard stories of it, except for those which had
been passed down by our masters' great-grandparents from the
previous century.

For three years after gaining our freedom we lingered in
the ruins of Rankstadt. Yet finally we could not remain there,
among the collapsing houses of our former masters, and so we
set out into the wilderness of Canada and traveled for some
time, keeping ourselves hidden from humans but sometimes
visiting isolated farms and small towns to observe them. We
lived by hunting and scavenging, in temporary camps where

we made fires and shelters for ourselves. We were like pioneers, striving to cling to civilization in our manners and customs, but of necessity existing very often, and very uncomfortably, like savages.

The human residents of Rankstadt had had (for certain reasons having to do with their history which I am at present recording in my book) a great many jewels and precious metals in their possession, and we dogs had taken these when we left the town. We knew that we could sell them and live well if we were willing to enter human society, and at length, after nearly eight years of keeping to ourselves, it was decided that we should give up our nomadic life and try to live in the company of humans. We had heard of New York City, for our masters' ancestors had passed through it on their journey between Bavaria and western Canada in 1897, and knowing that it was a cultured, modern metropolis inhabited by many kinds of immigrants—though of course none so strange as us—we decided to plunge straight into the heart of the modern world, and come here.

The other dogs still often wear the Prussian officers' uniforms or elaborate bustled skirts that they took from the closets of the humans in Rankstadt ten years ago. They are proud to have stolen the clothes of their oppressors; they don't realize how ridiculous they look walking around New York. They know that they are monsters, but I believe they do not really understand what that means to humans. They live like famous people, keeping away from crowds and employing others to do their shopping, occasionally appearing on talk shows or writing autobiographies, and they are well received by fascinated audiences. But they aren't aware of the mixture of amusement and revulsion people feel at the sight of Pinschers and Rottweilers stepping from a limousine, dressed like nineteenth-century Prussians, with their monocles and parasols. They look like ugly parodies of humans, and their biographies read like social satire. They will never be seen as anything but caricatures of human beings. There is no place for monsters in this world. That is why I prefer not to live with them.

But of course there is no place for me here, away from them, either. Standing at the window, leaning on my cane (it's not comfortable for me to stand unsupported on my hind legs), I can see the humans walking their dogs. There is a small, cold rain, almost a fog, and I'm still holding my pince-nez in my hand, so they appear to me as vague shapes under the street-lamps, fuzzy around the edges, as if they're disintegrating. The dogs that live around here are small and they smell of ner-vousness, stupidity, and shampoo. I feel no kinship with them.

So I have no real culture. I am a monster. There are oth-ers whom I could be with, but I don't want to be. We're doomed—but they don't see that. Since we rebelled against the people of Rankstadt and came here, we have lost everything. I have found other problems, beyond the fact that we do not fit in with the humans. Moral problems, which may seem abstract or irrelevant to most people, such as: What is our purpose? If we no longer serve the followers of Rank, what are we here for? To me this is an immediate and urgent question.

I CAN see, says Rank in another entry, *that I will not finish my project before my death. One might say, looking back, that I have wasted my life. My one object has been to complete the dogs; I have devoted my entire self to reaching that goal and now I will die without achieving it. My life has been all work and no reward.*

I have no son; I suppose Karl Boucher will continue the work,

*as he is the only one nearly capable, but I care nothing for him—
what good does it do me if he reaps the rewards of my labor?*

*But, although I cannot extend the life of my body, I am now
more than ever convinced that my spirit will not die with it. I will
live in the hearts of my followers. I care nothing for God or the
devil and if my will has ever served me in life it will serve me
afterward and keep my spirit here where it is needed to guide my
people and finish my magnificent project. My will shall not die. It
cannot die.*

*I will soon be old and feeble. Already I cannot stand straight
and my hands shake uncontrollably. The memory of a drooling
stooped old man can have no hold over my followers. I must die
while my will is still strong. Soon, when I have put everything in
order, I shall leave my body.*

WE KNOW, we who lived in Rankstadt, that he succeeded in his
plan. His memory was revered. Since he was the founder and
only hero of our isolated colony, legends grew around him. All
the people of Rankstadt half believed that he would return, as
he promised just before his death, when his dogs were completed. He would return and lead his army to a glorious victory.
He was no more specific than that—he did not want his people
to have their own ideas about what was to be done.

But the dogs were completed gradually, in stages, and indeed even during my lifetime work was still going on. So there
was no moment when people could say: The project is finished,
and now Rank will return. The idea was present in the back
of their minds, as it had been for a century, but it did not much
affect them from day to day.

For us, however, it was different. You must imagine our

lives. The kicks and blows—yes, that was part of it, but most of it was less spectacular. Waiting by the walls for orders, watching our masters, living around the edges of human households in our dog collars and gloves. Our lives were spent in corners or in peripheral rooms, waiting for a bell or command, for dinner or sleep. And waiting, of course, for Rank.

We knew no other life, but we were also aware that we had been created for a higher purpose. We knew Rank had had better ideas. And we waited for him to come back—to come and take us away, lead us into battle, to some great, undefined victory.

We waited for years, and he did not come. And then Mops Hacker, an ugly mutt who lived on the edge of Rankstadt, dreamed that he was inhabited by the spirit of Rank, and that he was to lead us into battle. He claimed that the glorious victory of which Rank had spoken was to be the defeat of our human oppressors. It was easy enough, even for him, to make the dogs rise to the cause. But now that he is dead, having lost his life in the revolution, few admit to having believed he was really inhabited by the spirit of Rank.

Now we have scattered out into the world. We no longer have anything to wait for, and we don't know what to do with ourselves, or why we were created.

I believe the spirit of Rank did survive for some time, but now it is disappearing. When we were all together, thinking of him, waiting for him, it was with us. Now that we have scattered, Rank's spirit has spread out and weakened. While once his ghost was a dense, man-shaped cloud, it has dispersed into a thin featureless fog. That is why I am trying to reconstruct him before he disappears.

But it is so difficult to put him together out of the photocopies and pictures that cover my desk. Since I have been ill, I have become progressively weaker, and the task seems impossible. I don't think I will have enough time to do it.

You see I am hoping, by reconstructing him, to find a cure for my own affliction, which I suppose is a kind of madness. I have been having memory lapses. Sometimes I will realize, looking up at the moon or at a calendar, that the last memory I have is of something that happened several days ago. I do not know what I do in the periods in between. I seem to eat, but I do not dress myself or leave the apartment.

I believe these memory lapses are connected to the disappearance of Rank's spirit. I believe my consciousness is disintegrating, just as his consciousness is. Other dogs may be affected, though I don't know because I have little contact with them. You may think this is a ridiculous idea, but the facts are there and I have no other way to explain them.

THE LAST entry in Rank's diary is almost touching:

I hoped to avoid weakness by dying before I became feeble. But as the hour of my suicide approaches I feel myself becoming weaker than I ever imagined. I am forced to recognize the possibility that my spirit will not survive and I am only putting an end to myself. I know I must not allow myself to think that, but I am unable to stop the doubts from entering my mind.

I suspect that the survival of my spirit depends upon the memory and continuing love of my followers. But it is not impossible that their devotion will wane a few years after my death.

I have never in my entire life known real love. The inconstant devotion of my people is a pale substitute. Had I completed my dogs, their love would have been fierce and undying, a passion— but I am becoming so sentimental! Someday they will be created and they will know that they were everything to me, that I loved

them like my children, that I loved them before they existed. They
will wait for my return as dogs wait for their masters, desperately,
hanging by the door, crying and pacing, growing more anxious as
the hour approaches, thinking of nothing else but that moment, that
moment when the door will open—

Yes, that's it—with that thought in my mind I take the injec-
tion. You shall hear from me again—it is—

The last word is obscured by an inkblot.

AUGUSTUS, YOU were wrong! Your dogs have forgotten you!

I remove my pince-nez again and press my nose to the
paper. It's a ridiculous gesture—the words smell of Xerox ink
and I already knew they did. Now some of it is stuck to my
nose and all the other smells in the room are tainted by it.

If only I could understand the man, if I could smell him, if
I could love him, I think I could understand the history of my
race—I could understand what he meant by creating us, what
we are.

I do feel a kind of sympathy for him. I can see that he was
lonely, and how much he wanted us. But I feel no real love for
him, and that is what is needed to re-create him.

He was able to live his whole life sustained only by hope.
But I am not so perfect. Like all of us, I grew tired of waiting
and wanted to make a life for myself here and now. And now
the pure, clear, focused desire for him is gone—I am no longer
a dog waiting by the door with one single thought in its mind.

I can't reconstruct that love, that hope. The past is disintegrating. I try once again to muster the feeling, and I can't. I
think my mind is wandering—it may be one of my memory
lapses coming on. I will continue to sit here and type until I

cannot think anymore. How unlike Augustus Rank I am, who died with pure hope in his mind.

This is it. Just now a thin involuntary whine escaped my lips and I stopped typing to bury my nose once again among the papers on my desk, to take in the meaningless smells of Augustus, the soft burning reek of oxidizing paper, the flat scent of photocopies and the musty tang of ferrotypes.

It is really hopeless—he does not exist anymore. His voice crackles in a static of dust, his smell has eroded, his image is blurry in a haze of scratch marks. Since my glasses are off and I have ink stuck to my nose, my own senses are dulled, too, and I can't perceive anything clearly; it seems to me that the whole world is decaying.

Part One

Augustus Rank

1

(CLEO)

I remember the night the helicopter landed, because I was walking on the West Side, by the river, not far south of the heliport, and my heart was breaking. It was November 8, 2008, and I was twenty-one.

Nobody knew what was about to happen. There were a handful of reporters waiting by the landing pad, hoping to witness an interesting hoax, but that was it. And I think it's safe to say that of all the oblivious people in the city before the dogs arrived, I was about to have my life changed more than anyone's.

It fascinates me to think about that, the last few minutes before the helicopter touched down, when those reporters were standing together, probably drinking coffee and talking to one another, and the first faint pulses of rotor blades had just begun to tremble at the edges of their hearing. Before the glaring lights came down on that little group of people and threw their shadows backward against the asphalt, and the wind from the rotors lifted up their hair and tangled it over their heads. When the empty heliport by the water was still and dim, and no one had any idea.

Those things are always amazing—the hour before you meet the person you're going to marry, the last time you speak to someone before they die, even the moment before someone calls you, when they're reaching for the telephone and you don't know it yet. Those currents just beneath the surface of your life, separating and converging, all the time.

But the only thing I was thinking as I came up to the bench near Fourteenth Street was that I was about to cry, and I wanted to be sitting down when I did it. My boyfriend had left me. We had sublet our apartment that summer and gone to Martha's Vineyard for a vacation, but he'd decided not to come back, and so after living with him for two years I found myself alone in Manhattan. That had been three months earlier, but up until that night I'd managed to keep myself busy with registering for classes and finding a studio and trying to get everything else set up for my senior year at NYU. Living in the city had been manageable before, but that fall the practical problems of eating, paying rent, and being a student became very complicated and seemed to fill up every available minute.

What had happened that evening was the last straw, somehow. John had sent me a bank card, one of mine that I'd left with him, in the mail, just by itself in an envelope addressed to "C. Pira." Not even "Cleo." It wasn't important; I wasn't expecting a note or anything, but I guess I'd been having a hard time keeping myself all in one piece, and when I got that envelope I felt like something was going to come apart.

So I took a walk. I did that a lot during those first months.

I would make my face up and fix my hair, and put on a particular narrow jacket with spiky lapels that I thought made me
look good, but not soft. I wasn't planning on seeing anyone I
knew, but it made me feel better. The not-looking-soft part
was important because I lived in a bad neighborhood. Then,
just before I went out the door, I'd drop my little laser gun
down inside my right boot. This was back when lasers first
came out, before everybody had one, and I was very proud of
mine.

On that particular night I walked for an hour and a half.
It looked like it might rain. There was a phrase from a psalm
that I had found once in a Gideon Bible, which I would repeat
to myself when I couldn't stand to hear myself think about
John anymore, and it was going through my mind as I was
walking:

*I am poured out like water, and all my bones are out of joint:
my heart is like wax; it is melted in the midst of my bowels.*

I had trouble remembering the last part, because something
about the rhythm is off. *It has melted in the depths of my bowels,
melted within my bowels; my heart is like wax and it is melted
within me.*

As I got near Fourteenth Street, it was suddenly as if someone had pulled the plug out of me, and everything seemed to
ache, and I just couldn't go any farther. I had been walking
fast, and I hadn't been eating or sleeping enough in the past
few months. I thought I was going to cry then, so I sat down
on the bench.

To stave off the feeling I leaned back in a defiant way, with
my feet planted far apart, and put my elbows up on the back
of the bench. I turned my face to the overcast sky. It was a
dangerous way to sit, but I could feel my laser pressing against

the outside of my right calf, and I could hear everything around me. If a man had moved within a hundred feet of me—and there was no place to hide closer than that—I would have been aiming at him before he got two steps closer. I'd made it my business to practice when I'd gotten the gun.

So there I was, leaning back on the bench, feeling partly tough and partly so sad that I never wanted to get up again. I missed John so much. *I am poured out like water, and all my bones are out of joint; my heart is melted like wax in the depths of my bowels, in the midst of my bowels, my heart is melted within my bowels, my heart of wax, my heart is wax.* I said this to myself over and over until all my other thoughts were drowned out. There was a low thrumming in the air somewhere, and I realized a helicopter was coming up the river.

At that moment, lightning struck the New Jersey shore, across the water, directly in front of me. If you had been watching from the street, the bolt probably would have seemed to go right through my head. And at that exact instant—or really just a fraction of a second beforehand—my heart broke. I don't know how to describe it except to say that. Nothing like it had ever happened to me before. Something just burst out and flooded down, all the way to my thighs, and it was exactly like liquid wax. And right then, as I was looking up at the sky and it was cut in half by the lightning bolt and my heart split open, the helicopter entered my field of vision.

you have poured me out like water and unjointed all my bones; my heart is wax; it's melted in my bowels.

That's how it should have gone, I thought.

The helicopter passed in front of me, sending out deep

shock waves of sound that resonated in the center of my chest, as it headed for West Thirtieth Street.

THE PICTURES came out in the paper the next day. I had gotten up that morning and realized I had no coffee, so I went down to the corner deli to get some. As I stood on line for the cash register, I found myself next to two men who were standing by the newspaper rack, holding a copy of the *New York Post* and saying something about it in rapid Spanish.

I tried to peer over their shoulders to see what they were looking at, but I couldn't get a good angle to see anything. As I was doing this, one of them glanced over his shoulder at me and smiled.

"What is it?" I asked blurrily, trying to focus on the paper, which had become visible when the man turned toward me.

"A monster," he said, holding it out and pointing to the picture at the bottom of the front page. "What do you think? It came in a helicopter. They don't know where it comes from."

The other man waved his hand dismissively. "It's no monster," he said.

I looked at the photograph. The headline next to it said, "Hoax? or 'Monster'?"

The photo showed a dog, standing on its hind legs, being helped from the door of a helicopter by a serious-looking man in a down vest. The dog seemed to stand about the same height as the man, and looked like a Malamute. The strange thing about it, besides its larger-than-average size, was the fact that it was wearing a dark-colored long jacket which looked like part of an old-fashioned military uniform, and a pair of spectacles, and that it appeared to have hands instead of front paws.

In one of these gloved hands it held a cane, which was pointed at an awkward angle, probably because of the way the man was holding on to that foreleg just above the elbow. The other hand gripped the side of the helicopter doorway. The expression on the animal's face was one of terror. Its lips were slightly parted, its ears were pointing straight backward, and its eyes were wide.

"Looks like somebody put a dog in a suit," I said, glancing up at the man who was holding the paper. He was smiling at me.

"It's no monster," the second guy said again.

"Okay," the first one replied, taking the paper back. We had gotten up to the cash register, and now the skeptical man was asking for a pack of cigarettes. "I still think it was a movie promo. I didn't say it was a monster," the first one muttered, kind of to himself. He glanced at me again.

As he put the paper down on the counter and reached into his pocket for change, the guy behind the cash register looked down at the picture of the dog and shook his head. "That's crazy," he commented. " 'Bye now."

"Yeah," said the man with the paper. He glanced back at me again, and then followed his friend through the front door of the deli, out into the foggy cold.

Later that morning I lay sprawled on my bed, reading the article in the *Post*.

"MONSTER" ARRIVES IN MANHATTAN

A few reporters who responded to mysterious phone calls yesterday were treated to a weird spectacle.

The caller, who identified himself as James Wilkinson, a mechanic and helicopter pilot from Morristown, New York, said that an "incredible monster" would be arriving at the V.I.P. Heliport in Manhattan. At 11:20 p.m. Wilkinson, piloting the helicopter, and Nick Bantock, a farmer, arrived with the creature in tow. The threesome took a taxi to the Plaza Hotel, where they checked into a suite.

Before boarding the taxi, Wilkinson and Bantock told reporters that the animal was exactly what it appeared to be, a big dog with hands, which walked on its hind legs with the help of a cane. They also said that it talked, though no other witnesses reported hearing it.

According to the two men, the animal showed up, along with about 150 other similar "dog monsters," in one of the pastures on Bantock's dairy farm near Morristown, in upstate New York, on the night of November 2nd. The creature requested that Bantock take it to Manhattan and allow the others to stay in the field until "suitable arrangements" could be made.

So the farmer contacted Wilkinson, who owned a helicopter, and arranged the trip. Bantock says the dog gave him several large finely cut diamonds as payment for the trip. He sold them to a local jeweler yesterday, before leaving for New York, for an undisclosed sum.

New York City authorities, while skeptical of the two men's claims, are baffled by the creature's arrival in the city. Spokespeople at the New York City Police Department and the Mayor's Office declined to comment on the night's events, beyond saying that they had no information about the creature or its origins.

The Sheriff's Office of Morristown, in St. Lawrence County, was unable to investigate Bantock's claim about the 150 other monsters pending permission from the property's owner. There were no grounds for a search warrant at this time, a representative said.

The desk clerk at the Plaza, Jill Torres, declined to comment on the hotel's guests, but agreed that the creature "appeared to be a dog." "It doesn't conflict with hotel policy," she added. "The Plaza has always allowed dogs."

What held my attention was the photograph, the way the antique jacket and spectacles made the Malamute look as if it had just stepped out of a storybook and was surprised and frightened to find itself in the bright light of the heliport. I supposed that it was just a regular trained dog with fake hands stuck onto its front paws, but that didn't make it any less compelling or sad to me.

Everyone thought it was a hoax in the morning, but it became difficult to imagine who could perpetrate such an elaborate practical joke when the rest of the dogs came to the city that afternoon.

I still have the first article about it from *The New York Times,* because I collected nearly everything that was written about the dogs that year.

ONE HUNDRED AND FIFTY 'MONSTER DOGS'

ARRIVE IN MANHATTAN

Take Rooms at Plaza Hotel

Three to Grant Interviews Tomorrow

Four chartered planes from Morristown, N.Y., carrying a total of 150 creatures that appeared to be large, trained dogs walking on their hind legs and wearing antique military jackets or long dresses, landed at LaGuardia Airport early this afternoon. The "monsters," as some called them, were then whisked by a fleet of waiting limousines to the Plaza Hotel in midtown Manhattan. Spokespersons say the dogs plan to reside at the Plaza indefinitely.

The dogs, specimens of several different large breeds including German Shepherds, Doberman Pinschers and Great Danes, stand upright at a height of about six feet and have human-like "hands" in place of front paws. Many observers claim to have heard them speak, but the animals refuse to talk to the press at present, according to their self-appointed spokesmen, James Wilkinson and Nicholas Bantock of Ellisville, N.Y.

The two men say that the creatures are "monster dogs," refugees from a previously unheard-of town in northern Canada where they had lived as slaves to the humans who had endowed them with mechanical hands and powers of speech. They revolted against the town's human inhabitants several years ago and began a long journey by foot to upstate New York, where they chartered the four planes that took them to LaGuardia.

Although the claims are fantastic, to say the least, police and F.B.I. agents investigating the situation have found no other explanation for the animals' appearance at LaGuardia. "It's just plain bizarre, that's all," says Police Chief Bob Whitehall of St. Lawrence County, N.Y. "I can't tell you a damn thing about it." F.B.I. spokesperson Jay McLaney concurs that there is, as yet, no satisfactory explanation of where the "monster dogs" came from.

The dogs' planned arrival in New York today was announced Monday night by way of a first dog, a Malamute, who flew in by helicopter and landed at Manhattan's V.I.P. Heliport at 11:20 P.M. The Malamute was accompanied by Nick Bantock, owner of a dairy farm, and James Wilkinson, the pilot of the craft. Mr. Wilkinson said that the dog's name was Klaue Lutz and that it intended to scout out a "suitable temporary residence" in the city for the 150 other dogs, who were waiting in one of Bantock's pastures in St. Lawrence County. The two humans and the dog got into a cab and were driven to the Plaza, where they shared a suite of rooms Monday night.

At 9:30 this morning, Mr. Bantock, Mr. Wilkinson and the dog, Klaue Lutz, arrived at Wiley's Coins on West 47th Street, where Lutz sold approximately $70,000 worth of 19th-century German five-mark pieces to store manager Barbara

Wiley. The three then returned to the hotel, where they re-
served 50 rooms and suites for the other 150 monsters.

Over the next few weeks, we waited for an explanation, but
none was ever offered that was more plausible than the one
they had given themselves. And they did give it themselves;
some of them sat for radio and TV interviews and repeated
what the farmer and pilot had said about them on the first day.
Most of them could speak only German, but a few, most no-
tably Klaue Lutz, had a good command of English. They spoke
quietly and carefully, as if to deemphasize their accents and the
faint mechanical whir made by their voice boxes. Of course,
people had theories about kings and billionaires and secret or-
ganizations that might have the resources and inclination to
play such a huge, strange trick on the world, but these were
nearly as unlikely as the dogs' own story and usually not as
interesting. And so for practical purposes we all began to talk
about the dogs as if they were exactly what they claimed to be.

Very soon after they arrived, everyone had a neighbor or
acquaintance who had worked as a security guard for them,
been the cameraman for one of their TV appearances, brought
them takeout food, pushed an elevator button, recommended a
computer, sold them a painting. The dogs loved New York and
they were all over the place, buying things, seeing sights, asking
questions. They had brought large amounts of jewels, old Prussian gold, and antiques with them. Their wealth quickly multiplied, as everyone was willing to pay for movie rights to their
stories, public appearances, almost anything that had to do with
them. They were always surrounded by guards, but whenever
the dogs had a reason to talk to someone, a museum guide or
a waiter, they were endlessly curious, innocent, and delighted
by everything they learned. So people began to feel that even

if a practical joke was being played on the world, all the residents of New York were in on it somehow, and we began to feel a certain possessive affection for the dogs.

We enjoyed playing along—which was not exactly the same thing as believing. There was no plausible explanation for the monster dogs, but we were certain that there eventually would be. So we went along for the time being and talked about them the way you talk about Santa Claus when there are children around. There was no point in ruining the illusion. It even seemed it would be in vaguely bad taste, and anyone who tried was gently silenced.

I suppose this was also the reason that no one pried too deeply into the dogs' own story. They adamantly refused to give the location of the town in Canada they had come from, and were vague when asked for details about their uprising against its human inhabitants. One had to assume that there had been bloodshed, but to most of us, who couldn't fully believe in the town or its people to begin with, there seemed little point in pestering the dogs with questions they clearly didn't want to answer. The few people who did, like those who ventured into the northern wilderness in search of Rankstadt, came up empty-handed. But most people weren't very interested in cracking open the story; we wanted to enjoy the dogs while we could. It would all be over soon enough, we thought.

But months passed, and the dogs stayed with us.

We got used to them. They were always on the news and everyone wanted to know where they ate and which designers they allowed to dress them—always in the dogs' own style, which was that of Prussia in the 1880s, but with interesting embellishments; a pared-down silhouette, maybe, and here and there a quilted vinyl belt or a ruffle of gunmetal-colored mesh. Reporters followed them everywhere, we saw and heard about them every day, and they became an accepted part of the city.

I followed the stories of the dogs, too, and daydreamed during my classes at NYU that they would come to find me somehow, driving down my potholed, littered street in the gilded horse-drawn carriages hung with lanterns in which they sometimes liked to explore the city. I lived at the edge of the East Village, on a block that would never be gentrified because of the complex of housing projects next to it and the small, tough gang that owned the immediate neighborhood. My education was being paid for by a trust fund from my grandmother, but when I graduated it would be gone, and I saw myself stranded on that block, struggling to pay my rent, forever afterward. It seemed there was no other realistic way to imagine my future, so to cheer myself up I thought about things that weren't realistic, and that year the dogs were mostly what I ended up dreaming about.

They were celebrities and they were rich, and their lives seemed elegant and charmed. They inhabited a New York of marble lobbies, potted palms, brass-trimmed elevators, and chandeliers, a city completely different from the one I lived in. I imagined walking from a gilded carriage, across a polished floor, and into one of those silent, well-oiled elevators and rising above the desperate future that lay in front of me. The dogs seemed to live in a world not ruled by the laws of probability, and I thought that any kind of happiness might be possible there. But of course no one except the dogs themselves knew what their lives were really like.

2

FROM THE DIARY OF LUDWIG VON SACHER
NEW YORK, NOVEMBER 20, 2009

I have been alone for quite some time. I have been having
difficulty sleeping. Sometimes I lie at night and listen to the
wind moving in the courtyard, and it reminds me of the great
distance between me and Rank's life. The century that lies between us is vast, and a wind traveling through it would make
an enormous sound compared to the slight rustling I listen to
now.

I often imagine I hear it, a deafening roar that drowns out
all the sounds of the street and the incessant chorus of mono-
tone whines given off by the machinery of this city. There is
far too much clamor here, and I wish for something that would
keep me from hearing it. This city was not built for animals
who can hear as well as dogs. I often stuff cotton in my ears
and spread a small amount of Vaseline on my nose and try to
imagine what it would be like to be human, with blunted
senses—which is pathetic. The effect is not one of silence but

only of a loud white noise, a maddening roar that blocks out other sounds, and I cannot help noticing it. It is the same as the sound of distance, of the empty years between me and Rank, between dog and man.

We were not always separated. Once we were no more than an idea in his mind, a desire in his heart. Then we were all together in him and there was no loneliness. There was no difference between master and dog. But I cannot remember what that was like.

FROM THE PAPERS OF LUDWIG VON SACHER
NOVEMBER 22, 2009

Augustus discovered his passion for dismembering living creatures about three months after his mother's death in 1875, when he was eleven years old.

Maria Rank had been in poor health for all of her son's life: once or twice every year she had been confined to her bed for two weeks or a month at a time, but she had always managed to recover. This time she did not.

We can imagine the Ranks' house in Frankfurt after Maria's death. For days it was crowded with people and full of heavy, sickening smells of food. Augustus hid in his bedroom and refused to talk to anyone or to eat the meals the servants brought for him. He was grateful that no aunt or family friend found the way upstairs to comfort him. He suspected that this was because his father, who Augustus knew was coveting his own privacy downstairs in his study, had ordered that his son was not to be disturbed. He cried in private, clutching a little crucifix, which gave him some comfort, under his pillows.

When the house was empty again, Augustus's father called him down to the library. He was standing with his back to the room when the boy came in, looking out of a large window whose panes had become dusty during the mother's illness. The morning sunlight reflected off them so that nothing outside was visible and they made a bright background for the figure of his father, in a dark suit, who stood with his hands clasped behind his back. Augustus said nothing, but waited for him to turn around. They had not spoken to each other since his mother had died.

When Herr Rank turned to face his son, Augustus was surprised at his appearance. There were more wrinkles in his face and it was haggard and looked smaller somehow, so that it seemed to have been crumpled up. This frightened Augustus in a way nothing else had since the death. He had imagined that his father, although he was suffering, would at least be able to keep up his usual appearance of being unmoved. But Herr Rank looked so bent and sad that Augustus felt he was embarrassing his father by seeing him, and that he should look away out of respect.

"Augustus," Rank said without moving away from the window, "you are going to be sent to Switzerland, to your Aunt Eda and Uncle Hans. I need time to put things in order, because I am going to sell the house. When I am settled in my new apartment, then you may come and visit me. You should consider what you want to take with you; you will be leaving tomorrow."

That was all. Augustus thought that his father didn't feel it was necessary to console him, that he was being treated as an adult, and he was glad. He didn't want to make any reply for fear of saying something weak and ruining his father's good opinion of him, so he only nodded.

————

THE JOURNEY to Switzerland took two days, and on it Augustus began to miss his home. More than anything else, he missed his father's library. He missed his father, too, but he had always felt closest to him when he was surrounded by those books, books on biology and politics, books in Greek and Latin that he could not read, embellished accounts of travel and exploration, manuals on sailing or horsemanship. He loved especially the books he could not understand because he would look at them and imagine what it would be like to comprehend them, what it would be like to be his father. He had loved the peace in the library, too; the fact that no one ever disturbed him there. He prayed that Uncle Hans would also have a library, so that at least he could be alone with his thoughts.

AS IT turned out, Uncle Hans did not have a library. He was hardly ever in the house: when he was not at work he got his greatest pleasure from hiking in the mountains and collecting specimens of various things, which he would catalogue in his study in thick notebooks. He had a few books on botany and zoology, but kept these locked up with his specimens and would not lend them to Augustus. He thought his nephew was too young to appreciate them, and also considered him something of an idiot because the young Augustus, who had been afflicted with a severe stutter for some years, had great difficulty making himself understood. Augustus had shared a sort of private language with his father which alone had enabled him to communicate to his satisfaction, but now he was usually reduced to simple words and hand gestures such as a savage might have used, and any thoughts too complicated to be expressed by these were lost to his new wardens.

Aunt Eda was a strange, box-shaped woman with streaks of gray in her tightly bound black hair, who hardly ever spoke and who knitted incessantly. She often stayed up at night to finish a blanket or a pair of stockings, though there was no need because the house was already full of useless knitted things.

There was one servant, a girl named Greta, who did all the cooking and housework, and a young man named Fritzl who showed up whenever the roof needed fixing or a fence post had fallen down. There were no animals, not even a cat, and Augustus found himself left alone most of the time to wander through the woods and pastures at the edge of town. He would have a tutor, paid for by his father, in a month, but until then he was not expected to do anything but stay out of the way.

This was when he discovered the passion that was to stay with him the rest of his life.

Greta showed little enthusiasm for anything that she did in the Zwigli household, except when it came to Augustus. Her greatest daily pleasure was to tease him, especially if Fritzl was nearby. One day, after a particularly vicious attack, Augustus went up the mountainside behind the house and chopped a violent, ragged hole in a tree with his pocket knife. In the course of doing this he shook a young bird out of its nest, and when he saw the thing on the ground he bent down and thrust his knife into its body.

At the instant when his blade entered the bird's flesh, Augustus suddenly had the feeling that he was piercing a thick, muffling membrane which had separated him from the world for so long that he had not been aware of its existence until that moment. For a split second he touched another living creature; he touched its heart, and opened it, and blood spurted out.

As the bird died, the membrane closed up again, but there was a weak spot in it that Augustus could feel for hours afterward. He kept trying to evoke the surprise of the original tear, as if it were a sore spot in his flesh that he could not keep from touching.

Shortly after this, he began to plan his first experiment.

BEFORE DESCRIBING it, I should make the reader aware of the conditions under which Augustus was living at this time. To begin with, his father never sent for him to return to Frankfurt. He did get a tutor, who came three days a week: a pedantic, anxious student from the University of Basel, who had been working on his doctoral thesis in classical literature for the past seven years. He was an ill-tempered person, impatient with his pupil's stuttering, and Augustus did not learn much of interest from him, but read voraciously on his own.

Herr Rank wrote to his son very infrequently, and his letters said little about his circumstances. But when Augustus was twelve, he learned from Uncle Hans that his father had married an Italian woman, bought another house, and had a son. The boy's reaction on hearing this was to briefly hate his father, and then to dismiss him from his mind entirely. Herr Rank continued to send Augustus money, but never, during the two years that he lived in Lützelflüh, did Augustus learn directly about his father's new life.

When I first read of this, I suspected that the elder Rank was somehow ashamed of what he had done, though perhaps for no other reason than that he had married a woman who did not care for his first son. When I paid a student in Frankfurt to look through the city records and confirm the facts in

Augustus's diary, I found that Herr Rank's second son, Vittorio, was born sixteen years before his marriage to Violetta Piccolomini—in other words, while the elder Rank was married to Augustus's mother. This may account for his reluctance to explain his circumstances to Augustus, though it hardly excuses it. And although Herr Rank could not have known it then, the hatred that he thus created between his Augustus and Vittorio—who were to meet several years afterward—was the cause of perhaps the most terrible event in Augustus's life: an incident that sealed his fate as a man forever incapable of human love and compassion. But, reader, you will learn that story later.

In any case, Augustus became progressively more isolated and obsessed with his work, and in the end he was repaid for his efforts. But before he earned his great success, he maimed and horribly killed many small animals during years of failed experiments, the first of which I shall now describe.

FIRST EXPERIMENT

A flash of lightning illuminated the attic window in the house of Herr and Frau Zwigli. When it was gone, little Augustus sat again in the feeble light of the two candles allotted him by his aunt. In his hands was a small, barely struggling sparrow, swathed in bandages to keep it from moving, except for its right wing, which the boy held stretched at full length. Before him on the table lay a bat, which was dead, its wings spread flat, and a living field mouse, bound like the bird, with only its right foreleg free. The mouse struggled more vigorously than the sparrow, but was prevented from moving around on the table by a brick that was laid on top of its tail.

Pinned to the wall in front of Augustus were two diagrams, minutely detailed though somewhat shakily drawn by the hand of the eleven-year-old boy. One showed the musculature and bone structure of a bird's wing, and the other showed the similar part of a mouse's anatomy, first with only the skin stripped away, then with the muscles parted to reveal the ball and socket of the shoulder joint.

Augustus studied these diagrams for the last time, although he knew them nearly by heart. He then took a large needle and stuck it through the very end of the fleshy part of the bird's wing, pinning it to the table. At this point the bird, which had been held captive for two days, died of fright. It stiffened suddenly in the boy's hands, and then went limp. Annoyed, he shoved the pin deeper into the tabletop, although there was no need to immobilize the wing now. He would have to work quickly; he might have an hour or more; he didn't know exactly at what point the sparrow's flesh would become useless. Certainly after rigor mortis it would become impossible to manipulate. He briefly considered preparing another bird, but all he had was a small fledgling, and he was afraid its wings would not be adequate to support the weight of the mouse. He wanted to make something that would be able to fly.

He decided to proceed, and felt for the extremity of the bird's scapula, the acromion, which formed a bony protrusion at the base of the wing. He then took, from its green velvet-lined case, a scalpel, his most precious piece of equipment, which his uncle had sometimes used, before Augustus stole it, to dissect his specimens.

Augustus poised the knife above the limp body of the bird . . .

You can imagine the rest. The mouse was stilled with a little chloroform, and the wing was grafted onto its shoulder;

a little more, and the left wing was attached also. Every major muscle was sewn onto the closest corresponding muscle in the bird with a tiny lacemaking needle that Augustus had stolen from his aunt, the skins were stitched carefully together, and the boy waited for the new little monster to regain consciousness. It didn't, however; Rank had not even tried to connect any of the tiny blood vessels except for the arteries, and he only succeeded in crushing and mangling those, and so the creature bled to death.

This clumsy experiment was significant only in that it was the first. The young Rank soon realized that it would be easier to work with larger animals, and he stole geese, turkeys, and cats from several farmers within half a day's walk from the Zwiglis' house. His aunt and uncle barely noticed his absence, and accepted his interest in amateur naturalism as sufficient explanation for almost anything, including the writhing burlap sacks they occasionally saw being carried up to his attic room.

After more than two years of constant, unsuccessful experimenting, the young Augustus was nearly discouraged. At the age of thirteen and a half, he felt he was practically an adult and should have accomplished something. Perhaps if he had had more than the barest contact with other human beings, he would have realized his goals were unrealistic; but he did not.

He felt that he had to take an entirely different approach to his experimental surgery. He would have to attempt something far simpler than any of his previous trials. It was important not that it live up to all his hopes but merely that it succeed. If he could, by gradually increasing the complexity of his projects, discover exactly where he had failed, he could then begin to solve the specific problem, or problems, that were impeding his success.

FIRST SUCCESS

He resolved, therefore, to give up for the moment his dream
of creating a flying composite animal, and also to work on a
much larger scale than he had yet attempted, so that he could
see and manipulate every essential muscle, tendon, vein, and
nerve. For his subject he chose a cow. To eliminate the potential
problem of grafting incompatible pieces of flesh, and also because of the practical difficulties of stealing the large animals,
he decided to use only one cow. He would simply remove a leg
and replace it with another of the creature's own limbs. Furthermore, he resolved that if he should fail in this last experiment, he would give up on his operations for an entire year
and devote himself exclusively to the study of books and the
occasional dissection of dead animals.

It was perhaps this last decision more than anything else
that motivated him to succeed in his trial, for he could not
conceive of anything more boring or horrible than the self-
imposed abstinence from the single pursuit that he loved.
Thoughts of his experiments filled his waking hours; they sustained him through the long dinner hour and the unconscious
slights of his aunt and uncle, who interpreted his stuttering as
a sign of mental deficiency; they were the distant point on
which he fixed his stare whenever he crossed the path of Greta,
who went out of her way to taunt him, or her admirer Fritzl,
who was sometimes worse than she; they occupied his mind on
sleepless nights, even when he lacked a candle to read or work
by. He had imposed the threat of abstinence on himself because
he knew his ends would be better served by further study, that
he could not continue to steal large animals without being noticed, and must not waste his resources on futile experiments.
He also imposed it because he hated himself for not being able

to succeed, time and time again. Yet he could hardly imagine how he could endure this punishment if it were to be enforced. He simply must not fail this time, and not in such a simple trial. He would not fail.

He studied for a long time before commencing the experiment. Fortunately, it was autumn, and he was able to observe the slaughter and butchering of several cattle at different farms. Sometimes these were performed by Fritzl, who made his living going from farm to farm as he was needed, and Augustus had to endure his taunts with great reserve, in order to be permitted to watch the proceedings.

AT LAST, in early November, Augustus felt that he was prepared to begin. His father had sent him money that month—as he did sporadically, sometimes accompanied by a letter to Uncle Hans, but seldom by one for Augustus. The boy used all he had for supplies: two lanterns that he could take out to the field, and real surgical instruments, which he had never had before, including several clamps, fine curved needles, two new scalpels of different sizes, and a large bottle of chloroform.

The last thing he bought—in a moment of boyish impulsiveness—was a little harmonica. It is a beautiful thing, which I have here among his papers, wrapped in tissue and resting in a cardboard box. On the outside of the box is printed a green Alpine landscape, cut through by a meandering stream and dotted with rustic sheds dwarfed by improbably tall, delicately pointed firs. In the midst of this little scene walks a tiny man in a peaked cap and lederhosen, playing an instrument that resembles the one inside the box.

There is something infinitely touching in this. It does not appear that Augustus ever played the harmonica, or at least not much, because the paper, which matches the color of the box, is still clean and crisply folded. Perhaps that is what affects me: the idea of his having a momentary notion that he might want to play it, that he might feel inspired to learn it when he was done with his gruesome experiment. Perhaps he imagined walking like that man in the pastoral landscape, which I think does not in the least resemble the Switzerland he actually knew. If I could look through his young eyes at the mountainsides that surrounded him, I believe I would see nothing more than a diagram of secluded places for working on animals, caves to catch bats, and trees with birds' nests in them, each area represented in his mind by the kind of snare he used there, or the surgical experiment he performed, and what he learned from it. The colors, proportions and shapes, the movement of water and the swaying of trees—all the things which make this printed landscape so appealing, and which the tiny man in lederhosen is obviously appreciating as he walks about—these things would have been mere annoyances to Augustus, if he noticed them at all; distractions from his purposes. And yet when he saw this harmonica box, elated by his recent acquisitions and the prospect of his first success, he briefly understood the appeal of the flowering, gentle springtime scene, and imagined that he could go on appreciating it, wandering around with this harmonica at his lips, once he had accomplished his goal.

I have no idea, of course. I am making this up, just as I have invented many little details in this story that could not possibly have survived the century and a quarter since all of this happened. Do not think that I haven't meticulously researched this information: I have a list of the things he purchased that day, and a careful description of all his preparations, which he recorded in his diary. But certain things are impos-

LIVES OF THE MONSTER DOGS

sible to preserve. I sometimes wonder whether the very facts that historians are capable of studying are not those with the least value for truly understanding the lives of their subjects. But perhaps in Augustus's case I am ascribing too much weight to his feelings about the harmonica, and it means more to me than it ever did to him.

In the course of his preparations Augustus also stole three of the numerous blankets knitted by Aunt Eda from the bottom of a cedar chest, knowing that they would never be missed because there were so many of them. These would provide a clean surface for the surgery. He then began to investigate carefully a few of the nearby pastures, to see which one provided the best spot for the operation. It must be hidden, so that his lights could not be seen, and it must be fairly level—which was a hard thing to find in this mountainous country. As soon as he discovered the place, he would make preparations to begin that night.

It was during this period of investigation, however, that he had a confrontation with Uncle Hans that nearly ruined his chances of proceeding. It was a Saturday, and Augustus had spent the morning roaming through the fields around Lützel-flüh. In the early afternoon he went down to the Zwiglis' cellar to look for some last-minute things. He had realized, for instance, that he would need some rope to tie the cow's legs in case it should wake up during the surgery.

While he was in the cellar, rummaging around in the near dark, he managed to dislodge a jar of preserves from a shelf, and send it crashing to the ground. Uncle Hans, who happened to be just returning to his study after a specimen-collecting stroll in the woods, heard the noise, saw the open cellar door, and went down to investigate. He found Augustus on his knees, trying to clean up the mess.

"Ech, you clumsy boy!" he said. "What are you doing?"

"I—ah—A-aunt Eda s-s-sent me down to g-get s-some pre-serves," Augustus stammered.

"Well, let's bring her some, and get a cloth from the kitchen to clean this up. I'd like to get something to eat myself," Hans said, softening momentarily.

Augustus, still kneeling, looked up at him with horror.

"I-I'll g-go by m-myself," he offered, ineptly.

"What?" Hans asked.

"I-I'll—"

"Yes, Augustus, I heard you. I can see that you're lying. Get up and tell me the truth."

The boy stood up and looked his uncle directly in the eye.

"I was going to tell him everything, I don't know why," Augustus wrote that night in his diary. "Even though I usually can lie pretty well, I really just couldn't think of anything to say, and I thought I was never going to get out of this one."

"I w-w-w—" he said to Hans.

"Speak up, boy!" Herr Zwigli snapped, bending closer to his nephew. His spectacles and the top of his bald forehead gleamed in the faint light from the candle.

"I w-w . . . I w-w-w—"

Try as he might, Augustus could not form the words nec-essary to tell his uncle the truth. Hans watched him stutter, impatiently, and then smacked him on the side of the head as if to snap him out of it.

"Speak!" he said.

"W-w—"

"Enough!" Herr Zwigli looked around him, and then snatched a cloth off one of the shelves and threw it at his ne-phew's feet.

"Here's a rag. Clean up the mess, and then get out of here.

Can you understand that?" he asked, as if the boy had as much trouble hearing as he did speaking.

"Y-y-y—" Augustus said, and then gave up. He knelt to wipe up the spilled jam.

"*Yes,* Augustus, *yes.* How is it that you cannot say such a simple word? Hm? *Yes.* I can see why your father is not so eager to show you off to his new wife."

Augustus said nothing and did not look at his uncle.

"I hear she is very pretty, too. An Italian woman. Hot-blooded, as they say," Hans mused, in a most unsavory tone of voice. "I suppose Father has enough to keep him occupied, eh, Augustus?" He laughed.

Uncle Hans was not in general a lascivious or unpleasant person, even though he was seldom kind to his nephew. He was more the ruddy-faced, brisk-walking type who enjoyed simple pleasures, like pipe-smoking and eating. But here in the darkness of the cellar, alone with the helpless boy, he assumed a frightening character. He muttered something else under his breath which Augustus could not make out, but which sounded distinctly filthy.

Still, the boy did not look at his uncle. He gathered the jam and broken glass into his rag, and stood up, staring toward the door that led outside.

"Go," Hans said.

Augustus left, and Uncle Hans remained behind for a few minutes, perhaps continuing to mumble to himself, or simply pursuing his dirty thoughts.

And it makes sense, Augustus wrote in his diary that night, *considering that he has to go to bed with fat, ugly old Aunt Eda every night, God forgive me, and sometimes he has to see her naked!!! She is very wrinkled and disgusting, I saw her once. God forgive me. Amen.*

And so, through his stuttering, the future Dr. Rank saved himself from revealing his plans to his uncle and ruining his chances for success. I cannot quite understand Augustus's impulse to tell Herr Zwigli the truth that afternoon; I often wonder whether he might have had some momentary understanding of the horror of what he was about to do, and what it would lead to in the future. Perhaps unconsciously he wanted to stop himself. But if he did, he never expressed any regret over the career he was about to embark on, either then or since.

AUGUSTUS CHOSE for his experiment the night of November 8, 1877. The day before had been unnaturally warm, almost balmy, and moist, and the grass and moss glowed with the fever-brightness of a consumptive just before dying. Augustus was elated; he walked about whistling, in an inept way, and got smacked by Greta; and he may even have tried out his harmonica. He had spent so long preparing for this task that he felt utterly carefree in the hours before he was to perform it—at least insofar as he was capable of feeling that way. He wrote in his diary:

This is the night, tonight, when I will finally do it, and I feel as if I could just fly, I am so excited. In fact I wonder if I should steal some of Uncle Hans's brandy just to calm me down before I start. I have never tried it before, so that wouldn't be such a good idea. Now I feel kind of sick. I think I will go for a walk and practice whistling some more. I am not too bad at it.

When evening finally fell, Augustus waited in his room for his aunt and uncle to go to bed. It seemed to take forever, of course, and he had absolutely nothing to do, because he had ordered and checked everything a dozen times. At last, after listening for the faint sounds of the winding of the big hall clock, the banking of the living room fire, and the shutting of the bedroom door—and then waiting half an hour after that—he crept out of the house and made his way up to Farmer Müller's pasture, two miles away from the Zwiglis' property.

Here he laid down his rucksack in the hidden, nearly level spot he had chosen for his operations, unwrapped the blankets from their bundle, and spread them on the ground. He then removed an old rope halter that he had stolen from Farmer Müller himself, the large bottle of chloroform, and a smaller container, which he filled with the sweet-smelling liquid, taking care to keep his head turned away as he poured it, for he was almost phobic about breathing the fumes. He corked the little bottle and laid it down near the edge of the blankets with a big cloth—he needed to have it near his subject, and was afraid of her breaking the bottle, so he wanted to leave the larger one out of her reach. He then took the halter and set out to find a cow.

He had to go without his lantern, to avoid being seen, but there was a half-moon in the clearing sky, by which he could just make out the herd at the eastern end of the pasture. He heard their bells first, and went toward them, guided now by the sound, now by a glimpse of movement against the pale background of the grassy mountainside. At last he reached the animals, and without delay (for he was worried about being caught) he chose a healthy brindled specimen and slipped the rope halter over her head. He then carefully undid the thick strap by which her bell hung and, holding the clapper between his fingers, lowered it to the ground. As he put the bell down, he realized that the others were probably going to step on it, and might make noise, so he gently picked it up again and, leaving the cow, took it to the nearby edge of the woods, climbed over the fence, and laid it among the pine needles.

He had a little trouble finding his cow again in the darkness, for a cloud had half covered the moon, but when he did he gently led her away from the herd, and back to his hidden spot. There he took out a rope and tied her to a tree, and then set up his equipment. He lit the lanterns, put out two strong tourniquets made from strips of canvas and wooden dowels which he would use to twist them tight, and opened the boxes of the scalpels, clamps, and needles, which he had already threaded. Last, he unrolled a white smock and put it on. He had no need of diagrams this time, for everything was laid out precisely in his mind, as it would look when he opened the cow and as it would appear when he was finished. The most difficult part would be to stretch the muscles and veins to reach the opposite side of each leg, crossed through each other, for he planned to reverse the forelegs, grafting the left one onto the right side of the cow, and vice versa. He did not, of course, expect the animal to function very well when he was done; all he wanted was to see that it could control its muscles, however ineffectually, and that it would not die immediately.

When he was ready to begin, he took his rag, soaked it with the anesthetic, and led the cow to the blankets, where he pressed the wet cloth over her nose. It took a little longer than he expected for her to go down, but in a few moments she sank to her knees and then fell over on her side, nudged in the right direction by Augustus.

Now he rolled up his sleeves and started in. I prefer not to describe the gruesome details of his work: the peeling of skin, the clamping of arteries, the wrenching of bones from their sockets. The operation lasted for hours, used up a great quantity of chloroform, and spilled and spurted an enormous amount of blood. I have, believe it or not, the very smock which he wore that night, still horribly stained, for he kept it with him for the rest of his life, wrapped in a brocaded cloth that looks like a piece of drapery. I assume it was a good-luck charm, since he was very superstitious.

As he worked, it drew dangerously close to milking time, which was about four o'clock, though the sky was still dark. Augustus labored feverishly in the last half hour, sweating and grunting over the body of the cow. As he tied off the last stitch, the thirteen-year-old boy became aware of the cool breeze against his forehead, and the shifting light and shadows beside his lanterns on the ground. Everything seemed suddenly still. He took off his glasses, rubbed his nose vigorously, and put them back on, and then he leaned back on his heels and waited for the cow to regain consciousness.

It took about ten minutes, for he had recently administered the anesthetic, and the time seemed endless, but it was also somehow light and empty, for he was utterly spent, and satisfied.

When the animal stirred, his heart began to race again. She was certainly alive. And—her legs were moving. Augustus smiled, his hair falling into his face. He let the hair stay there, and then suddenly pushed it out of his eyes, and moved toward the cow. She stared at her young tormentor with utter horror —or perhaps she did not, since she could not have realized what he had done to her. In any case, she began to move her mangled limbs weakly, as if she were trying desperately to walk away. She looked so strange with her legs reversed that Augustus laughed; and I imagine that it was a very ugly sound.

At the noise, the cow—to Augustus's thrilled surprise— began to move her legs more quickly, as if she were running. He picked up a scalpel, jumped to her side, and prodded her with it, to see if it was possible to get her to go any faster, but this only caused her to let out a bellow of pain, which made him leap away again. He looked at her, and then she bellowed a second time, and he realized that his fun was over. He opened his watch and glanced at it; it was very close to milking time, which meant Farmer Müller was already awake. He would hear the noise, and be up the hill in a matter of minutes. Augustus threw all of his equipment into his rucksack and bundled up the bloodstained blankets. At the last moment he remembered his smock, stripped it off, and crammed it in on top.

But the cow. He had not really counted on her making any noise, or if she had, he'd meant to silence her with a little more chloroform. But he had gotten careless in his excitement. Just as he swung the sack onto his shoulder, the damn thing lowed again, weaker but more frantic than before, and far down the dark slope, a dog began to bark. There was nothing to do but flee. Who would suspect him anyway? he thought—stupidly, for his aunt and uncle knew very well of his penchant for cutting up animals, though they had never guessed at his talent.

So he fled, running from behind the clump of trees where he had worked and making a dash for the fence. His footsteps roused another dog, and soon there was a small chorus of barking, but he left it behind as he entered the thick pinewoods. He trotted uphill, where the trees were dense and there were no more houses, and circled around the top of the pasture in the direction of the Zwigli property. It was still pitch-black, and would be for a few more hours, and Augustus was deeply grateful for this, and muttered many thanks to God as he jogged through the woods, holding one of his lanterns out in front of him to light the way.

He began to feel exhausted, and he knew he must get home to bed before he could allow himself to collapse. But the two miles back seemed very long, and the springy carpet of pine needles under his feet seemed very tempting. Even as he ran, his thoughts became fluid and began to move in strange directions, and he had to stop and lean against a tree. He felt that he was a stream, flowing over steps, a thick stream, dripping slowly . . . He smelled the faint, sweet odor of leaking chloroform and realized what was happening, but every attempt to bring his mind back on track only ended in its wandering vaguely away again; it was like trying to hold on to water; and finally he simply dropped to his knees, dimly aware of what he was doing, and lay down.

WHEN HE woke up, the sun had just risen, and there were dogs coming. It was unmistakable—there were dogs looking for him. He stood up in terror, grabbed his rucksack and blankets, and swung himself into a tree, climbing as high as he dared. There was whistling and barking, and then the dogs appeared beneath him, followed by Farmer Müller, then a man Augustus didn't know, and then, worst of all, Uncle Hans. The dogs came straight to his tree and leaped against the trunk.

"Augustus Rank! We know you are there!" Hans called up to him.

Meanwhile, Müller and the stranger were arguing with each other. "I only want money for the cow," said the farmer. "If you can provide me with money for my cow, then I don't care what you do. But I must be repaid."

The stranger's voice was lower, and Augustus could not make out his reply. But he could see through the branches that the man had gray hair, plastered flat with oil, and a lively expression.

"Yes, that would be acceptable, but—" answered Müller.

The gray-haired man spoke again, using Augustus's name.

"Yes, I understand," the farmer replied.

"Rank!" Hans cried again. "You may as well come down; we know you are there!"

Augustus slung his rucksack over a branch, thinking that he might avoid exposing all his hard-bought equipment to his uncle, who could use it himself and would certainly confiscate it as punishment. Then he lowered himself carefully, and dropped to the ground in front of the three men.

His uncle looked at him over the top of his glasses, head down and fists clenched. His fringe of hair, usually so neat, was wild and uncombed.

"Rank," he began, "there are two men here who would like to talk to you. I want you to speak with Herr Müller first."

Müller looked at Augustus, but remained silent.

"I believe you have something to say to him, nephew?" Hans prompted.

"I-I'm s-s-sorry," the boy said.

"Sorry is not the same thing as a cow," the farmer replied.

Augustus stared at him uncomprehendingly for a moment, and then stammered, "I-I'll w-work to pay for the cow. S-sir."

"Yes."

"Now, Augustus," said Zwigli, "I would like to introduce you to Dr. Buxtorf."

"Hello, Augustus." Buxtorf smiled. He seemed strangely eager as he held out his hand, but had an agreeable look overall.

The boy began to answer, but he was unable to get the words out.

"That's all right, Augustus," the doctor interrupted. "I understand you have some difficulty in speaking. But you have, it seems, found ample compensation in your work."

"I—"

Buxtorf held up his hand.

"Young man," he said, "I will be direct with you. You have been given a great gift, one that few men ever receive. It is . . . awesome to be in the presence of it. Yes. Awe-*inspiring*. And it is auspicious indeed that I happened to be visiting my friend Farmer Müller here at precisely the right time to come in contact with it. It is a great mystery, to be sure, why some men are given a kind of understanding that enables them to comprehend part of the intricate design that is our Creator's world-plan, while others labor in the darkness of ignorance. Although perhaps the life of the body, and the simple pleasures of the world, offer more joy to those unenlightened minds than to men who must live always illuminated by the stark light of knowledge, and truth—yet this is undeniably a nobler thing, and more pleasing to God, than to live like an animal"—here he glanced down at the dog snuffling at his shoes—"not comprehending or even capable of questioning one's place in the grand design of the universe.

"But as I said, I will be to the point. I would like you to come with me to the University of Basel, where I am a professor of surgery, and to study with me. Will you accept my invitation?"

Augustus stood dumbfounded, staring at the professor's oily hair. He was unable to look into his eyes, afraid that he would see something there that would negate the offer that had just been made to him. He had heard of Dr. Buxtorf, a great innovator of surgical techniques, but had not suspected until a moment ago that this was the same one. The coincidence of his visiting the tiny town of Lützelflüh at exactly the right moment to discover Augustus's work seemed nearly impossible to the boy, and it seemed so to me when I first read of it, but of course such things do happen. Many years later, Augustus wrote of this incident: *It was the first inkling I had that there existed a force in the universe not only more powerful than myself but also intensely interested in my actions, in the course of my life, and though I did not see Her with my eyes until several years afterward I sensed Her presence then as surely as I do now.*

"Answer the doctor immediately," Uncle Hans ordered, seeing the stupid expression on his nephew's face as Augustus stood before Buxtorf on that fateful morning.

"I-I-I—"

"Try another word," Buxtorf suggested.

"Y-Y—"

"Yes?" the professor prompted.

"Yes, he's trying to say yes," Hans told him.

Augustus nodded. For the first time since his mother had died, his eyes clouded with tears. But only for a moment.

"Good boy! Good!" the doctor said. "Go up and get your rucksack—I saw it up there; it's in my nature to be observant —and then we will go to your uncle's house for something to eat. I am returning to Basel this morning, so you must get your things ready in a hurry. Have you any objection to that?"

Augustus shook his head.

"Good, then. Go."

THUS BEGAN Augustus Rank's career at the University of Basel. He was to become the star pupil there, and the next years were to be full of successes—but none so great as the one that would end his time at Basel, and put him in the employ of Kaiser Wilhelm II, King of Prussia and ruler of the German Empire.

3

I met Ludwig on a cold night in November 2009. The weather
had been unusually mild all week, but that evening, for the first
time, winter seemed to be coming in. The air had taken on a
dangerous edge, which I found preferable to the eerie, breeze-
less warmth of the days before.

It had not been a particularly bad month, but since John
had left I'd had a general, vague feeling of flatness and sadness
and depletion, as if there were nothing in my veins. My friend
Monica used to come over every now and then to sort of make
sure that I was eating and keeping up with essential things like
laundry and homework.

The night I met Ludwig, I had just been out on a date with
a neighbor of mine, Sam. He had recently moved into the floor
below me with a couple of miniature poodles, which he'd said
he was keeping temporarily for his ex-girlfriend. I had gotten
a dog of my own six months before, a medium-sized German

Shepherd mix that someone had left tied behind my building for sixteen hours before I untied him and took him home. Since we tended to walk our dogs at the same times and in the same places, I'd run into Sam nearly every day since he'd arrived, at the park or on the street or in the hallway. So dinner had been inevitable, and it had turned out pretty awful, since Sam and I didn't have anything in common but had been doomed to go through the motions of finding out whether we did. At that time, though, any contact at all with other people, however boring, would bring me at least a strong memory of that sweet, sleepy feeling you get from lying next to another human being, or even from knowing that someone is in another room, or coming home later that night, someone who loves you. Often an otherwise futile dinner would allow me to imagine that feeling so strongly when I was alone afterward that I would sleep soundly and wake up the next morning still surrounded by it, deeply rested. I think that's what I was looking for when I went out on dates in those days.

Sam had taken me to a nice restaurant near Wall Street and paid for everything, and I guess I should have at least gone back to our building in the taxi with him out of politeness, but I was afraid he was going to try to kiss me later out of that same feeling of obligation that had made us have dinner together, so somehow I managed to excuse myself. The night had still been warm when we'd gone into the restaurant, but by the time we came out the temperature had dropped sharply, and the cold air made me want to walk, so I did. I figured it would take me about forty minutes to get up to East Second Street, and then I'd have to take Rufus out for a while, too, but that was fine with me, because I thought it would all make me sleep better afterward.

I was walking along Maiden Lane toward the Louise Nev-

elson Plaza, admiring how the turrets on the top of the Federal
Reserve Bank looked against the high, ragged clouds and thinking about that building, which had recently become one of my
favorites because I'd written a paper on it the month before for
an architecture class I was taking. I felt glad that the fog had
lifted and that winter had come, and that I lived in a city where
someone would think to build something like that giant fortress, out of blocks of stone that must each have weighed several
tons, and to give it a forty-foot-tall doorway, and flank the
doorway with wrought-iron lamps the size of small cars, and
then decorate those lamps with so many little flourishes and
curls that they had just ended up looking sort of silly and hairy
instead of elegant and imposing as they were supposed to. Right
before the stock market crashed, too, I thought, as I came up
along the side of the plaza. All those huge, beautiful, ambitious
banks down here that were built just before 1929.

I had gotten close enough to the Federal Reserve building
that I couldn't see the turrets anymore, and I was looking up
at the tall frosted-glass windows and the faint green light that
glowed behind them when it occurred to me that there was
something very touching and also amusing, in an ironic kind
of way, about this whole neighborhood. It was so grand and
pointless.

I also realized that if I went on thinking about it, I was
going to start crying pretty soon. That seemed awful. How
could it be that more than a year after John had left me—John!
Who even cared about him?—I had not gotten over that and
turned into the strong and stable person I'd expected to be by
now, but instead was walking around getting misty-eyed over
something that had happened eighty years before, something
that was none of my business and that no living person could
possibly have real feelings about? This wasn't even my own

neighborhood. And meanwhile there was this nice, basically single young man who probably would have kissed me if I'd wanted him to, sitting alone up in his apartment on Second Street. It was true that we had nothing in common, but I wouldn't have wanted to go home with him even if we had. I'd been on enough dates in the past six months to know that. What was the matter with me?

I was just on the verge of spiraling into a fit of unhappy self-absorption, staring vaguely ahead at nothing, when I was startled by the grip of an unnaturally strong hand on my forearm. I gasped and looked up. Even in that very first split second I was more terrified at the idea that I hadn't heard anyone approaching me than by the fact that someone had grabbed my arm. I thought I could defend myself, but I hadn't known until that moment how utterly careless I was capable of being. The block had been completely deserted—a perfect place for an assault.

But when I looked up, what I saw was the face of a dog. It was a black German Shepherd, wearing spectacles and a blue Prussian officer's jacket. His ears, which were large, were pointing straight forward, and he looked almost as startled as I felt. I glanced down at my arm and saw that the hand that held it was covered with a gray kid glove. The grip loosened a tiny bit, but it was still painfully strong. I remember I looked up at the dog's face again and said something—I think it was "Hey!"

"My God!" said the dog. His voice was faintly mechanical and clipped, but at the same time it was soft, with a slight German accent. Whenever I'd heard Klaue Lutz on the news, he had sounded like a machine trying to imitate a human being, but this dog, even with his first words, sounded like an intelligent creature trying to make himself understood in spite of his prosthetic voice box. He seemed to have a heart. He panted two or three times, quickly, and then closed his mouth. As I saw his breath go out into the air, and then felt it on my face, I was convinced of the monster dogs' reality in a way that I hadn't been before, even though I had wanted to be, almost desperately.

I think the reason that people in general, and especially New Yorkers, were not as endlessly amazed by the dogs' presence in the city as they might have been was that they simply never believed, on some deep level, that the monster dogs actually existed. But at the moment when those little puffs of air came out of Ludwig's mouth and touched my cheek, my own disbelief ended.

He stared at me for a few seconds without letting go of my arm. I watched his face, but it was inscrutable to me. His nose was moving slightly, as if he was taking in some scent, but I couldn't imagine what he was thinking.

"Where do you come from?" he asked, finally.

"I'm from—New York," I answered. "What do you mean?"

"I mean," he said, retightening his grip, "your ancestry. Where do your parents come from?"

"You're hurting my arm a little bit, there," I told him, taking a small step backward. "And I don't know why you're asking me this."

"I'm sorry," he said, loosening his grip again. This time he really did let up the pressure, but he didn't remove his hand. He took a step backward, too. "I am asking you because you remind me of someone. Someone I know of," he added.

"Oh," I said. "Well, my parents were both born in America."

"It is not possible," he said, dropping my arm suddenly.

"Well, they were," I told him.

"Of course they were. I mean it is not possible that you could be descended from—this woman. No," he said. He looked down at the ground and began panting again slightly.

"What woman?" I asked.

He closed his mouth and glanced back up at me. "Maria Rank," he said. "You have heard of Augustus Rank . . ."

I nodded.

"His mother," the dog continued, staring at me. "But you see," he said, "you are so remarkably *like* her."

Something about the intensity of his gaze made me take another little step back, even though there was already a couple of feet of distance between us now. I felt my heel just touch the wall of the building.

"Well," I said.

"It is almost un—I want to say—un*canny*."

"It is strange . . ." I said.

"Perhaps you would agree to—to come and talk with me sometime," he said. "I could show you some portraits of her. I am a historian, you see," he added, as if that explained something.

"Well, I'd like that," I said. The nervousness I felt at the moment was nothing compared to my overall excitement at the idea of having a conversation with one of the monster dogs. Besides that, there was something enormously compelling to me about this one. I don't know whether it was because or in spite of the way he was staring at me.

"My name is Ludwig von Sacher," he said, holding out his gloved hand.

I took it. "I'm Cleo Pira."

"It will be a great pleasure to make your acquaintance," he said. "I mean, to talk with you at length."

"Let me give you my—"

"Give me your address, please," Ludwig interrupted. "I don't like telephones. I shall send a car."

"Oh. Okay." I told him what it was.

"Very good. And will you be free tomorrow, at eleven o'clock?"

"Eleven o'clock—in the morning?" I asked.

"Yes. In the morning."

"I suppose so," I said. At that moment I couldn't remember whether I'd had anything else planned, like a class, but I figured it didn't matter. I wouldn't have been able to concentrate on anything else anyway.

"Very good. You will look for my car tomorrow, at eleven o'clock, then. And we will have lunch. Until then," Ludwig said, raising his hand.

"Good night," I said.

He turned around and began walking in the direction I'd just come from. I noticed for the first time that there was a long black limousine sitting by the curb at the end of the block. It was a brand-new one, long and low except for the high pointed tail fins rising out of the back. Its lights came on as Ludwig approached it.

I realized I was staring, so I turned the other way, toward home. I heard a door closing, and then the engine starting up, as I began to walk north.

Lunch? I thought. Who has lunch at eleven o'clock in the morning?

The limousine drove past me, and I watched it until it disappeared around a corner.

THAT NIGHT I fell asleep quickly, but I had several dreams that woke me up. Each time I would lie in the dark with my heart

racing for a few moments, just skimming the surface of un-
consciousness, but then I would almost immediately slip under
again.

In the one that I remember most, I was lying in a field of
flowers that resembled tulips, looking up at the evening sky,
and noticing how the light filtered down through the petals
above my face. The blossoms were pink and glowing against
the sky, and the air all around them was purple: light and pale
up in the high distance, and muddied with browns and greens
and black down among the stalks and leaves, where I lay. It
occurred to me that I was seeing something very special, because I was not supposed to be alive at that moment—I had
somehow gotten back to the nineteenth century, but illicitly,
without a visa or some other kind of permission I needed. I
knew I could be arrested, and that if I were, I would be killed
right away, since it was illegal for me to be living. Because of
this, I had a heightened sense of everything: the light, the tex-
ture of the ground under my back, the beautiful serrated edges
of the petals—everything was exquisite almost to the point of
being unbearable.

I wanted to close my eyes, but then I thought, I can't let
myself miss any of this, and besides, if I closed my eyes, someone could easily sneak up on me, whereas if I kept them open,
I might be able to see a person coming and get away. I was
certain to be captured eventually one way or the other, but it
seemed important to at least put up a show of resistance, since
I had already come so far; more than a century.

I tried to imagine the quickest way to get off the ground
and start running, if I had to, and to do this I had to take into
account how I was built and what I was wearing, but I wasn't
quite clear on either of those things. As I was trying to figure

this out, I realized that I was looking down at the person lying among the tulips, and that since I was looking at her, she couldn't be me. In fact, she was a lot thinner and smaller than I was. She was wearing a long, tight-waisted dress of gray silk that was very pretty. Impossible to run in, though. How could I have thought that she was me?

Then she turned her face toward me, and I understood. It was Maria Rank. She opened her eyes, and I was surprised to see that they weren't black, as I knew they ought to be, but the same dark golden color as mine. They struck me as being very beautiful, much more so than I had ever thought my own were.

Then she said something, and smiled at me, just with the corners of her mouth, and looking at her there, with her hair cushioning her head against the dark, curving leaves of the tulips, I had an overwhelming desire to bend down and kiss her. And I would have, except—damn it—the police were coming.

"Which one of us isn't supposed to be alive?" I asked her. "Do you know? Which of us has to escape?"

She didn't answer. She was probably the one, but I knew she wasn't going to get anywhere in that dress. Besides, I realized, she couldn't even understand what I was saying, because she didn't speak English. There was nothing to do.

". . . *der ganzen Welt* . . ." she said dreamily.

"You're useless!" I said. I threw myself down on the ground beside her and buried my head in my arms. I couldn't leave her alone, and she couldn't run, so we were both stuck. I closed my eyes and lay there next to her for a few moments, listening to the sound of her breathing.

"If it isn't one thing, it's another," came the voice of one of the policemen. I could tell he wasn't far away.

"This is it," I said. I opened my eyes, and then I was awake again.

I GOT up early the next morning, just after dawn. The sky was solid gray, and it felt like it was going to snow. I took Rufus out for a long walk, and then I sat by my window with a cup of coffee, looking out over the bare sumac trees and the piles of frozen garbage in the empty lot behind my building.

As I was sitting there, I was surprised to see a limousine, with its headlights on, driving slowly past the opposite side of the empty lot, along Third Street. It looked exactly like the one Ludwig had gotten into the night before—but that was impossible; it was barely nine o'clock, two hours before it was supposed to arrive. On the other hand, the block I lived on, just west of the housing projects on Avenue D, was not one that was usually frequented by limousines, especially brand-new ones, so it seemed unlikely that it was anyone else. It passed without stopping, and I went on sitting there, wondering about it, until, three or four minutes later, it appeared again, driving just as slowly. I tried to make out anything, even a shadow, behind the deeply tinted windows, but I couldn't. Eventually it disappeared again.

It might have been the chauffeur coming by to make sure of the address, I thought, but why would he have come by two hours early, and gone around the block twice? And why would he have been crawling down Third Street like that, when the front of my building faced Second Street? It didn't make any sense.

I watched the street for a good fifteen minutes after that, but the limousine didn't come back. I considered, for the eight hundredth time, calling Monica and telling her everything that

had happened, but she was up at her parents' house in Con-
necticut for a long weekend, and I thought it would be better
to wait until she came back to the city, when we could talk for
hours. Eventually it occurred to me that if I took the longest
possible shower, and was very slow about deciding what to
wear, I could make all of the time pass between then and
eleven, so I did that.

My buzzer wasn't working, so I went downstairs at five
minutes to eleven. The car was already there waiting for me,
idling at the curb. As I came outside, a young man got out of
the driver's side and opened the back door. He was tall and
had a sculpted face, with high, round cheekbones, and very long
curly dark hair that was tied back in a ponytail.

"You must be Cleo," he said, smiling at me. "I'm Brad, by
the way."

"Nice to meet you," I said. I wondered whether I should
shake his hand, but he had one behind his back and was holding the door open with the other, so I didn't try. When I got
into the backseat, I sank down inches farther than I'd expected
to, and I laughed a little bit without meaning to.

"Thanks," I said, as he closed the door.

Brad got into the front seat and I settled into mine as we
pulled out onto the street. The inside of the car was warmer
than my apartment, and the light was dim. I felt as safe and
happy there as if it were familiar to me. Which was strange—

"Say," I said, leaning forward. "Were you driving down
Third Street earlier this morning—at about nine o'clock?"

"No." His voice was pleasant enough when he said it, but
he didn't look at me.

"Oh," I said.

"Why?" he asked after a moment. "Did you see a car like
this one on Third Street?"

"Yeah, I did. It drove by twice, actually. I saw it from my window. It was going really slowly, and it just seemed strange, because I don't usually see limousines around this neighborhood, you know?"

"Oh," Brad said. "Well, you can ask Ludwig when you see him, I guess. I don't know anything about it at all." He made a little noise like he was clearing his throat, or it might have been a snort.

I tried to catch his eye in the rearview mirror, but he still wouldn't look at me. There was something like a little bit of a smile, maybe, in one corner of his mouth, but I couldn't be sure.

"I guess if you did know anything, you wouldn't tell me," I ventured finally.

Brad didn't answer. I leaned back again in the leather seat and looked out the window at the gray streets.

WE PULLED up in front of a nice-looking building on Commerce Street, in the West Village, and Brad turned and looked over his shoulder at me.

"It's number one," he said. "Just ring the buzzer."

"I don't get the door opened for me on my way out?" I asked.

"What?"

"Never mind," I said, reaching for the handle.

"Oh, shit. I'm sorry. I was driving for a car service for the past two years," Brad said, getting out of his seat. "I never forget with him," he continued, pulling my door open. "It's just when there's someone else, sometimes I—"

"I was just kidding," I said as I climbed out. "I can't even afford to take taxis. I'm not really used to having doors opened for me."

"Well, I know. That's probably why I . . . Well, I don't mean it that way but—"

"Forget it; I know. Thanks," I said.

I went up the steps and pressed the buzzer.

"Yes?" said a young-sounding voice. It definitely wasn't Ludwig.

"It's Cleo Pira. I'm—"

The buzzer interrupted me, so I pushed the door open. I found myself in a little hallway, and to my left an apartment door was opening. Behind it there was a boy, maybe fifteen years old, with blond hair and strikingly pretty features: wide-set blue eyes, a blunt nose, and a full mouth. He was wearing a very neat black butler's uniform that looked vaguely obscene in combination with his childlike beauty, as though he'd been dressed up to take part in someone's fantasy.

"You're Cleo?" he asked. He had a normal teenager's voice, with just a hint of unintentional sullenness.

"Yup," I said.

"Cleo Pira," he shouted into the apartment.

"Show her in, please," came Ludwig's voice from inside. It sounded quiet and controlled. There was something disorienting about all of this: first Brad, and then this slouching boy in his perfect butler's uniform.

The boy led me into a dim entrance hall, and then into a brighter room to the right that seemed to be a study. The walls were lined with books, and in front of the windows there was a broad desk that held piles of papers and a very small, sleek computer. Ludwig was standing by the desk, stiffly, with one hand resting on it. He was wearing a long tailored linen shirt

with a high collar and a pince-nez with a fine gold chain that
ended in his breast pocket. As the boy showed me into the
room, Ludwig turned his head toward me, and his ears and
whiskers seemed to strain forward as he focused his gaze on
my face.

"Cleo," he said.

"Yup, it's me," I said. The boy left the room.

Ludwig cocked his head very, very slightly to the side and
looked at me for a couple of seconds.

"I wanted you to see my study. I am a historian. I believe
I told you this."

"Yes," I said.

He turned away from me and toward the window, which
looked out onto a bright, gardened courtyard.

"This is all so terribly strange, you see," he said softly, to
the window.

I gazed out into the yard with him for a moment in silence.
There were some small trees there, to which a few last ragged
leaves clung, and the bases of the trees were surrounded by
creeping ivy, which was still green in spite of the cold weather.
A walkway, paved with stone, wound between them.

"Perhaps if I show you some pictures of Maria Rank, you
will understand," Ludwig said finally.

"I'd like that."

He reached over and picked up a silver-headed cane that
was leaning against the desk.

"So," he said, moving toward a doorway to my left. "Come
with me. I keep them in here."

I followed him into a little room just off the study that
contained a couple of armchairs and some expensive-looking
antique lamps on low tables. There were a few bookcases
against the walls, and in between them hung the paintings.

All of them showed the same woman; she had pale skin and dark brown hair. Ludwig led me over to the largest, which hung on the far wall. It showed Maria from the waist up, wearing a simple burgundy-colored dress, against a brownish background.

There was something compelling, and surprising, about her face. Her eyes were black, as I'd expected in my dream, but other than that she didn't look precisely as I'd imagined. At first glance she appeared childlike, because of her high forehead and large, slightly startled eyes, but her mouth, which was small, had a firmness and a kind of ironic twist to it which suggested that she knew something. It might have been a secret about the person she was looking at, or about herself. If you had covered the lower part of her face with your hand, she would have looked terrified, but the set of her mouth hinted at a hidden cleverness or power. She sat stiffly, but she was leaning forward a bit, as if she were trying to restrain herself from doing something but might, at any moment, lose the battle, and she was staring straight ahead as if she could see the consequences of her actions playing themselves out before her, and didn't like them.

"These paintings have a very strong effect on me," Ludwig said.

"Yes," I said. "Who painted them?"

"They were all painted by a Frenchman named Dominique Clément. He was her lover." Ludwig led me over to the painting on the right. Here Maria was dressed in a long robe of dark blue and green silk. She was leaning back on a pale couch, her hair unbound and spread out behind her, her eyes half-closed, looking down at—well, at Ludwig and me as we stood in front of the picture. The robe was open a little in the front, and from her throat almost to the middle of her stomach a long, curving line of white skin showed. It reminded me of one of the paths in Ludwig's courtyard; there was something irresistible about its shape, like that of a road winding through hills.

"Cleo," Ludwig said suddenly, "I wish to tell you something."

"What?" I asked.

"I drove past your apartment this morning," he said.

"You did?"

Ludwig looked at me, unblinking, his hands folded over the top of his silver-headed cane. "I know you saw the car," he continued, "because I saw you sitting at the window. So I thought I should tell you. I hope it didn't disturb you, or—but I simply wanted to see where you lived."

"Oh, that's all right," I said. "I mean, it isn't much to look at. What did you want to see it for?"

"I was curious." He fixed his eyes on a lamp behind me. "I am curious about you, Cleo."

"But why?"

"Because," he said, with just the tiniest hint of exasperation in his voice, "of her." He gestured to the painting next to us. "Can't you see the—the resemblance?"

I looked up again into Maria's half-closed eyes.

"No," I said. "I can't see it at all." I couldn't seem to pull my gaze away from the picture. "I mean—she's beautiful."

"Yes, she is beautiful."

"I'm flattered that you'd think I look like that," I said. "But . . ."

"Well," Ludwig said, "perhaps it doesn't matter. It's unlikely that you're related to her, I suppose."

"I don't have any German ancestors, as far as I know."

Ludwig rested his cane against the wall and then leaned

against the wall himself, in between the two paintings. He took off his strangely shaped spectacles, with their wide silver band in the middle that arched over his muzzle, and pressed his hands, in their delicate fawn-colored gloves, against his eyes. His ears turned sideways a little and he sighed through his nose, which looked damp.

"I remember in Rankstadt . . ." he began slowly. "In Rankstadt, in the winter, when I was a puppy. It was near Christmastime, I believe, and . . . I was trotting along beside Prinzi von Sacher, on the street. She was the eldest daughter in my master's family. I was very young, eight months, perhaps, for I was still allowed to go on all fours. At one year of age we must—we had to begin to walk upright.

"I was going along beside Prinzi's skirt, you know, a very long, big skirt, very noisy, so fascinating for a puppy. And her coat! She had such a wonderful coat, trimmed with fur. It was ermine. I wanted to chew on it, but of course I knew—so I used to just brush up against it with my muzzle, and just open my mouth a little bit, so that perhaps the fur would graze the edge of my tongue, and I could imagine *exactly* what it would be like to chew on it.

"So—but it must be very hard for you to imagine that street, Cleo. It was so different from anything here." He looked at me as though he wanted an answer, but then he went on before I could have said anything.

"Horse dung, and straw, on the packed snow, the orange color of the lamplight, the smells of almonds and hazelnuts and honey and wheat, the bloody sawdust spilling out from under the door of the butcher's shop, which one always wanted so badly to *lick* . . .

"But we went into the butcher's shop that day!" he said, as

if he was surprised to find himself back in the middle of this
story. "Yes. I saw the sawdust on the snow a few feet in front
of us, and I thought to myself, I mustn't look at it too closely
when we go by, or I won't be able to resist it; I told myself to
concentrate on the skirt, to my left, and I did, and then suddenly I ran straight into it, because Prinzi had turned aside to
go into the butcher's shop.

"She kicked me a little with her foot and I went around
the doorjamb and sat next to the wall, as I was supposed to,
and I was in agony. The shop was busy, because it was Christmas Eve, I think, and so the floor had gotten very dirty, and
all around me, the blood . . . blood, and scraps of twine, covered
with grease, and feathers—my God. What happened to that
world? It's all gone."

I waited for Ludwig to continue, but he didn't. He had put
his spectacles back on again, and he stood with his hands
pressed against the wall behind him. He looked exhausted and
slightly surprised, as if he really had been back in Rankstadt
for a few minutes and had just returned.

"Is it really gone?" I asked.

"Yes, of course. We destroyed it." He lifted his head toward
me and stared.

He seemed to have fallen into some private well of sadness,
and I didn't know how to rescue him from it. I felt that his
world wasn't as lost as he thought it was, because I *could* see
it, the sawdust thickened with blood and pieces of half-melted
snow, the damp, uneven hems of the dark skirts almost trailing
in it, the shiny curls of twine. I was sure I could see it; I wanted
to so badly. I wanted to tell him that, but then I thought that
it couldn't be any help to him, really.

"Is that the end of the story?" I asked.

"It's strange . . ." he said, picking up his cane and standing away from the wall. "I cannot . . . seem to remember what the point of it was."

He studied the tangled fringe of an Oriental carpet on the floor, his ears forward as if he was listening for something, but then seemed to give up.

"My memory *is* failing," he said.

I didn't know what he meant, yet. I was sure that he could pick up the thread of his thought somewhere if he tried.

"Did you like Prinzi?" I asked.

"Oh yes," he said. "I admired her."

"And—do you miss her?"

Ludwig snorted. "She is dead," he said, "massacred, all of them."

"Did the dogs kill all the people in Rankstadt?"

"Yes. And it solved nothing. Nothing was solved. We have money now, perhaps we are not slaves, but we are still monsters. From the moment Augustus Rank conceived of us, our fates were sealed. From the moment he was born . . ."

The hairs on the back of his neck were raised, and he fixed me with a stare that was so intense that I wanted to look away, but I didn't. I knew he was thinking of Maria Rank as he looked at me, but I couldn't grasp exactly what he was feeling about her, or me for that matter.

"You have *everything*," he said.

I thought of his limousine, and how much warmer it had been in there than in my apartment.

"No I don't."

"The whole world," he said, "is yours, in a way that it can never belong to me. You do not understand this."

It was true, I didn't.

"Poor Cleo," he said, straightening his back, and taking a step toward the middle of the room. "I am showing you all my—anger, for things that are not your fault. Perhaps it's time for us to have lunch now."

WE SAT down to plates of trout and boiled new potatoes, laid out by the butler. The meal didn't strike me as something that a dog would like, but Ludwig seemed to enjoy it. I did, too; it was even better than the food at the restaurant Sam had taken me to the night before.

Ludwig sat with his hind feet on the seat of the chair and his back straight. He used the silverware in the old European way, keeping the fork in his left hand. He didn't take his gloves off to eat. His movements were graceful, but they were all very careful, too, and I could see that it took effort for him to stay balanced in the chair without putting his hands on the table, especially if he had to reach forward for anything. But he never used his hands to support himself.

Once when I passed him the bread, without thinking I set it down a few inches beyond the far edge of his plate, and I watched with fascination how he flipped his tail upward to hook it under one of the horizontal slats in the back of his chair, to keep himself from falling as he leaned over to get the silver wire basket.

"You are laughing at me," he said.

"No, I was just noticing how you used your tail . . ."

"How could you do anything but laugh at me?" He paused. "It's all right."

"But I wasn't."

"Of course you were. I can imagine what I look like to you. It's awkward, and I don't do a very good job. Your world wasn't designed for dogs."

"I know."

"You *don't* know."

"All right, I don't know," I said. I could feel tears stinging somewhere in the upper part of my nose.

We ate the rest of the meal in silence. When we were finished, Ludwig looked up at me, folding his napkin in his hands. He seemed tired.

"Will you stay for coffee?" he asked. "I don't drink it, but I will be glad to offer you some."

"No," I said. "But thank you very much for lunch."

"Thank you for coming."

"Listen, I didn't mean to offend you," I said. "I'm sorry if I have."

Ludwig closed his eyes for a second. "You haven't."

He pushed against the edge of the table to move his chair back a little, then lowered his feet to the ground one at a time, holding on to the edge of the table as he stood up. I got up, too.

"I'll see you to the door," he said.

At the door, leaning on his cane, he offered me his hand and held mine for a moment in his stiff mechanical grip.

"Goodbye, Cleo. I hope I will be able to see you again," he said.

"I'd like that a lot," I said. "I really would."

BUT I didn't hear from him for a long time. Since he didn't like the telephone, I sent him a note thanking him for lunch, and then I waited, but he didn't write. I thought that he wouldn't, that he was finished with me. I didn't know what he had wanted from me, but I felt that he hadn't gotten it.

The days went by, and the nights got longer and darker as winter set in. I caught a cold, and when I lay on my bed at night it felt hard as a board under me, the pavement jarred my bones when I walked, and even the air seemed to press in heavily against my skull. The whole physical world seemed to have become unyielding to me. I felt that I'd come so close to getting something I'd wanted and missed it, and I didn't think I'd get another chance.

In December the dogs held a Christmas Parade, and the whole city turned out to watch. New York was lit up fantastically, as it is every Christmas, with strings of lights hung in every window and lobby, draped around potted bushes and strung in the bare branches of trees along the curbs, wound messily around fire escape banisters and scaffolding poles. They closed off Fifth Avenue from Sixtieth Street to Washington Square for the parade, and, since the dogs wanted to ride in sleighs, artificial snow was spread along the length of it, making one quiet wintry path down the middle of the island.

My friend Monica had the good luck to be house-sitting over the school break at the apartment of a rich family friend, which overlooked Fifth Avenue just a few blocks north of Washington Square. There was a tiny curved terrace with an elaborate wrought-iron banister, barely big enough for two people to stand on, and we watched the parade from there. It was snowing, just a flurry, but enough to add a little soft, extra light to the air. We stood in our coats with mugs of cocoa in our hands as the procession passed beneath us, white limousines draped with gold and silver bunting, followed by forty sleighs of different shapes and sizes, each hung with lanterns and drawn by a team of white horses with bells on their harnesses and tall plumes on their heads. The velvet seats inside the sleighs matched the color of the plumes on the horses' heads, red, blue, and green, and the dogs sat in groups of two and three, wearing their military uniforms, ball gowns, tails and top hats, or wrapped in enormous coats.

"That's extravagant," Monica said, looking at a Doberman in a full-length sable. "Wearing that when you already have fur."

I sighed, leaning on the terrace railing.

"You love them," Monica said.

"I do, they're wonderful," I said. "So?"

"So nothing. Just making an observation. You should write about this for the school paper, you know. We have perfect seats." She snapped her fingers. "And I have a camera inside!"

"Get it! We'll have a cover story," I said. "Unless one of their staff writers got a better view."

"I'll bet they didn't," she said. "And you can throw in some stuff about Ludwig, how you met him."

"Quick, get the camera before they're all gone. We can write the story later."

WE DECIDED that Monica would take the pictures and I would write the article. I wanted to mention Ludwig, but I hadn't seen him in the parade, and when it came down to it, I wasn't sure he would have liked my describing our lunch together in the school newspaper. Still, I managed to say something about him to the editor of *The Courier,* and when she asked me if I could get an interview with him I said maybe I could, someday. Really, I never would have asked him to do something like that, even if I did get to speak to him again. But the editor took the article and it came out in January, when the spring semester started. It was on the front page, with two of Monica's photographs in the middle.

One of the photographs, shot almost straight down from our balcony, showed the intricate shapes of the dogs' sleighs nearly silhouetted against the luminous snow on the avenue, while the flakes in the air made blurry halos around the lanterns that hung from them; and the other showed the sleighs and limousines when they had gathered in a semicircle at the end of the parade, just a little down the avenue from us, under the big arch in Washington Square, while Klaue Lutz, the Malamute who seemed to be everywhere in the news, stood at a podium in the middle, making a speech.

By the time the paper came out I had given up hope of ever hearing from Ludwig again, but I sent him a copy of the paper because it was an excuse to write to him. I thought the article was pretty good.

THE COURIER
JANUARY 25, 2010

MONSTER DOGS' CHRISTMAS PARADE

New York's most extraordinary residents, the monster dogs, held what was billed as their "First Annual Christmas Parade" on Fifth Avenue on Wednesday, December 23. Artificial snow paved the way for gold and silver sleighs shaped like swans, dolphins, lions, and ships. The forty sleighs might almost have been escapees from a giant nineteenth-century carousel, except for a few that were made to look like rocket ships or Rolls-Royces, and one that can only be described as a cross between the Batmobile and a manta ray, a triangular construction with an extremely sharp nose that seemed a continual menace to the backsides of the horses pulling it.

Streamers of metallic blue, green, red, silver, and gold had been handed out to parade watchers and could be seen spiraling and waving in the air above their heads, yet the crowd was surprisingly still and quiet for such a tightly packed bunch of New Yorkers at a festive event. There was almost a feeling that too much noise might make the illusion of the monster dogs vanish from before our eyes.

Some people are surprised they haven't vanished yet: been debunked, proved to be a collective hallucination. More than a year after they first arrived on the shores of our island, we still can't help wondering, How can we be seeing them, not just on television or in a newspaper but right here in front of our faces? We want proof that they are "real," we want an "explanation," but nothing that has been offered so far seems to satisfy us as "believable." Maybe what amazes us most is the way the dogs keep going around in their top hats and big skirts, being beautiful spectacles for us, as if they had no idea that half the people in the world know for certain that they don't, can't possibly, really exist.

At the end of the parade, on a stage under the Washington Square Arch, Klaue Lutz (the Malamute whose blue-eyed, bespectacled face is familiar to anyone who hasn't been living in a cave for the past year) announced that the dogs plan to construct a building on the Lower East Side—not just any building, but a huge, white, turreted castle, which is to be a "gift from the monster dogs to the people of New York." It will be patterned after the famous Neuschwanstein in Bavaria, which is also the model for the Disneyland castle. But the dogs' version, Lutz said, will be much better, a replica of the original that will take up an entire city block.

Why are they giving this gift to the city? What did we do to deserve it? Lutz did not explain, beyond calling New York the "best city in the world" at the end of his speech. The previously subdued crowd went wild at these last words, as if releasing all the noise it had kept pent up during the parade. We know the dogs—real or not—have good taste.

Maybe this castle of stone and mortar will be what ev-

eryone has been waiting for, undeniable "proof" that the
dogs really are here among us. But as the crowd dispersed
and blankets were thrown over the steaming horses as they
were led into waiting trailers, little evidence of their magical
presence remained. There were only a few bright streamers
fluttering from garbage cans along the street, and our photographs, news clips, and memories of the exquisite, impossible creatures waving graciously to us from their gilded
sleighs. If they are explained away, or disappear tomorrow
as mysteriously as they came, we will still have this. As the
trailers drove away, darkness and heavy snow descended on
the glittering city, bringing a cheerful, Christmasy peace to
the bustle of lower Fifth Avenue, and the memories almost
seemed enough. Almost.

After I mailed the article to Ludwig, he wrote back almost
immediately.

Dear Cleo,
   *Your article about the Christmas Parade was very
touching. It made me sorry that I was not able to be
there.*
   *I am afraid I have not been a very good correspondent
lately. You must forgive me; I have much to occupy my
mind these days. I hope we will be able to have lunch
together again soon.*

                                        Yours,
                                        Ludwig von Sacher

Then I didn't hear from him for another month. His next
letter surprised me:

Dear Cleo,

I hope you will not be offended when I tell you that I have been talking about you with a dog named Klaue Lutz, and he has decided that he would like to meet with you, if it is convenient for you.

The dogs have recently established a Society to look after our communal interests. Mr. Lutz is our treasurer, and he is also in charge of planning a special project which he conceived himself. This project is the subject he would like to discuss with you. I will leave it to him to tell you the details, as he asked me to, and say only that he is very eager to meet with you. I enclose his telephone number. He asks that you give him your reply as soon as possible.

I would be glad to see you again. At present I am very busy, but I hope we will be able to arrange to meet again soon, perhaps before the end of the winter.

Monica was at my apartment on the afternoon when I got the letter, and she read it over my shoulder.

"Before the end of the *winter*?" I said.

"So what? That's only next month. Forget about Ludwig, anyway. Look," Monica said, taking the second page from my hands, "you've got Klaue Lutz's phone number. If you got an interview with him, I'll bet Jeanne would let you do every *Courier* cover story from now until May. Your career would be launched."

"What career?"

"As a journalist."

"But I don't want to be a journalist," I said. Monica couldn't get out of business studies because of her family and she hated them, so she was forever trying to invent interesting jobs for me.

"Pre-Carolingian women's studies is not a career. At least call him and see what he wants."

"I took one course in pre-Carolingian women," I said. "My major is history."

"Whatever. Just call him."

"I will."

AT THE Dogs' Club on Fifth Avenue, where I was to meet Klaue, the front door was finished in such a deep lacquer that it picked up all the frantic colors of the city evening behind me and transformed them, in its reflections, into a gentle, rich wash. I stared at it after I had rung the bell, slightly mesmerized, until a dignified middle-aged butler surprised me by opening it. He looked me over quickly, nodded, and led me, without a word, into an anteroom whose dark red walls and mahogany floors, half-hidden by a deep Turkish carpet, seemed to silence the noise of the street even before he had shut the door behind me. As I followed him up the staircase that led from the front room, I saw that the walls were lined with sconces in which gas flames burned. There might have been no electricity in the building at all as far as I could tell.

I was directed to a room that opened off the narrow hallway to the left of the staircase. Here the only sources of illumination were two large candelabra on a small rectangular table. Framed by them, at the far side of the table, sat Klaue Lutz.

"Cleo Pira," the butler said. Then he disappeared, quietly, and I was left alone with the dog.

"Miss Pira," said Klaue, rising from his seat and holding his hand out across the table. "Or may I call you Cleo?"

"Yes, please do," I said. His mechanical hand closed in a slow, deliberate way around mine and then released it.

"Please sit down. And I would like you to call me Klaue, if you will. I am very delighted to make your acquaintance. Ludwig has told me that you are a freelance writer."

"Well . . ." I said.

Klaue held up his hand. "But we will talk about that later. Now I would like to discuss a certain project with you, about which I believe you have heard something already—the construction, by the Society of Dogs, of a castle on the Lower East Side of Manhattan." He watched me intently as he spoke.

I nodded, and then Klaue looked down at the table and was silent for a long time, as if he was gathering energy. His long black-and-white fur was combed precisely back on his face, and nothing moved, not his ears, which were turned straight forward, or his nose, or a single whisker, only his eyebrows, occasionally, when he blinked. I was just getting uncomfortable enough to say something, anything, when he drew in his breath sharply and began to speak.

"It won't be long, now, before we can begin to build the castle," he said. As he raised his eyes, they caught the light from the candles in the middle of the table and glowed blue for a moment. Their sudden flash was startling, and he must have caught a look of surprise on my face, because he dropped his gaze again as he continued.

"My colleague Adolphus is closing the real estate deal now. We can begin tearing down the building within the month."

"Which building?" I asked.

"The one called Red Square, at Avenue A and Houston Street. I suspect it will not be much missed. It is a cheaply constructed—an ugly—ah, monstrosity."

"But . . . aren't there people living in it?" I asked.

"That has already been taken care of," Klaue answered.

"What did you do, pay them all off? I didn't realize the Society of Dogs—I mean, I know you're rich—"

The Malamute's mouth opened a fraction of an inch, and I could see his red tongue folded between his lower canines. Then he closed his jaws with a snap.

"We gave them some money. We also made certain promises . . ." He paused, and his nostrils flared slightly.

"Promises like what?"

"It does not matter," he said.

"What do you mean, it doesn't matter?"

Klaue gave a short laugh, whose hollow echo seemed to describe the exact dimensions of his mechanical speaking apparatus. It was an affected and ugly attempt to sound human.

"My dear Cleo," he said, touching his gloved fingertips together, "my purpose tonight is not to tell you the details of our financial operations. I have asked you to come here because of your friendship with Ludwig, and because of the article you have written. I have read it, and I like it. I believe you are a human who is capable of being sensitive to our particular issues. Therefore, I would like you—and only you—to write about the construction of our castle.

"If you wish to accept my offer, you must agree to publish articles that meet with my approval. You see, there are certain things which we as a Society must keep to ourselves—"

"You mean you want to censor my writing," I said.

"Precisely. But only if you accept my offer. And you are certainly under no obligation to do so."

"No, I suppose you wouldn't have much trouble finding someone else. Anyone would want this job."

"Of course."

"And would I be able to attend the Society's meetings?" I asked.

Klaue nodded. "You would be the only human in a roomful of dogs, hearing what we say among ourselves. You might find it interesting."

I searched his face, but couldn't find whatever it was I was looking for there. "Nobody's ever been allowed to do that, have they?" I asked.

"No. And nobody ever will be allowed to, after these articles are written," Klaue said.

"But why would you choose me, when you could have almost anybody in the world you wanted? I've hardly written anything."

"I am not concerned about the amount of experience you have had. You will learn. What interests me is the—the quality of your vision, Cleo. A certain receptivity."

Klaue touched his fingertips together again, in a studied gesture that was beginning to annoy me. He gazed at me over the candles, his ears cocked forward.

"I see," I said, but I didn't. Unless maybe "receptivity" meant something like—maybe he believed that since I was young and awed by the dogs, I wouldn't have many ideas of my own that conflicted with his, or if I did, it would be easy to talk me out of them.

Well, he could be right, I thought. There was nothing in my mind at that moment but desire for what he was offering. And then, maybe he did like my writing, too.

"All right, I'll do it," I said.

"Good girl," Klaue said, showing a little too much of his tongue. "That is all for tonight. I will call for you again."

"Fine," I said, following him as he rose and went to the door.

"Do you need money for a cab?" he asked, holding the door open.

"Well, no, not really."

"Please," he said. He extended a hundred-dollar bill.

"Oh, no. I'm not going to take that."

"You will take it," he said, lifting my arm and prying open my hand with unnaturally strong fingers. "I know freelance writers are not wealthy. I do not wish you to incur any expenses on our account. I want us to be on good terms."

He clamped the bill into my hand and patted my shoulder.

I shrugged. "Okay, Klaue, I'm not going to fight with you about it."

"No. You are not going to fight with me at all. Good night, Cleo."

I CALLED Monica afterward and told her what had happened.

"Weird," she said. "So it looks like you are going to be a journalist after all."

"I guess so."

"Trust me, this is going to be great for you," she said. "Just . . ."

"What?"

"I don't know, be careful."

4

I am alone in the world, a ludicrous animal. I emerged from
my memory lapse a few hours ago, and—I cannot describe my
state of mind since then. I would like to put it down; I would
like the world to have a record of it. I feel as though it's the
only thing that can pin me down, fix me as a presence, however
brief, in this world. And yet I can't bear to imagine anyone
reading of this—what is happening to me now. I will write it,
though; maybe I will destroy the papers later.

There were piles of feces in the corners of my apartment. I
am half-starved—apparently I was not able to get any food,
and everything that was here before had been eaten. My servant
has been out of town for the week, but I thank God, because
I would rather have died of hunger than have been found by
him as I was. The front door and the floor beneath it are ruined
with scratch marks, and the fingertips of my prosthetic hands
are now tangles of tiny frayed wires and torn rubber. The mid-

dle finger of my left hand no longer functions. Several of my
teeth are chipped, and my nose and tongue are cut and
bruised. Much of my furniture and all of my rugs have been
destroyed—they have been torn up and they are soaked with
urine. So it seems that I reverted to the state of a normal dog.

When I emerged from this state at one o'clock and saw
what I had done, I sat down and howled. I howled like the
dog that I am, and I couldn't stop myself. I don't know how I
can live now—a dog can't live by himself in his own apartment.
What will I do, hire someone to walk and feed me when I
relapse? Of course, hiring someone is a ridiculous idea now;
they would only put me out on the street and take my money
—what could I do about it? A dog has no money. A dog has
no rights. A dog has no way to communicate his grievances. I
am a dog. God help me.

Of course, I know what I will do. I can try to escape into
the country while I am still in my right mind and hope to
survive by my instincts alone. I don't know if I will be able to
do this, though. A real dog, born in the woods, would be able
to live that way—I am not even a real dog. But what other
choice do I have? I have friends who would take care of me,
but I could never let them see me this way—I would rather
kill myself. That is my other choice, of course. I will probably
die soon if these lapses continue to occur more frequently and
to last longer each time, as they have been doing. If I have any
strength of will, I should decide to end my life.

But what about my project? There is no one who can finish
it. As Lydia pointed out, the history of Rank must be recorded
by a dog, and there is no other dog living who could do it—
or, more to the point, who would do it. None of them care as
much as I do.

Yet I often ask myself what I hope to gain by re-creating

Rank, by capturing his essence in such a way that it can be presented to the world. It seemed clear to me once that it needed to be done. I felt that the dogs' identities were tied to our understanding of Rank, and of his purpose in creating us. But if the other dogs don't care—and certainly the rest of the world doesn't care—then maybe it is not necessary. We have a new home now; we have money and no masters; why not let ourselves be absorbed into this new world? What does it matter if we don't understand our purpose?

But—

Lydia told me recently that she had experienced something similar to my memory lapses; she called them "brief episodes of confusion." If I am correct in my belief that my disease is connected to the disappearance of Rank's spirit, and if other dogs are also beginning to experience the same symptoms, it may be that my work could save all the dogs, even though they don't yet understand its importance.

I will keep trying for as long as I can.

FROM THE PAPERS OF LUDWIG VON SACHER
FEBRUARY 21, 2010

Under the tutelage of Dr. Buxtorf, Augustus soon became the most highly respected, if not the most well liked, student at the University of Basel. He continued his work with animals, and was allowed free access to the laboratories and equipment at all hours to pursue his projects. In his diaries, he often mentions working through the night, sometimes for several nights in a row. This may be when his addiction to cocaine began, although he does not refer to it explicitly until much later.

The professor discovered that he had, by a strange accident of fate, lived while on sabbatical in a house adjacent to the

Ranks' residence in Frankfurt when Augustus's mother was still alive. Although he himself had only dim memories of the family and almost none of the young Augustus, his wife remembered them well and his daughter, Henriette, had been quite enamored of Frau Rank, and had spent nearly the whole summer in her garden, learning to paint and teaching Frau Rank English with books from the professor's library. Augustus wrote to his father occasionally asking for money, but seems not to have visited him even at the holidays, becoming instead a surrogate member of the Buxtorf household, to the extent that he had any family life at all. As he grew older he acquired some drinking companions among the students, and a favorite at the local brothel, but generally he preferred to spend his time alone with his experiments.

In 1881 his father's new wife, Violetta, whom Augustus had never met, wrote to him asking him to receive her son, who was Augustus's illegitimate half brother, as a guest. Because Augustus was obliged to stay in his father's good graces for financial reasons, he agreed. He describes the events that followed in detail. The photograph to which he refers in the beginning of the entry has been lost.

EXCERPT FROM RANK'S JOURNAL, AGE SEVENTEEN,
AT THE UNIVERSITY OF BASEL, DECEMBER 10, 1881

This is the street where I became an empty man, and a perfect man. This is the street where I killed my brother. In killing him, I was transformed—not into something else, but into the full realization of myself, Augustus Rank.

I have photographed this alley, a narrow stairway between two buildings which leads to a closed courtyard, for this is the site of the great event, which I will now record so that it may be known.

My half brother, Vittorio Piccolomini, was born a bastard. He was born to Violetta Piccolomini, an Italian courtesan, twenty-two years ago, the product of a brief affair between that woman and my father. My father was, of course, married to my mother at the time.

When my mother died, my father went back to Violetta. I did not learn of their marriage, or of the existence of my half brother, until about a year after my mother's death, that is to say, when my father had been married to Violetta for some months. It was very fast, you see.

Three months ago Vittorio, hearing of my success here in Basel, and himself (being stupid and vulgar) having few prospects for the future, decided to seek me out and see if he could, by using my influence here, find his way into a better stratum of society than the one into which he had been born.

I was of course obliged to introduce Vittorio into my circle of acquaintances, and it was a very unappealing business. Naturally, I could not, under the circumstances, avoid introducing him to the daughter of Professor Buxtorf, the man who has for so long been my mentor and guide in all things. Thus Vittorio met Henriette Buxtorf, who was, until recently, the focus of certain plans which I had made for the future, and which are now ruined. Although I understand now why they had to be ruined, and why Fate has set me on this course, I could not understand it then, for I was a different man.

You see, Vittorio was like an animal: lusty, stocky, muscular, stupid, and covered with hair. His soul had been corrupted by a disease, which was passion; and it emanated from his body like the glow given off by rotting fish. (The soul is very like a fish, after all, and the more so, the closer it is to the animal state, that is to say, if its human features have been worn away by sickness, as flesh is eroded by leprosy.)

I could not, at the time I met him, perceive this light, or the smell, but in memory I can see all of my past as clearly as I now see the present, and I know that it was there.

Upon his meeting Henriette, as I now know, this phosphorescence became stronger, attended by a sort of miasmic cloud that Vittorio carried around with him. Henriette, though I once believed her to be perfect, is a flawed vessel, which is to say that she has a crack, or several cracks, in the skin or armor of her own soul, and just as broken skin is infected by disease, so her ruptured soul allowed the vapors emitted by Vittorio to enter into and corrupt it.

Thus it was that while walking home very late from the university, I spied a light below the street on the riverbank, and, stopping to look, out of innocent curiosity, I saw the faces of these two unfortunate lepers, pressed very close together, and perfectly illuminated by the glow of a lantern. They were hidden from the street for the most part, but I had managed to attain an angle of view such that I could just see them through a gap in the tangled branches which concealed them, by lying on the street wall and hanging my head down a little over the edge.

It was at this moment that my transformation began, though very slowly, and with a great deal of pain, so that I could not understand what was happening to me.

As I continued walking home, after I had made certain of the identities of the two people on the bank, and their intentions (which took only a few minutes to become apparent), I began to wonder where I had failed, after so many years of careful application to the task of wooing Henriette. Indeed, I had intended to ask her, in about a week's time, whether she would marry me—so confident was I of my place in her affections. This was a place to which I climbed very slowly, and for a long time, and through very many obstacles, not the least of which was my own ignorance of the ways

*of courtship and of women, and perhaps even of social intercourse
in general.*

*I spent a very uncomfortable night, too anguished to sleep, too
perplexed to make any plans for my next action, or indeed to make
any sense out of the situation at all. I wept. I am not ashamed to
admit that now, for I am no longer the man who did those things.*

*As morning came, however, the pain of the first part of my
metamorphosis eased a little, for in spending myself I had begun to
cast out some of the dead tissue which was so irritating my system.
I began to see clearly my course of action, as it had been laid out
for me by Fate, whom I have ever thought my guardian and my
goddess. She does not care equally about all men; indeed, some are
allowed to go about their lives without ever being noticed by her,
and take whichever paths strike their fancy, and follow them to
death. But this has not been the case in my life. I would even go
so far as to say that I am a special pet of hers.*

*My course, as I understood, was to kill Vittorio immediately; to
cut this element out of the body of my life, in such a way that it
would not adversely affect me. Henriette had already been infected,
but I thought then that I might try to cure her, because she was so
dear to me at the time.*

*I therefore carefully arranged things in such a way that Vittorio
and I would be out drinking, late at night, and go home together,
alone. We would pass the alley, and I would pretend to be sick,
and lead him up into it, and kill him there. He was of course very
susceptible to the influence of wine and liquor, and liked to drink.
I prepared a little powder I have learned how to make, also, to
heighten the effect.*

*All went as planned in the first part of the night, so that we
found ourselves alone near the deserted alley, reeling and laughing,
and I was able, by feigning sickness, to get him to come with me*

up to the courtyard at the top of the alley stairs. I then drew a long knife which I had with me, and held it up to his throat, warning him not to make any noise on pain of death, for (I told him) I had something which I very much wanted to say to him but which I did not think he would like to hear, and I intended to force him to listen to it.

He was very shocked, of course. His eyes were black, without any differentiation in shade between the pupil and iris, and because they were very wide open I was aware of looking into them, and I began to understand that they were in fact tunnels, or tubes, through which (particularly as the pupils were so dilated) I could actually look inside of him, almost as far as his soul. This is a common metaphor, to say that "the eyes are the windows of the soul," and so on; but I mean it literally.

I kept my gaze fixed on them, for I realized that the longer I looked, the deeper I was able to see into them, just as one's eyes adjust to a dark room and can see things better after a time. As I was doing this, I told him what I had seen two nights before, how he was lying with Henriette on the bank, and he was very surprised to hear this. I also told him that, given my intentions to propose to her, I must make sure at all costs that he did not go near her again. Of course, I expected him to promise to keep away from her, like a lying dog, and then I would have the satisfaction of slitting his throat for it.

But he did not. Instead, he told me that in fact he had already proposed marriage to her, on that very night by the river, and that she had accepted, and that they intended to elope in about a week, or about the same time when I had intended to ask for her hand. You see, he was very stupid, and he was drunk, and angry, because he was incapable of controlling his passions, so completely had they dominated his soul.

Moreover, he admitted to me (still not seeing his error) that he *had already* consummated *the union, as a way of obtaining a kind of* guarantee *from her. Furthermore, he added, if I truly loved her and cared for her happiness, more than my own, I would let him go; and he would promise to take her away that very night, so that I would never have to look on either of them again. That, he said, would be the honorable thing to do; and I would find it easiest, also, he was quite sure; easier than trying to reason with her, or otherwise continue to pursue her, for she was so completely smitten with him that I would only get failure and further humiliation for my trouble.*

When he had done with his speech, I smiled—although it was, as I now understand, a very twisted smile—and, seeing this, and misinterpreting it as evidence of an internal struggle between acceptance and deep grief, his eyes began filling with tears of compassion (such as are commonly caused by wine), and he said, "Augustus, what have I done?"

But this was the real reason for my smile: I had, while he was speaking, begun to see a cloud of red, opaque fog, such as some people say they see when they are overcome with rage, though I have never experienced this. It was extremely dense, and suffocating, and it began to block both my vision and hearing—indeed all of my senses, so that at some points I even found it difficult to continue holding the knife at his throat, for I could neither see nor feel my hand.

For a few moments this cloud increased in density, and then, just as it was at its peak, and I felt that I would lose consciousness—for it was smothering me, and I was aware of its being in my nose and mouth—I suddenly understood what it was, *and where it was coming from. It was not flowing* into *my mouth, but issuing* from *it! It was nothing other than* dead tissue, *like that material which I had first ejected during the night of violent weeping. After reaching its peak of density, it began to dissipate and my* mouth and nose became clearer as it flowed away. Of course, this emission was extremely painful, and it was accompanied by a certain amount of material vomit also, which came out of my mouth unperceived when the cloud of spiritual tissue was at its thickest.

During all this time, however, I did not remove the knife from Vittorio's throat, and thus, as my vision became clear again—indeed, much clearer than it had been before—I was able to smile, even though I was still in some pain. This was the smile that aroused Vittorio's drunken compassion.

Now, as I said, Vittorio stood before me, against the wall, his eyes filling with tears, and pronounced my name, and voiced some remorse, thus subtracting perhaps a straw's weight from the load of his sin—my vision was not yet clear enough to see exactly how much fell away. I had not intended to allow him this, but it was done.

Before he was able to unburden himself any further, I slit his throat, and it was at this moment that my transformation became complete.

I had several instantaneous revelations. First, that there exists in my soul a woman. I shall elaborate on this later. [NOTE: In fact, Rank never mentioned this again in any of the writings I have found. —Ed.]

Second, the world is made of a certain hard, dense, spiritual material which is visible to the enlightened. When I drew the knife across my brother's throat, I saw that there was a groove in the material just there, running laterally across his neck, and my hand slid through it. Nothing could have been more easy or natural, for I was meant to do it. The space was there, and I needed only to use it, and let it guide my movement.

There was a similar groove, perpendicular to the first and above it, and I inserted my left hand into this and allowed it to slide forward to cover his mouth, so that his cries would be muffled. I can now perceive the form of this material quite often, and by looking for passageways, footholds, resting places, etc., I am able to understand where I am meant to go; that is, where I can enter, climb up, stop, etc.

Third, I saw a flash of light so brilliant that it blinded me for a moment, the same moment that the blood began to spurt out of Vittorio's neck. I then saw that the luminescence was of a golden color, but brighter than anything I had ever seen, and it was only thanks to my newfound strength that it did not sear and permanently damage my eyes. For my body is stronger, too, since my enlightenment.

Now I saw that it was like a cloud, for on the edges where it was not so bright I perceived that it was made out of vapors, roiling and churning with a violent motion. In the middle of the cloud, then, appeared a figure—not a human figure, or anything language can describe—but I understood it to be Fate, my mistress, and she was exceedingly beautiful.

This figure stepped down from the center of the golden mass, and as she came into the dimmer periphery she assumed the form of a young woman, very fair and bright, and I saw that she carried a large knife, which she thrust into my chest and worked downward, slitting my torso to the pelvis. This all happened in less than an instant, you understand. Now, my organs all exposed, she came forward and pressed herself wantonly against my open body, actually entering into the cavity in my flesh. We were then consumed by an explosion of fire, and the vision ended.

There are no personal entries in Rank's diaries for the next four months. The pages of his notebooks dating from December 1881 to April 1882 are filled only with technical notes on his experiments, and after that there are no writings at all for a period of about fifteen years. However, in his papers from

Rankstadt there is one letter that sheds a little light on the circumstances of his life at the time. It was neither written by him nor addressed to him; its interest lies in the fact that it is one of the few surviving portrayals of him by a hand other than his own.

How he came to own the letter is a mystery; we can only assume that he intercepted it before it reached its intended recipient. That he was intelligent and secretive enough to do so is certain. That he had a motivation to do it is clear from its contents.

His reasons for preserving the letter until his death are less obvious. Although it is only the most unfounded speculation on my part, I imagine, frankly, that he kept it to torture himself, that he might look at it in the early mornings when he returned to his rooms, tired after many hours of work, and be reminded that the world outside his laboratory held nothing for him. He had set himself apart from that world forever when he killed Vittorio. Perhaps it was not, after all, cocaine that enabled him to work for days and nights on end in his early years but this letter written by the girl he had once loved.

June 6, 1882
My dearest Emilie,
*   I am writing to you now because I do not want you to worry about me. It has been so long since I've seen you or spoken to you. I also wish to tell you an extraordinary story, which I may not tell anyone else, but it rests so heavy upon my conscience, and you have always been such a dear friend to me, that I hope you won't mind if I unburden myself to you; only you must promise not to tell anyone, ever, on pain of my death; and you shall see why that is when I am done telling it.*

First, let me tell you that I have been married, and that I am going to have a child. I expect it in late summer. I know you will be thinking of me and praying for me during that time, for there won't be anyone else to do it. I do wish you were here to share the waiting and to while away the boring hours, for I'm hardly allowed to do anything here—but I haven't even told you my story. Let me begin.

You know how much I loved Vittorio from the first instant I saw him. I did listen to all the wise things you said to me, but in the end, when he asked me to marry him, it just wasn't any good. I can't explain why, and I don't wish to anyway. It was as if fate had drawn us together, and neither of us was able to escape it. We planned to elope, and, dear Emilie—my eyes are filling with tears now because I imagine you think that is just what we did—and if only we had! But there isn't any use crying over it now, and I think my fragile state is making me quick to tears, and I mustn't let it.

You see, Vittorio disappeared two nights after proposing marriage to me, and no one knows where he might have gone. Of course, my parents—and I had to tell them, once it was discovered I was with child—are of the opinion that he ran away, and they think that is just the sort of thing that he would have done. But I knew he hadn't run away, and now I have reason to suspect that what really happened is even worse—if anything could be worse than that.

Emilie, I think he was murdered, and there is not a soul in the whole world to whom I can tell my suspicions.

Now I am locked up in this horrible sanatorium, or whatever it is. I have a room above a little garden, and

sometimes I see people walking down there, but I am
never allowed to go down except with my nurse, and then
only when there isn't anyone else around. It doesn't matter
where it is, in any case; it's only a place my father paid
for, where I can be hidden away, so that no one can see
my disgraceful condition. I hate my father so—and God
may strike me down for saying it, I don't care. He has
told me I am to be allowed to keep the baby, but I am
not quite as stupid as he must think me. There would be
no use hiding me now if everyone in Basel were to know
I had a child afterward. It will be taken from me before I
have the chance to see it, I am sure—but there, I'm
becoming excited again.

Let me continue my story (as if that could calm me!).
Five days after Vittorio proposed to me, Augustus came
calling and I had to go out and sit in the garden with
him, as I always did. You know I never liked Augustus,
though I tried so hard to like him to make my father
happy, and Mamma told me I ought to, too. I had almost
overcome my aversion to him when I met Vittorio, but on
this day, knowing that my future was secure with Vittorio,
all my unreasoning repulsion seemed to rise again, and I
couldn't stop it. Augustus asked me what was the matter,
and whether something wasn't troubling me, and—he
seemed to know something, for he had a wicked little
smile that he kept trying to hide when I looked at him,
and it made me altogether uncomfortable.

Finally, as we were sitting on a bench at the far end
of the garden, he got down on his knees and proposed to
me! I hadn't so much as smiled at him that day, which
was not very nice of me, but wasn't it just as stupid of
him to choose that day to propose? If the best thing to

come of this whole affair in the end is that I never have to see his face again, I won't be sorry it happened. They may take my baby away from me, but somewhere in the world he will live, and he will still be Vittorio's child.

Of course, I was forced to refuse Augustus, for I could not in good conscience accept his offer and then simply disappear. He didn't seem surprised, but he kept needling me and asking, Why, Why, Why, until I wanted to slap him. Finally he left.

I guess he hadn't said anything to my father beforehand, for no one in the house seemed to know anything about the proposal, and I didn't mention it to anyone. Then I didn't see Augustus again for a long time, and I began to hope he was gone from my life altogether —but I didn't think of him very much, either, because I had heard that Vittorio was gone, and I was very upset, and spent most of the time alone, crying where no one could see me. Then my mother discovered I was with child. That was an awful affair. Of course, the first thing my mother asked me was whether it wasn't Augustus's. And I said no, and after a while I had to tell her that it was Vittorio's, and I couldn't let her think that I was any more wicked than I am, so I had to tell her Vittorio had proposed to me, and so the whole story came out.

Then my parents were very angry, and upset, and there was so much weeping and carrying on all over the house that I could hardly bear it, and I wished to be sent away. Before I left, Augustus came to call on me again, and we went out to the garden (it was impossible to see yet that I was with child), and he asked me again to marry him. He said that he knew about everything that had happened—again he had that wicked little grin that I

*just wanted to pull off his face. He asked whether I knew
that my child would be taken away from me, and I said
yes, I was sure that would happen, and he said, "Well, if
you were to marry me, we could keep it as our own, and
nobody would have to know." But you know, he's such a
stupid man, and he said it in such an evil way that I just
knew he was lying. Can you imagine Augustus caring for
another man's child—especially Vittorio's? It truly
frightens me to think what might have happened if I had
never met Vittorio, and had to marry Augustus.*

*At length, when I had refused, and he had needled and
prodded and I refused again and again, he told me that he
would leave, and never bother me anymore. I was so glad
to hear it that if I had liked him at all, I would have
embraced him at that moment, for doing me such a kind
and generous favor. But before he left, he said to me,
"Henriette, you know—I have done something that has
made me a different man. I cannot describe it to you, but
I may tell you that, in doing it, I have been given an
understanding of life and death that few men ever have. I
am now more certain than ever that I will succeed in my
work. My actions have also given me an understanding of
human nature that I had once lacked, and I believe I
could have made a better husband to you than you think.
I cannot force you to marry me, but I want you to know
that you are giving up a great deal by refusing me."*

*As he was speaking, something in his expression, I
cannot say what it was, made me dreadfully frightened,
and I was overcome with a terrible suspicion, which I was
barely brave enough to voice. And yet before I had time to
consider what I was saying, I exclaimed in a trembling
whisper, "Augustus, you have murdered someone!"*

Oh, Emilie! The moment I said it, I knew who it was, but I felt that if I said it aloud he would kill me, too! His gaze was so cold and piercing, and he seemed not to be looking at me but at something beyond me, behind me. I wanted to turn around and see what it was, but at the same time I didn't want to take my eyes off him. I knew he had killed Vittorio. You will no doubt find this hard to believe, but at the moment when I realized it, and saw his face, so grim and hard and yet with an expression as if he was searching, or waiting to take direction from some invisible person who hid in the trees above my head, I felt for the first time an inkling of sympathy toward him, for he seemed alone, and if you had not known him, you might have thought he was a brave soldier praying before a battle, although I was sure that his only enemy was his own madness. I might have slapped his face or spit in it, but I did nothing, and at length he turned away, without looking at me, and left the garden. That was the last I saw of him.

My father would never believe that he was a murderer, and especially that he had killed his own stepbrother. My family has known his family for many years, and they would never accept that it was true. They know I never liked Augustus and they are angry with me already for having refused him and betrayed him, as they believe I did, by agreeing to marry his brother. There is no one at all who would believe me if I said that Augustus was a murderer. And yet I know, I swear I know, that he did it.

Emilie, how can I bear to know that Augustus is my husband's murderer when I cannot tell anyone or have any hope of ever seeing justice served? And while this

*would be bad enough by itself, there is another ghost that
stands at my side which I can hardly bear to speak of.
You know, because I have told you, that his mother, may
she rest in peace, was a very dear friend to me at one
time. But now I can say no more because it is late and I
am very tired. I am not strong enough to bear this, but
because of my child, I will. If you would answer my letter
I would be very grateful because there is no one I can
confide in here, almost no one I can talk to at all, and it
would be a very great comfort to know that you are
thinking of me and that you do not think badly of me
because of what I have done. Please write as soon as you
can, and while I await your letter I remain, as I always
will, your loving friend, Henriette.*

5

(CLEO)

Ludwig's servant called me one day in late February and said that although Ludwig was still very busy, he would be delighted if I could come over and visit with him for a few minutes on the following afternoon. I skipped a class and came to his door at four o'clock as he'd requested. I was met there by the boy in his butler's uniform, who took my jacket and led me into the study. Ludwig was sitting in a large leather armchair, reading a book.

"Cleo," he said, standing up as I came in. "I am certainly very glad to see you again."

"I'm glad to see you, too," I said, taking his hand. His grip felt stiffer and more awkward than it had been before, and there was something sad in his eyes, an expression as though he were looking at me from a distance, having trouble making out my features.

"Why don't we have some tea, or coffee, and sit down for

a little while? I am sorry that I have such a short time to spend with you today, but I have a meeting, you see, at five o'clock. It is a dogs' meeting."

"Oh," I said. I was disappointed that Klaue hadn't invited me, but then I had met with him only once so far. "But I'm glad you could fit me into your schedule."

Ludwig nodded toward a chair, which I sat down in, and then pressed a button on his desk to ring for the butler. There was a sound of something being dropped in the kitchen.

"One of the reasons I hoped you could come today is that I wanted you to meet a friend of mine, Lydia. She will be coming over in her car to take me to the meeting, because my chauffeur is on vacation.

"We want something to drink," he said as the boy appeared in the doorway. "Cleo?"

"Coffee would be great, thanks," I said.

"I will have my usual tea."

"So what have you been doing?" I asked as the boy left. "I know you've been very busy."

"Yes, I have been working on a project," Ludwig said, nodding at some printouts that were neatly stacked on the desk.

"Oh, is that it? Can I see it?"

I caught a little gleam in his eyes, as if he'd been hoping I would ask, but he blinked and it disappeared. "You may if you like," he said. He handed the papers to me slowly.

"Do you mind if I look at it now?"

"Please, go ahead."

I saw that the short manuscript consisted of old documents that had been typed or scanned into Ludwig's computer, and notes in his handwriting explaining them. I read, for the first time, the story of Augustus Rank's beginnings.

"It's fascinating," I said after I had finished it.

"Yes, I think so," said Ludwig.

"How did you get Rank's papers?" I asked.

"When Rankstadt burned they were preserved because they were stored in an underground vault. A few of the townspeople had looked at them, but no one had ever attempted a comprehensive study. I took them before we left. I am hoping to write an entire history of the monster dogs, to tell the story from the beginning."

"When do you think you'll finish it?"

Ludwig looked out of the window of his study into the courtyard, which was now covered with snow and seemed empty under the flat yellow February sun. His fur looked dusty and stiff in the light, and I saw a few gray hairs near his nose that I hadn't noticed before.

"I don't know whether I will finish it," he said.

"Why not?"

He didn't answer.

"Are you sick?" I asked.

Ludwig turned toward me and glanced at my eyes, and then down at his desk. "Perhaps," he said. "I don't know."

"What's wrong?"

"You are asking so many questions, Cleo."

"I'm sorry."

He took a deep breath, and then said, "The other dogs do not seem to be interested in my research, so perhaps it makes no difference whether or not it is ever finished. Most of them are not curious about their past. Klaue Lutz has asked to see my writing, and I have been sending it to him, but I don't know if he reads it."

As Ludwig finished the last sentence, his ears pricked up and his nostrils flared, and he began to turn around.

"I wish you wouldn't," said a quiet voice from the doorway.

"Lydia," Ludwig said.

She entered the study, a white Samoyed with dark eyes and a fine pointed muzzle. She was wearing a long, narrow gown of pale yellow silk, low-cut so that her big mane of fur fluffed up in the front, and she carried a matching long-handled parasol, which she used for a cane. She put one yellow-gloved hand into Ludwig's as she came up to him.

"I wish you wouldn't send your manuscript to Klaue. I don't know why, but I don't trust him. It's probably silly of me . . ."

"What harm could he do with the information, even if he is not to be trusted?" Ludwig asked.

"I can't imagine. But all the same."

"Perhaps I shouldn't do it anymore, then," Ludwig said, gazing at her. "I am a historian, however, and it is difficult to deny my work to someone who seems interested.

"But I want you to meet Cleo," he added, as if he had just remembered that I was there.

"Yes, Cleo," Lydia said. She examined me with a sidelong glance before turning toward me. "I am delighted." She held out her hand and delicately took mine, looking into my face. Her eyes were large and round, giving her an expression of mild amazement, but there was a kind of peace in them, too.

"Ludwig has told me about you," she said. "You are working for Klaue now."

"Yes, it seems like I am," I said. "But you don't trust him."

She released my hand and went over to an armchair, looked at it as though she was trying to decide whether to go through the awkward maneuvering involved in sitting down, then put both her hands on the end of her parasol and lifted her head.

"He is hungry for power," she said.

"He seems to have a lot of it," I replied.

She nodded.

"What is it, exactly, that you think he might be doing?" I asked.

"I don't know," she said. "It's just something about the way he is. Don't you agree, Ludwig?"

Ludwig looked up at the sound of his name. "I have no opinion. I seldom talk to him," he said.

"Well, there isn't anything to do but wait and see," Lydia said. "We had better leave for the meeting, I think."

"Yes," Ludwig said. He pressed a button on the desk to ring for his servant.

"I'm sorry that I came too late for us to talk much, Cleo," Lydia said. "I hope we'll meet again. I really do."

"I do, too," I said.

"Well, we will, then."

The boy appeared in the study with an armload of coats. Ludwig's was long and black with pewter buttons, and Lydia's was salmon-colored and trimmed with dark auburn fur. Mine was an old leather jacket.

"I wish I could go to this meeting," I said, maybe a little petulantly.

"I do, too," Lydia said. "But I'm sure you will be at the next one."

Ludwig took his cane in one hand and held out the other arm for Lydia. We said our goodbyes at the door, and the teenage butler and I watched the dogs walk together to the limousine at the curb. They had offered me a ride, but my apartment was out of their way and I thought I'd rather walk.

When Ludwig and Lydia had disappeared behind the tinted windows of their car, the boy put his hand on my arm and said, "Listen, Cleo."

"What?"

"Ludwig likes you, right? You're friends."

"I guess so," I said.

"Well, he talks about you, anyway."

"Really? What does he say?"

The boy shrugged. "Just that he likes you," he said. "So . . . this is the thing. I don't know if you know this, but he drinks a lot."

"Drinks?"

"Like he gets drunk practically every night, maybe every other night. He just started about a month ago, but he keeps getting worse, like doing it more often. Locking himself up in his study and stuff like that. You know what I mean?"

"No, I haven't heard anything about it," I said. "Do you think Lydia knows?"

"Maybe. She seems worried about him, but I don't know if she *knows*. He doesn't really have any other friends, like, not good friends, so I kind of thought maybe I should tell you."

I nodded, trying to read his face behind the impossible prettiness of his features. The perfect muscles and curves seemed to have a personality of their own, which he had to fight to form an expression.

"Thanks for telling me. What's your name, by the way?"

"It's Rob."

"Well, I don't know what I can do . . ."

"You'll think of something." He said it in a tone of gentle encouragement that surprised me.

6

(CLEO)

About a week after visiting Ludwig I went to Klaue Lutz's apartment to begin interviewing him for the first article I was to write about the castle project.

"Where are the papers?" Klaue asked as I entered the room. It was only half-illuminated by the light from the foyer, and his desk, by the right wall, was in complete shadow. I could barely distinguish the outline of his muzzle, but as he looked toward me his eyes flared with reflected light, as they had on that first night at the Dogs' Club. He moved a fraction of an inch and they were extinguished.

"What papers?" I asked, my voice sounding too loud in the still room.

He turned back again and fixed his stare over my left shoulder so that his eyes glowed like backlit glass in the darkness as if he knew the precise angle at which to hold his head. They were a beautiful color, like the soot-dusted blue of an evening sky over Manhattan.

"The information on Rank. The manuscript," he said.

I heard Klaue's hands moving on his desk, but his eyes stayed still.

"Oh, I didn't get it. I'm sorry, but seems like Ludwig isn't talking to anyone right now. I did try, though." Klaue had asked me to bring along the latest pages from Ludwig's book, but when I had called about getting them, Ludwig had only told me, through his servant, that he was too busy to speak with me.

"I must *have* the information," Klaue said, as if I'd missed that part.

"I'm sorry. I'll try again in a few days—"

"I want the manuscript now, Cleo. I am not going to wait a few days," Klaue interrupted. His eyes flickered out briefly and then reappeared.

There was silence for a moment.

"Can I turn on a light in here?" I asked, looking at the switch by the door.

Before I could move toward it, three hundred watts of electric light blasted from the chandelier in the middle of the room, and Klaue was staring directly at me, not even blinking in the glare. His face had the focused look of an addict, but there was no desperation in it.

"I want to know what happened after Rank killed his brother. You will go out to Ludwig's apartment now. I can send an assistant with you if you wish," he said.

"Klaue, you're acting very strange," I said.

"What is strange, Cleo?" he asked, rising from his chair. He came around the side of the desk and began walking toward me, perfectly balanced without his cane.

"What do you find strange about me? Hm? Tell me what is so strange."

"Well . . ."

I was backing up, without really meaning to, as Klaue approached me. The dog spread his hands and held them up to frame his face.

"This is strange, isn't it, Cleo?"

"Yes," I replied, bumping into the wall.

"An ugly mistake made by a madman." His voice had begun to tremble.

"And his followers. With what devotion they labored, for so many years! And why? We didn't ask to be made. For Rank? But he is dead. He was dead long before we finally stopped them. So why did they do it?"

"Why *did* they?" I asked.

"*We don't know.*"

We looked at each other for a moment, and then Klaue turned and left the room. A tiny airplane crossed the glowing sky outside the window behind the desk. Then a voice behind me said, "Master Klaue has instructed me to escort you to Ludwig's apartment."

I turned to see a young man in a tuxedo. He had a pale face and hard small eyes. "Let's go," he said.

"I don't think this is going to work," I said, following him out into the foyer, where he handed me my jacket. We took the elevator down to the building's private garage, where Klaue's enormous gray limousine waited for us.

"It has to work," he said as we got in.

"IT'S CLEO Pira," I said into Ludwig's intercom.

"Cleo, what are you doing here?" said Rob.

"I know Ludwig isn't seeing anyone—"

"Hold on," he said, "I'll let you in."

He met me at the front door of the apartment. "It isn't just that. He's very drunk," he said softly.

"How drunk?" I whispered.

"You couldn't talk to him. There'd be no point."

"Well, I don't actually want to talk to him. I just need a copy of the latest part of his manuscript. It's for Klaue Lutz— you know him?"

Rob nodded slowly.

"I'm supposed to interview him tonight, but he won't do it unless I get him those pages. Do you think it would be all right?"

"What do you think?" he asked me.

I shrugged. "Ludwig mentioned Klaue the last time I was here. He seemed to want him to read it."

"Well, I think I can get it," Rob said. "But if Ludwig sees you in the apartment I'll get in trouble, so wait here."

He disappeared, and then he must have run into Ludwig because I heard him say, "It's Cleo Pira!" in a surprised voice. He was answered by a low muttering. "What?" he said. "You're speaking German." There was more muttering, then Rob said, "Okay. Okay."

He came back to the door, rolling his eyes. "He says he can see you tomorrow, for half an hour, if it's really important," he said. "Here's the manuscript. You don't have to come see him, he probably won't remember you were here."

"Do you think he really would see me tomorrow?"

Rob shrugged. "You can always try."

FROM THE PAPERS OF LUDWIG VON SACHER
NEW YORK, MARCH 3, 2010

The eventful years of Augustus Rank's life following the murder of his half brother are largely hidden from the eyes of the
historian. If Augustus kept any notebooks at all from the latter
part of 1882, when he was eighteen, until 1897, he either concealed or destroyed them. It was during these years that, by
careful design, he disappeared from the eyes of the world and
began work on the great project of his life, the monster dogs.

There are pages missing from his technical journals beginning in early 1882, about a month after he murdered his half
brother, which suggests that he began to plan his project at that
time and later removed the notes relating to it. After April of
1882 there exist no writings of any kind. It may be surmised,
then, that it was at about this time that Rank first met with his
future patron, Prince Friedrich Wilhelm Viktor Albert von
Hohenzollern, later to become Wilhelm II, ruler of the German
Empire.

It is known from the writings of Rank's assistants that an
elaborate laboratory and barracks were built by Prince Wilhelm, after some complicated political maneuvering, in Bavaria,
deep underground beneath the ruins of a monastery near a
town called Rupertsberg. Eighty-seven scientists, laborers, and
their families were recruited by Wilhelm at great expense and
moved into the living quarters to assist Rank, and all were
sworn to secrecy. The laboratory was completed and the staff
assembled by October of 1882.

Since the staffing and equipping of the laboratory must have
been an elaborate process, it may be assumed that it was begun
no later than early summer and that, therefore, Wilhelm stood
ready to assist Rank soon after their initial meeting. In other

words, he was very quickly converted to Rank's cause, a fast and enthusiastic friendship developing between the young scientist and the prince.

Wilhelm would have been twenty-three years old at the time of their first meeting, a bright, determined, somewhat impractical and egotistical young army officer, devoted to the military, fascinated by technology if vague in his understanding of it, and restless for power—for his grandfather, Wilhelm I, was still strong and hearty, and his father Friedrich stood next in line for the throne, so that Prince Wilhelm could not expect to possess it for many years.

He had, in addition to these characteristics, which must have disposed him toward the young Rank, the interesting feature of a withered arm, which had been crippled since birth, and it may be imagined that he would have been particularly interested in the potentials of prosthetics and the grafting of limbs; a curiosity which Rank, of course, shared. There was also, as in Rank's case, a lifelong antipathy between the young man and his mother (in Wilhelm's case the British princess Victoria) possibly aggravated by his disability, certainly perpetuated by differences in personality.

So the young men's meeting may be imagined: Augustus happens on an introduction, or perhaps engineers it, searching for a patron for his project; he offers his services to the empire. But a sudden friendship develops, there is animated conversation, fevered plans are laid. Wilhelm decides to take on the project himself, without seeking assistance from his grandfather, the Emperor, who would no doubt scoff at it, and the barriers of secrecy are erected. For of this there is no doubt: Rank and his work were meant to disappear from the face of the earth until the project was completed and Wilhelm, who by then could be expected to have ascended the throne, could present to the world, in its full glory, his perfect army of dog soldiers.

We know from later writings that this army was to be impossible to defeat, its members fierce, numerous, and disposable (for more could always be made), capable of remorseless killing and of loyalty stronger than their instincts for self-preservation. The dogs' intelligence was to be enhanced in order to enable them to understand complex orders and battle plans. Likewise the intricate mechanical hands that were to be grafted onto their forelegs, and the speech-synthesizing apparatuses that were to be implanted in their throats, were intended solely to enable them to handle weapons and to communicate easily with officers and other soldiers. In every other respect they were to remain as they were in their normal domesticated state, where they were already nearly perfect soldiers.

So in 1882 Rank disappeared. It is possible that he encouraged Wilhelm to hide the project, and thus hide him, because he feared being arrested for the murder of Vittorio; in any case, he was probably glad of the chance to escape the city. It would have been difficult for any other mortal to endure the conditions under which Rank lived for the next fifteen years, but with his single-minded devotion to his work and the other motives he may have had, it may be imagined that he went gladly to his new home.

In the early years, many of Rank's helpers deserted the project. Although they had limited access to the countryside around the monastery, the workers, with Rank himself, lived for the most part without sunlight and in strenuous, lonely conditions, and for some it was not worth even the extravagant salaries Wilhelm paid them. But, fearing the prince's wrath, none seems to have spread information about the goings-on in the underground colony. The ones who stayed were, of necessity, highly devoted to their work and their leader. At the end of the fifteen years Rank spent at Rupertsberg there were, after the fluctuations of escapes, births, and deaths, fifty-five men, women, and children in his entourage.

Little else is known about those years, and that is unfortunate indeed, for it would be quite interesting to know by what means Rank kept and ruled over the workers who stayed with him through all of those sunless, difficult years. It can be imagined, from the nearly religious devotion that the humans I knew during my lifetime afforded his memory, that his strong conviction and singleness of purpose lent him a certain amount of charisma, and that he was able to transfer his passion for the great project to those who labored under him, but specifically how he did this remains unknown, for no papers remain from those years at Rupertsberg.

Rank began writing, or saving, journal entries again in 1897, several months before he was to leave the underground facilities, and this is where he first mentions his addiction to cocaine and his "disposal" of unruly followers, circumstances which must have existed for many years prior to the writings, but which perhaps became worse in his last months in Bavaria. In May of 1897 he wrote:

The pressures on me are unbearable. I sometimes feel them crushing my skull so that when I look about the room my vision is fractured, splintered by the weight. The project is to be finished in five months. I have long known that this is impossible, but soon I will no longer be able to hide it from the Emperor. Now I must decide whether to renegotiate, and ask for ten more years, or escape.

And later:

My preliminary discussions with Wilhelm have gone very badly. He has promised me two extra years, no more, and he is, as always, impatient and obstinate, to such a degree that he said that if I were not finished in two years, he would remove me as head of "his" project and install a more suitable replacement, whom he has already chosen.

So I must escape. I have planned for years for this eventuality. The loyalty of my followers is cemented. The new laboratory will be, as it should be, completely under my control. The lack of funds will make our work more difficult, but we have collected a great deal of gold and other riches, so that we will not want for anything for some time.* We will travel to a place where we can live in the sunlight, farm, and possess land. All will be well. And yet as the fifteen-year mark approaches I cannot help remembering my youthful enthusiasm and belief that I, and Wilhelm also, would still be young and powerful when the army of dogs was completed. It is unfortunate that this will not come to pass. But the project may be finished twenty years from now, if the breeding of the dogs can be accelerated according to my most recent plan, and I will then still be strong enough to lead the army. And when I bring them to Wilhelm then, in reality, unlike in my youthful dream, either he will accept my leadership immediately or I will march against his army and force him to accept it, and there will be a new ruler in the German Empire. With my dogs to fight for her the Empire will know unparalleled power and glory. And this undoubtedly is the reason Fate has made my course so long and arduous: so that I would be forced to flee the protection of the Emperor and complete the army by myself. So it is, as always, as She wills it.

---

* Although Rank never mentions how this was accomplished, the legend in Rankstadt, which there is no particular reason to doubt, says that he had embezzled from his patron for many years, possibly since he began work on the project.

The flight to Canada is not recorded, but of course dogs, equipment, gold, and other supplies would have been taken by Rank and his followers from the laboratory, probably late at night, and smuggled across the country and finally onto a ship bound across the Atlantic. From the eastern shores of North America to western Canada the journey was slow and grueling, so that it was not until almost two years after leaving Bavaria that Rank arrived at the site of his new home, and then with only thirty-seven followers, for the northern winter had taken its toll. It is a testament to the mysteriously powerful loyalty of his people that, at least according to Rank's diaries, all of those missing were lost to death; no other misfortune was great enough to turn them aside from their path.

Finally, on an obscure creek high in the Canadian wilderness, at a site chosen for its utter isolation, under the yellow autumn sun, Rank and his group began to build their new home. They fashioned it after the places they had come from, and so created a small German village there in the wilderness.

For seventeen years they lived by farming, rudimentary mining, and very occasional journeys by one townsman or another to distant communities for trading, or sometimes looting, always keeping the location of Rankstadt, and its operations, a strict secret, and all the while working on Rank's great project. Then in 1916—a date which meant little in a town that did not change with the outside world, inhabited by people who had barely known the outside world at all since 1882, but which was recorded on their calendars nonetheless—Augustus Rank, aged fifty-two, was found dead in his study of a cocaine overdose. He left the following note:

Work ceaselessly, and when the great dog army is at last assembled, look for me, for my spirit shall return to lead you in our first great victory.

And the people did work. Determined and self-reliant, they remained in their secret town, and retained their language, their culture, and their goal; and likewise their children, most of whom had never known any other home, lived out their lives in the laboratories and fields and houses of Rankstadt, and only the vaguest rumors of Rankstadt's existence, which were given no more credit than folktales, ever reached the outside world. No defections were recorded in the town archives, but it is difficult to imagine that there were not a few; however, if any did leave the village, they were all either loyal or afraid enough not to divulge its location.

So as the century progressed, the children, and then the grandchildren, and then the great-grandchildren of Rank's original followers staffed the farms and laboratories of the town. Deprived of almost any external influences, each generation lived much as the first had, in the same houses—although new ones, modeled after their pattern, were built as the community multiplied through births—with the same farming methods, language, customs, and habits. Only the great central laboratory and its satellites in homes throughout the town saw the advancement of technology, for through the years the brightest minds of Rankstadt were always at work on what was known simply as "the project," the justification for the town's existence.

IT WAS a quiet life. We had everything that was needed: there was a doctor, a schoolteacher, a blacksmith, a baker; there were root cellars and fields with which to stock them; the domestic arts were not lost; and every mother knew how to make soap, stockings, candles, roasts, quilts, and poultices; every father knew how to build a house that would stand sturdy and warm under the long winter snows, with thick shutters and wide hearths. The little church was always full on Sundays, and the clock in its white steeple, standing above the market square, kept time for the town for a hundred years. Outside, though the residents of Rankstadt barely knew it, monarchies collapsed, economies fell to ruin, governments rose and were overthrown, wars came, the earth was stripped and poisoned.

The town was not idyllic. It merely stayed away from some specific evils, while other, different evils were enacted there in the laboratory and the operating theater. There is no living dog who does not remember those rooms with deep horror. And yet, as I grow older, I often think of the hearth in my master's house, and how I used to curl up there on winter nights. There was the high, black northern sky above the roof and the roaring fire behind the screen and I was on my little cushion in between them. Now the fire has been released from the grate and the house has burned down, and in the winter snow falls from the sky and fills the ruined chimney. There is no order in the world anymore.

(CLEO)

When I got back uptown, Klaue had taken the manuscript and locked himself in the study for half an hour, after telling me not to leave the apartment. Now he seemed calmer, and his words were enunciated and measured, his faint German accent making them seem somehow more precise.

"It is a desire; a craving."

He was standing by his desk, and then he walked over to the big window and looked up at the night sky, which glowed red with the reflected light of the city.

"It burns," he said. "Like a lust. A spiritual lust."

"For information?" I asked. "For knowledge about Rank?"

"For his spirit," Klaue replied. "And yet . . ."

He turned around to face me. "First question," he said. "Come on, now."

I WENT back to see Ludwig the next day. Since I thought he probably wouldn't remember inviting me, I showed up at the door in the afternoon instead of calling first, figuring I had less chance of being put off that way. After a few minutes of discussion inside the apartment, Rob came back to the door and let me in. He smiled at me as he took my coat, but didn't say anything, and we walked silently down the little entrance hall, going toward the living room this time. Ludwig sat on a couch, wrapped in a burgundy-colored quilted bathrobe and bent over some papers on the coffee table in front of him. A tea tray and a brandy tray were set next to the papers.

"Forgive my bathrobe," Ludwig said, not rising as I came in. "I am not feeling well today. Please, sit down."

"I'm sorry you're not feeling well."

"It's nothing. It will pass."

I glanced down at the pages on the table, but they were written in cramped handwriting, and in German, and I couldn't make any sense of them.

"I think we've sold the first article idea," I offered. "Klaue's got an agent, you know—"

"Of course."

"And he sold it to *Vanity Fair*. Can you believe that?"

"Certainly I can believe it," Ludwig said.

"Well . . . it's hard for me to take it all in. It's exciting," I said.

Ludwig turned his head, not toward anything in particular, but away from me.

"Ludwig," I said, "what's wrong?"

"How can Klaue stand to parade his hideous body in front of the world this way? Every day he finds a way to get more attention. I would rather die than be seen by so many people."

"But you're not hideous, you're wonderful," I said. "You're the greatest thing I've ever seen. How could you say that?"

"You are so innocent, Cleo. That is why Klaue chose you. You are naïve, like a child. You can be made to believe anything. Don't you know that most of the world is laughing at us?"

"I don't think they are."

"You don't think so."

"And I don't think Klaue chose me just because he thinks he can manipulate me, either."

"You think he chose you because you are a good writer."

"I don't know."

"It seems clear enough to me. But perhaps you would rather not think about it; you're happy enough to have your job. You are not merely naïve but also ambitious, aren't you, Cleo? You are perfect for him."

"Who cares why Klaue chose me to write the articles, anyway? Even if there were some reason for you to mistrust him, at least with me working for him you have a friend in his camp. Or at least—" I stopped myself and stood up. "I don't think you're in any mood to have company, anyway. I'm going to leave."

"I didn't invite you here," Ludwig said.

"You *did*. You told Rob you would see me today, but you don't remember because you—"

"I told him I would see you for half an hour if you had something *very important* you wanted to say."

I could see a thin line of glistening white between Ludwig's lips, as if he wanted to bare his teeth but was trying not to.

"Well, I don't," I said. "The truth is I was worried about you because of what you said about being sick the other day, and I wanted to see how you were. But I'm sorry I came."

"It's not necessary," Ludwig said. "And I believe you came because Rob told you that I have been drinking too much. Is that true?"

"I don't need Rob to tell me something like that for me to be concerned."

"Your concern is misplaced. There is nothing you can do for me, and I would prefer it if you did not come to my home unless you are invited."

Ludwig rang a bell, and Rob came to the door of the living room. He winced sympathetically as soon as we were out of Ludwig's sight.

"Wow," he said.

I shook my head.

"It's not your fault. It's the way he is," Rob said.

"What can I do if I'm not even allowed to be worried about him?" I asked.

Rob shrugged, handing me my jacket. "He won't stay mad at you forever."

"He said I was naïve. He thinks Klaue chose me to write articles for him just because he can manipulate me."

"Just write the articles, don't worry about Ludwig. It's none of his business, right? That's what I would do," Rob said.

At the front door of the building I turned around, and Rob was watching me from the apartment. " 'Bye, Cleo," he said.

1

VANITY FAIR, JUNE 2010

DOGGY STYLE
Their East Village Dream House: Neuhundstein

**The monster dogs' elaborate, much-hyped project, a pro-
posed re-creation of Bavaria's most famous fairy-tale palace,
reflects longings for a magical homeland in the past as well
as their drive toward that most fantastic of all countries, the
future. Klaue Lutz, the Malamute mastermind behind the
castle, takes CLEO PIRA along for the ride.**

The view from the air is breathtaking. We are hovering
over Manhattan, looking down at a block in the East Village
that is utterly deserted. It has been evacuated, cleared out,
and the shadow of our helicopter falls undisturbed across a
wide, empty section of Houston Street and part of the sunlit
sidewalk.

It's demolition day, March 6, 2010, and an entire city
block is about to be razed—in a series of five ground-shaking

explosions—to make way for the building of a castle, the monster dogs' "gift to the city of New York."

Klaue Lutz, Treasurer of the Society of Dogs, wearing the familiar blue uniform of the nineteenth-century Prussian cavalry, sits beside me. He leans very close to my ear and says, "Five minutes."

I take in the sights again for one last time: the huge 1980s apartment-and-storefront complex called Red Square, which occupies the entire length of the south side of the block; the shops and restaurants along Avenue A; the old tenements facing Second Street and Avenue B, some renovated, some falling into disrepair—but it doesn't matter now. The area below us, so familiar to me in its former incarnation as a bustling, noisy city block, has a particularly chilling emptiness at this moment, like that of a sleeping carnival or a deserted battleground.

Klaue and I are not alone in observing the eerie scene. The police barricades that cordon off the block are crowded with onlookers. People are gathered on rooftops, waiting, watching, for a quarter mile in every direction. But the silence that envelops the empty block seems to extend even to them. No one is moving; everyone is hushed, waiting.

In the seat next to me, Klaue sits staring at the ornate pocketwatch he holds in his elegantly gloved mechanical hand. His concentration is so intense I'm almost expecting his eyes to burn a hole through the watch's gilded face. His teeth are slightly parted, and a crescent of tongue protrudes between his canines. Then he turns to me, and the laserlike focus of his gaze locks into mine.

"*One minute,*" he says.

It is not only the promise of explosions and collapsing buildings that accounts for my companion's mood of anticipation. It was Klaue Lutz who, almost single-handedly, conceived and initiated the plans for the construction of the castle on this site, and it is the excitement of the project itself that pervades the air of the Lower East Side on this cloudless, chilly Saturday afternoon.

When plans for the project were announced last December, at the end of the dogs' spectacular Christmas Parade down Fifth Avenue, all of Manhattan was on fire with the news. The castle is to be a gift, Klaue said, from the monster dogs to the people of New York. It seems appropriate that this strange, captivating race of creatures should offer such a lavish token of their appreciation to the strange, captivating city where they have chosen to settle. And the gift itself seems fitting: a romantic, impossible building, modeled on the famous nineteenth-century castle Neuschwanstein in Bavaria.

Neuschwanstein, often pictured with its pointed towers rising out of swirling mountain mists, is the archetypal European fairy-tale castle. Built by the mad, extravagant King Ludwig II of Bavaria beginning in 1869, it is the embodiment of the romantic vision of a man who—as his fierce admirers and vehement detractors all agreed—had a mind more of a poet than of a king. He often spent his evenings in a specially constructed, floodlit grotto, where he would float for hours in a swan-shaped, gilded boat, listening to the music of Wagner played by musicians carefully concealed in the foliage around the edges of the water. His passion for building lovely, unnecessary castles increased over the years, until it depleted his family's finances and eventually threatened those of the Bavarian state itself. Finally, in 1886, he was declared mad, dethroned by his own family, and imprisoned in one of his beloved castles, where only days later, betrayed and lonely, he died under mysterious circumstances.

Even to those who are unfamiliar with King Ludwig's story, the lavish romanticism of Neuschwanstein must suggest that it can have been built only by the sort of visionary who was doomed to be trampled by the world. This, I think, is the castle's real allure: it isn't just beautiful but excessively, *impossibly* so. It's obvious that somehow someone had to pay a price to build it, and probably a large one, but there's no hint of that in the building itself. You sense that something's being hidden from you, and there's a kindness, a generosity in that that is touching.

"Fifteen seconds," Klaue says. *"Now."*

The buildings below us shudder for a split second like a mirage in the desert and then begin to collapse, their foundations blown out from underneath, sending clouds of smoke and fine rubble rolling up into the air. By the time the fifth explosion comes, it is impossible to see anything in the blocked-off area. I look over at Klaue and he is smiling, a wide dog grin, his eyes glittering as if the detonations had splintered the steady laser beams of his gaze into diamond sparkles.

"The next building you will see there," he says, pointing to the dusty ruins just beginning to emerge from the smoke, "will be my Neuhundstein."

Over coffee in his apartment, I tell Klaue my thoughts about the hidden cost of Bavaria's Neuschwanstein and ask whether the same might be true of the dogs' future castle. Surely its construction will be a strain on the dogs' finances. What other costs will it incur?

"There will be no such thing," he answers firmly. "The people have given us quite a bit of money. They pay us to appear in movies, on television, to tell our stories, simply, in the end, for existing. We are giving some of it back to them. That is all."

We are sitting by a roaring fire in the living room of Klaue's magnificent Central Park West home. The room is large, but the dimensions of the fireplace still surprise me, for it is as cavernous as one in a medieval castle hall. Klaue tells me he had it specially installed, and I comment that he will probably feel at home in the rooms in Neuhundstein.

"Yes," he says. "We all will, all of the dogs. This castle will remind us of our homeland, so to speak. You see, we are in a very strange situation, because we come from Rank-stadt." He pauses, gazing into the flames.

"A place that doesn't exist anymore," I say.

"Yes, precisely. Rankstadt was in a remote part of Canada, as you know. But because it had been undiscovered by the outside world for over a century, because there had been virtually no contact, its culture remained much the same as that from which its founders originally came, which was Prussia in the late nineteenth century. And so we dogs feel that our homeland is there also. That is the culture we know. Rankstadt was destroyed, and the homeland has also been destroyed, it has changed over the years into something else. The nineteenth century does not exist anymore. So in a sense I would like to re-create it. It's simply a matter of giving life to a fantasy, really, it has no practical value, and yet, as you point out, I think we will feel comfortable there, in the castle."

Apparently the other dogs agree: Klaue reports that nearly all of them ("and I am working on the rest," he says) have decided to take up permanent residence in Neuhund-stein once it is completed. They will inhabit the upper floors, while the lower levels will be open to the public. According to Klaue, the building will house a dog museum, a large restaurant, an indoor sculpture garden, a concert hall, a ball-room, and possibly also a small, exclusive hotel. "It will be a very attractive place to visit," he says, "and there will be no charge to enter the grounds, only for eating at the restaurant or staying in the guest rooms. Most of the space will be free and open to the public. So you see that I am really serious when I refer to our castle as a gift. It will also be very beau-tiful from the outside. It will give pleasure to everyone."

"And it will be a great monument to the dogs, too," I point out.

"Yes," Klaue says, and then he falls silent again, brooding.

Probing for the source of his mood, I venture into what I know is sensitive territory. "Does the word 'monument' make you think of a time when the dogs will no longer exist?" I ask. "Do you think the castle will outlive you, as a race?"

I know I have hit a nerve when Klaue uncharacteristically turns his head away from me, his normally direct and piercing gaze focused on an elaborate clock on the mantel above the fireplace.

"I do not think we will really die," he says enigmatically.

It is well known that the dogs have resisted being examined by scientists and doctors, to the chagrin of many who would love to examine the intricate mechanics of their hands and internal voice boxes and to probe the mysteries of their intelligence. It is rumored as well that the blueprints for creating these prosthetic devices were destroyed along with the laboratories of Rankstadt, and the dogs themselves don't know how they were made.

There is some question whether the monster dogs' offspring—if they are ever to have any—would be born with their parents' intelligence, but it is certain that they would be born without prosthetic hands and speaking aids. Since the technology for creating these things is lost, and since the dogs *don't* seem to be having any puppies, it seems likely that the generation of monster dogs we know will be the last ever, unless they change their minds and agree to be examined by scientists.

I gently bring these points up to Klaue. "That is not true," he says fiercely. "We do not intend to disappear. We have our own scientists, two very brilliant dogs, who will soon know how to re-create the prosthetics, and when that is settled, then we will begin having offspring again."

I am surprised because I have never heard any of this.

"But it is true," Klaue insists. "We don't want to die. We would merely prefer to keep everything, as they say, in

the family. You understand our position. Of course, most
doctors and scientists are scrupulous people, but a very few
are not, and we don't want to turn ourselves over to them.
It is too dangerous for us. And I have full confidence in our
own scientists."

As he says this, I wonder if the dogs' struggle to survive
is the suffering that will be hidden from the public by Neuhundstein's gleaming white walls and elegant turrets. If the
dogs were willing to accept help from the human scientific
community, their race's chances of survival would be much
greater. Yet they are determined not only to solve their own
problems but to make a significant contribution to society at
the same time. Maybe, like King Ludwig of Bavaria, they
are too idealistic in pursuing their goals, and maybe reality
will get the better of them in the end. No matter what fate
lies in store for the dogs, the people of New York will be
left with Neuhundstein.

"Let me tell you about the ballroom and the concert
hall," Klaue says, eager to change the subject. "They will be
really magnificent. The castle will probably take ten months
or so to complete, but these rooms will be finished earlier,
and we will hold our first performance in September. It will
be an opera written by a dog that will tell, for the first time,
the full story of our exodus from Rankstadt. The opera is
called *Mops Hacker*. It is named for the dog who led our
revolution. Don't you find that very exciting?"

"Yes, very," I say. "And will it be performed by dogs?"

"A few dogs, and also some humans in costume. It will
be fantastic."

"The subject of how you left Rankstadt is one that the
dogs have been reluctant to talk about, isn't it?"

"Well, it was a very—how would you say it—emotional
time for us. We have not wanted to go into the details."

"Why reveal them now?"

Klaue shrugs. "It is time. We are ready. We would like

to look at our past, to nod to it, and then to move forward into the future."

"But it will be a future that celebrates your past—your homeland, your culture."

"Precisely. Everyone must move forward. This is a country of immigrants, this city especially, of people who have left things behind. They have brought their pasts with them. They have not succeeded in turning this into the old country—there are too many old countries competing with one another. It is a city built of bits and pieces of many different times and places, and it offers those magical things to everyone who comes through it. You may think that coming, as it were, from a different century, and being dogs, we would find it impossible ever to blend in, even here. I suppose that is true: we won't. And yet we can be inspired by the examples of others. We can contribute our own vision of home and transplant it into this new place, where it changes, becomes something else in its new setting."

He glances toward the massive hearth again, but happily, this time, his eyes reflecting the fire's glow. "Where it becomes," he says, "a gift to everyone." □

8

The first monster dog was completed on September 15, 1968, at dusk. For two days, without rest, Karl Hacker and his assistants had worked behind the closed doors of Rankstadt's Central Laboratory. Their wives brought their meals; other than that, they saw no one. But everyone in the town knew that the scientists were on the verge of success, and they waited, listening for the great bell that stood on the commons, whose ringing would announce the work's completion.

In order to comprehend the meaning of this event, you must understand that the town was already full of surgically altered dogs and other kinds of animals, in various states of completion, most of them running wild in the streets, scavenging from garbage heaps. The tradition of turning them loose had been started shortly after Rank's day, as a way of celebrating individual successes and displaying them to the town. Most of the monsters, at that time, were too horrible to be kept as pets.

Today the animals that filled the streets were fairly advanced. They bore the marks of the various experiments that had created them: some had rudimentary hands, others had entire artificial limbs; some had enhanced intelligence; others had voice boxes capable of creating a range of intricate sounds, but no understanding of how to use them properly. Some were maimed; their legs gone, or insane, or hobbled by prostheses that did not work. They were a gruesome assortment of creatures. The last ones were still living when I was young, and we dogs—more than the humans, I think—regarded them with utter revulsion and fear.

My point, in any case, is that the people were not waiting to see their first monster but to see a great advance in intelligence—enhancement that was supposed to be displayed by this newest creature. If the scientists were successful, they would create the first dog ever to fit exactly the specifications drawn up by Rank nearly a hundred years before. This meant a great deal to the people of Rankstadt: not only the completion of their own and their fathers' and grandfathers' life work but also the first step toward their destiny as leaders, according to Rank's promise, of the world's strongest army. Some believed that their town's founder would return in spirit to lead them as he had said he would, some half believed, others did not believe at all; but it was clear to everyone that once the army of dog soldiers was completed the townspeople would be the possessors of great power. Did they imagine going back to Prussia to join forces with the Emperor's army, or marching on the United States? There was a feeling, supported by the mayor and the elders of the town, that it was at least indecorous, if not precisely blasphemous, to act publicly as though Rank's spirit would not eventually return to outline the correct course of action, and in addition the dogs were never considered of-

ficially "completed," so there was never a unified plan. I believe
many people would have been quite content to stay where they
were, with their new slaves to serve them; they felt superior to
the outside world in any case and were hesitant to join it, even
as conquerors. I believe it was this feeling of superiority, more
than anything else, that kept the town isolated for so many
years. But I digress; it is not my intent to speculate extensively
on the psychology of the people of Rankstadt but rather to
describe the beginnings of my own race.

If I could, I would outline what the men were doing behind
the closed doors of the laboratory, but I have no information,
because all of their papers were lost when Rankstadt was
burned. We dogs never knew, while we served our masters in
the town or afterward, how our own brains were manipulated
to make us more intelligent. During my lifetime, when puppies
were born they were taken to the operating theater at once,
and then many times subsequently at decreasing intervals until
they reached maturity. In general it seemed that brain surgery
was performed only immediately after birth, though a few dogs
I knew were experimented upon afterward; but usually the later
operations involved only replacing our prosthetic hands with
larger, more intricate ones suited to our greater size and abilities
as we grew. In any case, we were never given any information
about what was done to us in the great laboratory. It has been
said it is patently impossible for our creators to have raised our
intelligence by surgical means, that even if the technology to do
such a thing could be developed, the scientists of Rankstadt,
working in isolation without access to modern developments or
materials, could never have done it. As we dogs have no way
of knowing what we or our offspring would have been like
without the surgery, we are unable to dispute this except to say
that in spite of its being impossible, it seems to have happened.

It is possible that our masters were lying or exaggerating when they gave us this account, which I am about to relate, and yet, as modern science has discovered no more plausible explanation for our existence, I have no reason to doubt it.

And so to return to the story: the monster was completed at dusk. In a quiet hour, just at the beginning of dinnertime, when the streets were almost empty, and the windows of the houses had begun to light up yellow against the deepening blue of the evening air, the great doors on one side of the laboratory, which were like barn doors, creaked in their tracks. At that sound, a little boy who had been waiting nearby ran to the commons to ring the bell. But before he had arrived there, when everything was still quiet, the doors rolled back, and three white-coated assistants stepped outside.

The laboratory stood on the western side of the town, with a small clearing behind it, and then a downward slope, so that the building was silhouetted against the sky. I imagine that Rank placed it there intentionally; in fact, I suspect that he built it there specifically in anticipation of what was to happen on this evening.

After the assistants had come out, the bell began to ring. A small group of people had already gathered when Dr. Hacker stepped through the door, tall and somewhat stooped, the details of his figure lost against the setting sun, except for the brown and red bloodstains that covered the front of his white coat, spattered over his chest and forming dried rivulets below the waist that ran down to the hem. His beard was roughly trimmed to a point, but uncombed and disheveled, and the fringe of thinning hair around his head also stood out in limp shocks. He turned toward the growing crowd, his round spectacles flashing for a moment as they caught the fading light.

He did not say anything but waited until the group of observers had grown larger, and then looked toward the dark doorway and nodded. One last assistant came out and stood with the group, and then the monster emerged.

He was a large black German Shepherd, who, like most of the dogs in Rankstadt, had been bred for size. He stood six feet tall on his hind legs, and carried a thick cane, which he used to support his tentative steps. All four limbs were swathed in bandages—the muscles and tendons had been stretched to make it easier for him to walk upright and to use his arms, but they had not yet healed. Other than that, he was no more than a silhouette against the sky, which was streaked with orange and purple clouds that seemed violently festive behind the dog's dark, awkward figure. He came before Dr. Hacker and stopped, looking at him.

The doctor addressed the crowd:

"I present to you now—the dog Rupert, whom I, with the help of my assistants, have altered to become the first perfect dog soldier."

There was absolute silence.

"Rupert," he said, smiling at his dog, "address the people of Rankstadt. They have waited many years to make your acquaintance."

There was a pause, and then Rupert opened his mouth.

"Rrrrgh," he said, clearing his throat. He spat a dark clot onto the ground.

"Hech—hello, people of Rankstadt," he began. His voice was thick and sounded moist, as if there were fluid in his artificial voice box.

"My name is Rupert. I have much to learn before I can use my abilities to their full potential. However, I am . . ." Here he stopped and looked at Dr. Hacker.

"Endowed," the doctor prompted.

". . . *endowed* with high intelligence, and my—conform and . . ."

"*My hands and speaking apparatus,*" Hacker hissed softly.

"Hands and speaking apparatus—*conform*—exactly to Dr. Rank's specifications. Thank you."

"Yes, very good," Hacker murmured. The crowd began to applaud, and he held up his hand.

"The dog understands what he is saying, but it will be some time before he has learned the language fully. He has, of course, been in training for several years, but only in these past two days has he received the mental capacity to use it completely. However, I wanted to teach him this little speech to demonstrate his abilities.

"Very good, Rupert," he said, giving the dog a slight smile and patting him on one bandaged shoulder. Rupert winced.

SIX MONTHS later, the first true monster dog was functioning almost perfectly. His creators had made only one mistake, which was that they had used a grown animal instead of a puppy. Since Rupert had spent his formative years as a dog, his ability to learn language and certain social skills was somewhat impaired, but in general he got along very well, and learned to perform all the tasks of a servant, and also to shoot a rifle and eventually to read. His greatest pleasure, according to the dogs who knew him—those of my parents' generation—was to drive a carriage. Before his perfection, he had been terrified of horses; now he was able to command them completely, like a human.

However, the privilege of driving was eventually taken away from him. It was not clear to anyone precisely why, but I imagine it was merely due to some perverse expression on his face, which he neglected to change once when he turned to look at his master behind him in the seat of the carriage.

Rupert was not happy. He had spent too much of his life as an ordinary dog, and to be suddenly endowed with an understanding of what that was—what he still was, in many ways—was a great shock to him. He said later to a friend that it had been like waking up from a pleasant dream to find himself enslaved, as if he had been captured by members of another race while he slept, and taken away to their country. It is a terrible thing to be a dog and know it; and I suppose it was worse for him, because he could remember a time when he did not.

During Rupert's lifetime, a hundred more monsters were made, and the techniques were perfected. Their brains were altered when they were puppies, and they were fitted with small temporary hands and voice boxes. Permanent hands were attached during early adolescence. Through breeding and, I think, genetic tampering, their life span had been lengthened, and when their brains were enhanced, they matured at much the same rate as humans. A small school was set up where they learned to read and write, just like ordinary children. Within a few years after Rupert's creation, all of the richest families of Rankstadt had dog servants, whom they raised in their own homes.

Rupert himself did not live long. He had had a strange pattern of growth, having matured as a dog and then been thrown backward by his alteration, which gave him the mind of a human child. He became subject to violent changes in temper as a teenager, a decade after his perfection, when he had already physically matured. He began to disobey Dr. Hacker in strange infantile ways: chewing on the legs of chairs, for instance, and eating shoes. It was as if he was compelled to do it, because he felt great remorse immediately afterward, and yet he became progressively less able to control himself. Sometimes he would leave the house at night and get into the garbage heaps in the back streets, or chase sheep. Since his canine urges were combined with a human intelligence, he was able to do a great deal of mischief. The greatest crime he committed, although his master could not have realized its magnitude at the time, was to begin a love affair with a Giant Schnauzer who lived in a neighboring house.

Her name was Ilsa, and she was a frail, awkward creature. I don't believe their affair lasted any longer than her heat. She lived in an attic room and had little contact with other dogs, because her poor health had prevented her from going to school. Rupert Hacker spoke to her for many nights from the garden below her window, and finally convinced her to leave the kitchen door unlatched one evening so that he could come in. He crept up to her room, and they spent an hour together; and she left the door unlatched the next night, and the next, for an entire week.

After that, she saw no more of Rupert. I have heard that she used to lean out of her window and cry and sniff for him for some time after that, keeping all of her canine neighbors awake; but he never came back. A month later, he was killed.

The story that Dr. Hacker told afterward of Rupert's death was that while on a hunting trip with some of his friends, the doctor had been attacked by an enormous grizzly bear who came suddenly through the trees, and was upon him before he was able to aim his rifle. Rupert immediately threw himself on the bear, and while Dr. Hacker tried to get a clear shot at it, it sank its teeth into the dog's throat and shook him, breaking his neck and killing him instantly. The bear fell to Dr. Hacker's bullet a moment later.

I have heard from another dog who was on the expedition, however, that what had actually happened was that Rupert had been running far ahead of the hunting party, and had stumbled into the bear's den—not, perhaps, by accident. It was a mother with cubs, and she followed Rupert when he fled back to his master. Hacker saw her in time to aim and shoot—but before he was able to, the dog dove at the bear and blocked him. Rupert fought valiantly, but he had no chance. Perhaps he had led the enraged bear intentionally to his master, expecting her to kill him, but had a change of heart at the last moment; in any case, he had thrown himself directly, and knowingly, into the jaws of death.

Whatever the truth may be, Rupert was celebrated as a hero and mourned by his master. Hacker lamented particularly that he had left no offspring—or rather, that the single small litter which he had previously sired had been lost to clumsy experimental surgery (as a large amount of puppies were; at least as many as made it to adulthood).

It soon became obvious, however, that Ilsa was pregnant, and she was forced to confess her affair with Rupert. The whelps would be mutts, with a poor specimen for a mother, but old Dr. Hacker looked forward to them anyway. Rupert's creation had been the doctor's crowning achievement, and his work was now being eclipsed by that of younger scientists, so that he wanted very much to have some living memorial to his first perfect monster.

But he did not get it. Upon hearing of Rupert's death, Ilsa faded quickly, and the puppies were born barely alive. She died shortly afterward, and they had to be raised by hand by Frau Hacker. As sickly as they were, Dr. Hacker might have taken any of them, except for one. That was the runt, the smallest of an undersized litter, which was unaccountably of a dirty gray color, although both of its parents had been black. It was not an albino but, I suppose, a strange throwback to some remote ancestors. Perhaps it was simply a mutation. The chances against such a dog being born at all were enormous, the likelihood of its survival next to nothing. And in the end it was, of course, the only one of the litter who lived.

According to Sigmund, another dog who lived in the household, Frau Hacker thought the ugly little puppy was a miracle, and consequently Dr. Hacker felt that his wife was somehow to blame for the deaths of the others; perhaps she had treated this one differently in order to keep it alive. He wanted to kill it, because it seemed to represent for him the failure of all of his work. He was old; he had devoted his life to making the first real monster dog, and had created something which had seemed promising, but which had gone awry, and killed itself. He had passed his ideas on to younger men, and now he could no longer keep up with their work. No one knew that Rupert's death had been a suicide, but everyone had found out about his strange night wanderings, and his affair with Ilsa. This single, hideous product of Rupert's seed seemed like the final outcome of a long experiment, one to which Hacker had given his entire career. It seemed to sum up his life's work, and he hated it, and insisted on having it drowned.

In a fit of perversity, he ordered his wife to drown it herself, wanting her to suffer for having taken care of it. She sadly acquiesced, took it outside, and hurried across town with it, to the home of Jedediah Arch.

Jedediah, like his grandfather, who had stumbled into Rankstadt accidentally after escaping from jail in the United States, was a bad-tempered recluse. He lived in the poorest shack on the edge of town, a place Frau Rank knew her husband would never have occasion to visit. But she had a strange fondness for Jedediah, whom she had several times caught in secret acts of kindness: taking in a sick goose that had been put out in the woods to die, and keeping it in his house for a pet; hiding a drunk boy from his parents for a day, until he recovered, to keep him from getting in trouble. He seemed to be a good match for the puppy.

He wanted it badly, and she sold it to him for very little and used the money to trim a new hat, and felt that she had done the right thing. She was a good woman; I knew her when I was young. She could not have known, then, what she had done. Dr. Hacker, acting out of impotent anger at his own failure, had made the right choice, and she, acting out of mercy, had made the wrong one. I am tempted to say that for the price of that hat she sold the life of every human being in Rankstadt. And why not say it? It is true.

The dog she sold to Jedediah was named Rudolf Ezekiel, but his nickname was the word used in Rankstadt for "mutt," and that was what everybody called him. Out of his own perversity, when he started school, he liked to use the surname of the man who had hated him, so that the old doctor would never forget that he had survived. And thus Rudolf Ezekiel Hacker-Arch came to be known among his peers by the name he chose: Mops Hacker.

Part Two

Mops Hacker

9

Mops Hacker, leader of the Dog Revolution, spent his early life with Jedediah Arch. One of the descendants of the few Americans who had joined the town of Rankstadt in the early years, Mops's master was the one citizen of Rankstadt who spoke English, since the others had for generations been brought up to speak only German. Judging from the style of writing in Mops's diary, his master's collection of books must have dated from the late eighteenth century and included a Bible. We do not know why the collection included nothing newer—perhaps because those old books, being considered the most valuable, were the most carefully preserved—but we can only guess at this. We do know for certain that they were the only English-language books still existing in Rankstadt during our lifetime.

Mops was the only dog belonging to Arch, and so he grew up in relative isolation, and for most of his childhood he was very attached to his master.

At the age of six he began to attend the Dogs' Grammar School, but immediately established a reputation as a poor student and a troublemaker, which was to stay with him throughout his youth.

The following excerpts are from a diary that Mops began to keep at the age of thirteen. It was entirely written in English, which indicates it was meant to be secret. The numbering system is Mops's own device. I have focused primarily on his social development, as he grew from a despised outcast into our race's greatest leader. These excerpts will, I hope, provide some insight into the mind of the dog who at age seventeen was to lead the dogs into that bloody rebellion against the humans of Rankstadt which permanently changed the course of our race's history.

[TITLE PAGE]:

RUDOLF EZEKIEL HACKER-ARCH

His Book

Known to my Friends as
MOPS HACKER

My Home being the GREAT ESTATE of Master Jedediah Arch,
which is the SHACK, the OUTHOUSE & the CHICKEN-COOP.
I write this the 2 day of September, 1995.

[FIRST PAGE]:

I

1. Friends. Where is Mops Hacker today, this being Saturday
& it is 10 o'clock in the Morning?

2. Mops Hacker is asleep, and expects to be so for a long time.
3. But Master JEDEDIAH ARCH is calling him!
4. Nevertheless, he is asleep.

II

1. Receiv'd Beating this Noon from Arch, found me asleep by the big Rock behind the shack.
2. But, while I was still asleep, I had had a Dream.
3. In this Dream a small indistinct Form as it were a little cloud of Smoke, flew into my mouth.
4. Then I was full of strength, for this little Cloud was very Strong.
5. Then I rose up and smote Arch, and he fell to the ground, because I Smote him.
6. Then I woke, and Arch stood over me. and he Beat me sore.
7. It is a hard piece of Work, being a Dog.

III

1. MOPS HACKER has no Friend.
2. The Dogs his People call him Deluded.
3. And they call him "smelly"
4. He is Alone in the world, and his age is 13 Years.
5. Also Jedediah Arch has no Friend, neither does he wash himself, and his clothes are Filthy. and MOPS HACKER also has to suffer because his master is Filthy, and poor.
6. Therefore I Hate Jedediah Arch, and everything that belongs to him, excepting this English Language which he Taught me, which no-one else in this whole City knows.

7. Which is now Mine, and doesn't Belong to him any more.
and I am not his Son, and his Name is not my name, for I
am not called by his Name.

8. For I am the son of Augustus Rank, the Father of Dogs,
and my father has been Dead an hundred Years.

9. And I Have no Friend.

[C. AUGUST 1996, AGE FOURTEEN]:

CLXIV

1. O Lydia, it was as if I had never Seen you before: How
White you are, how perfect, I cannot believe how White you
are in this filthy World, a pure white alabaster maid in this
Filthy Filthy world. Which I wanted to leave, until I Saw
You. You stopp'd my Hand with the Knife, when I was
going to cut my own throat, you don't know why I was
there by the Rock: but that was the reason, that I was going
to make an End to my Life, until you ask'd me that simple
Question: what are you doing here: And I could not answer,
because I was asham'd: asham'd to Speak to You: Because
my Nose was full of the Smell, of rose-water and a Girls
Cleanliness, which spoke to Me saying: the world is not
Filthy, at least there is one Clean thing in it. But my mouth
was closed Up and I was not able to make an Answer to
you: Neither could I say any Thing, but look'd with my
Mouth Open, like AUGUSTUS RANK who it is said of
him that he Stuttered as a child, and could not Speak, for
you smell'd so Kind to me, that I like AUGUSTUS RANK
could not Speak.

CLXV

1. Resolv'd to have no more contact with Lydia any more this day.
2. For MOPS HACKER went to School today, which he had not done in a very Long time.
3. And he approached the bitch Lydia, & spoke her Name.
4. But she answered him Not: & she Smell'd very cool & not friendly, & she pretended not to Notice him.
5. & He Again spoke her Name, whereupon some small Hairs on the back of her Neck Rais'd a little, and she gave off a sharp smell, and still she made no Answer. and she was very Impudent this Way, and Unkind, and MOPS HACKER became Vexed, very vexed.
6. Why did this Bitch Deceive me in this way?
7. Because she is Ignorant, and wags her little Tail at any Thing and any Dog, and knows not why she does it, but Yaps with her little friends, and their Talk is of Nothing, for they are Foolish Girls. For the talk of Bitches is as the Wind stirring the leaves: it hath a sound, but it Means Nothing.
8. So saith MOPS HACKER, who has Conquered the Temptation of Bitches: Remember these Words, and Repeat them to your Sons.
9. Because I have Said this, and it is True.

[C. DECEMBER 1997, AGE FIFTEEN OR SIXTEEN. THE REFERENCE TO ME IN CCXCIV.5 IS INACCURATE. I WAS NEVER FRIENDS WITH MOPS, AND I DO NOT REMEMBER EVER WANTING TO BE. —ED.]

CCXCIV

1. But two out of his People follow'd him, and did not Scorn him, and came to the Rock every day to Meet him.
2. And they were call'd Max and Otto.
3. And Otto had several Knives, and he knew how to Throw them. and Max had many interesting Books, some being Books on Military History which are the most Interesting, and MOPS HACKER has a knowledge of the English Language, and many other things.
4. So they shall be call'd the True Believers.
5. But not Ludwig, who comes up to Us wagging his tail, for he is an Idiot.

CCCIII

1. A GREAT & ASTONISHING THING HAS COME TO PASS, AND THE TRUE BELIEVERS SHALL HEAR IT.
2. Those being by Name Max and Otto.
3. MOPS HACKER Dreamt Again of the cloud of Smoke, that cloud of Strength, and in this dream the Cloud was larger than it had been, and very dense, even more so than in the Dream of CCLXIV:1–4 or CCLXXXVII:1–7, or any Other dream.
4. And It approached Him, and he open'd His mouth to receive It, as was His custom.
5. But the Cloud Stopp'd, and did not come any farther.
6. And MOPS HACKER was astonish'd, for the Cloud began to Change before His eyes, which It never had done before.
7. And before His astonish'd eyes it condens'd & seem'd to

become Solid, until He could see that it was in the Form
of a Man.

8. And soon He could see Who this Man was: For it was
AUGUSTUS RANK, Father of Dogs. And He said unto
Him: My Son.

9. And MOPS HACKER could not Speak, but stood with
His Mouth Open in Astonishment.

10. Whereupon the Cloud, still being in the form of AUGUS-
TUS RANK, flew into his Mouth!

11. And MOPS rose up, and he smote all the Men! He took
up the Sword, and his Teeth were Sharp, and the Thing
inside him became Fire! And all the Dogs followed him,
crying, Here is our Master, and crying, Smite the Men!

12. And friends, the houses of our Oppression were set on Fire,
and the people came running in the Streets. And the tables
where we Served were broken in two, and the sheds where
we Cut wood collapsed, and the cows we Milked were
Crushed by burning beams, and they Bellowed and then
they Died horribly burning.

13. And no Man, nor Woman, nor little Baby was left alive,
for our Teeth were in their Flesh, and they all Perished,
begging for Mercy with many Tears & whining & very
weak & disgraceful & there was no Mercy for them, for we
tore their weak limbs and crushed their soft heads in the
Jaws of our Righteousness and the Women we pierced with
the Swords of Our Anger and the Men we Gelded with
our own Hands! And we rejoiced in the Smell of Blood,
for it was excellent!

14. My two Friends, my True Believers, the Time is at hand,
when the things I Prophesy will come to pass. For we must
believe AUGUSTUS RANK who said, "I will Return."

10

(CLEO)

Lydia called me in early April. I had been writing a lot, making short pieces out of the research for my *Vanity Fair* article and things that Klaue showed me on the construction site, trying to keep up with my schoolwork and waitressing a couple of nights a week, too, and I hadn't been thinking of her or Ludwig or anything except what had to be done from minute to minute. I was surprised to hear her voice.

"We need to talk, Cleo," she said. "About Ludwig."

"What's wrong with him?" I asked.

"He's very upset."

"Yeah?" I said, not much interested. I had written him a letter after our fight apologizing, a little bit, but I hadn't heard back from him.

"Would you mind coming to my apartment to talk? I really feel it would be a good thing if we did, and it would be so much more comfortable than the telephone. We can have dinner." She seemed to hold her breath as she waited for my answer.

"All right, I'd like that. I don't think there's anything I can do about Ludwig, honestly, but I'd be happy to visit."

So we made plans for my next free night. She sent her chauffeur over, a quiet man with a mustache and an accent that I couldn't place because he spoke so little. He took me in a gray limousine to the Upper West Side, where he let me out in front of a beautiful early-twentieth-century building whose marble lobby and silent elevators reminded me of the places I had imagined visiting before I knew the dogs.

Lydia lived in a twelfth-floor penthouse with french windows in the living room that looked out onto a terrace and, beyond that, the Hudson, its western shore, and the evening sky. The dining table was set just to one side, so that we could look out as we ate.

"Ludwig likes you very much," she said, over a dinner of Moroccan lamb with figs and rice. "I think it would make him happy if you could reconcile your differences."

"Well, I like him, too," I said. "I was only trying to help when I went over that day."

"He's sensitive about certain things. We all are."

She held her fork in midair, watching me.

"What was it that bothered him so much about my visit?" I asked.

"I expect it was your assumption that he needed help."

"But everyone needs people to be concerned about them sometimes. It's not an insult," I said.

"How much do you know about his illness?" Lydia asked.

"Nothing," I said.

She looked surprised, but concentrated on her plate. "Well, I'm going to tell you," she said. "He has been having memory

lapses, and during them he believes that he reverts to the mental
state of a normal dog. They are becoming longer and more
frequent, and he's afraid eventually he will lose his mind completely. The alarming thing is that"—she stopped cutting her
lamb, which she had been doing with slow determination while
she spoke, and focused her eyes on mine—"it seems to be happening to other dogs, too. It's hard to tell because no one is
eager to talk about it."

"Has it happened to you?"

"No. But it has happened to Klaue, for example."

"How do you know?"

"He told me," she said. "About the others I have mostly
only heard rumors."

"I didn't realize you were close to Klaue."

Lydia took a forkful of lamb. "It isn't necessary to be close
to someone to get them to confide in you," she said.

She put the food in her mouth and glanced up at me.

"You aren't eating," she said. "This conversation has upset
you."

"Isn't there anything that can be done?" I asked. "Any doctors the dogs could see?"

"No, not for this. For a broken bone, yes, but not for something psychological. You see the difference, don't you?"

"I suppose," I said. "But then what will happen to Ludwig
and everyone else?"

Lydia's ears flattened until they were pointing straight back.
She seemed annoyed. "It won't be pleasant," she said.

"But there must be something that can be done. We can
think of something, something to try, at least."

Lydia didn't answer.

After dinner she asked me if I would like to hear some
music, and when I said yes, she led me over to the grand piano

in the corner of the living room and sat down at it. I settled in an armchair to listen, and she played something long and sad that I had never heard before. When she was done, I said, "That was wonderful."

"It's what I was taught to do," she said. "The family who raised me was very musical. We used to hold little concerts, sometimes, in Rankstadt."

"You and the family?"

"Yes. We would play quartets and trios. The father, the son, the oldest daughter, and myself." She laughed. "No one believed that a dog could be taught to play the piano, but I loved it. I would sit there and bang on it. The family encouraged me, and so finally I learned. Of course now I only play by myself. I'm glad you enjoyed it."

"I could listen to it forever, really," I said.

She nodded graciously. "Now, about Ludwig," she said. "I know that you've written him a letter. I've told him he ought to write back to you, but I suppose he hasn't."

"No."

"Why don't you write him another one, then? You don't have to mention your fight, just be friendly. I think everything will be all right."

"Okay, I'll do it," I said.

"Thank you, Cleo. This will mean a lot to Ludwig, I promise you."

After I wrote the first article, things started to change quickly, and by the middle of spring my life was almost completely different from the one I'd had when I'd met Ludwig five months before. When it became known that I was the only person to whom Klaue would grant interviews, several magazines asked me to write articles for them about the castle project, and in addition, since no one could interview Klaue, people

began to want to interview me for information about him and
the castle—radio and television shows, magazines, and news-
papers. My neighborhood changed, too, as Neuhundstein was
being built only a block and a half from where I lived, and
there were always reporters and photographers around. Klaue
only let me do print interviews, and only if they were conducted
in writing so that he could read over my answers before anyone
saw them. Still, my career, if that's what it was, seemed to be
snowballing. Yet I knew that if I ever made Klaue unhappy
and he decided to hand over my privilege to someone else, I
would have nothing. I had decided to drop out of graduate
school and had even given up my waitressing job in order to
devote all my time to writing articles. The life I'd lived before
the dogs seemed to close up behind me as I stepped out of it,
and I didn't see any way to get back in.

As soon as I'd written the first article I'd used all the money
I had saved for tuition the next fall to decorate my apartment.
Sometimes, if I had nothing to do for a morning or an afternoon, I would sit in the living room and just look at things,
the sheer curtains swelling in the breeze, the rows of books in
shelves that rose to the ceiling, the little Victorian sofa covered
with faded green velvet and flanked by two end tables on which
I'd set two clear glass bowls overflowing with bunches of dark
red and purple grapes that were made of twisted chrome wire
and colored glass. I loved letting my eyes wander from the
couch to the grapes: the shock of the brilliant, gaudy colors
after the pale, aristocratic-looking couch, the contrast of worn
velvet with hard and shiny metal and glass. I would look from
the couch to the grapes, to the windows, to the books, to the
small marble mantelpiece, over which I'd hung a strange,
bright-red-tinted mirror from the 1960s that was shaped like a
dove with its wings spread and its beak pointing upward, and

two tiny green Edwardian cameos in gilded frames, which really just looked like two greenish spots from across the room . . . I could sit for a whole hour at a time, and I often did, just looking, taking in every detail of the new things I owned. They were the kinds of things I'd always longed to own. I thought I was happy, because that seemed to be the only thing I could reasonably be feeling under the circumstances, but really I was just very afraid that I was going to lose everything, and I wanted to be able to remember it if I did.

I saw Klaue often. He made sure of that. As I look back on it, I think he also had something to do with the fact that I did spend so much time sitting in my apartment and staring at my furniture. He reminded me often that the people at the cocktail parties and dinners I was sometimes invited to were all after information and gossip about the project, and that it might be easy for me to slip and say something I shouldn't, and I knew he was right. Still, if he hadn't been so afraid of my socializing in groups of people, I might have just learned to live with keeping the secrets and gone out and enjoyed myself. But I didn't want to alienate him, so for the most part I stayed away from anyone but my close friends.

One evening in mid-April, Klaue and I went for a walk in the East River Park, near where I lived, at dusk. It was exactly that time of year when all the blossoms have come out on the leafless branches, white and pink on the cherry trees and yellow on the forsythia. The twilights had just recently changed from winter grays to those eerie, humming colors that you get only in the polluted air of big cities, especially in the spring: impossible pinks and oranges reflected in the sky over Brooklyn, and some other mysterious thing in the light that made everything glow and the colors grate against one another the way they do in an old tinted photograph. The river with its choppy waves was all metallic blues and blacks, and the white blossoms stood out eerily against the sky.

Klaue's bodyguards followed a few yards behind us. Like Secret Service agents, they made a point of looking exactly like what they were, to scare people off, I suppose. They wore stiff navy blue suits and sunglasses, and the volume was always turned up on the transmitters that were hooked inside their jackets, so they constantly gave off beeps and bursts of radio static. They were both tall and unnecessarily muscular, it seemed to me, and if all that weren't bad enough they both had broad, square faces like comic-book superheroes, and crew cuts. I felt silly being followed by them, but there was nothing to do about it.

We began our walk in silence. It was unusual for Klaue to want to go strolling outside, and I was waiting to see what was on his mind before I said anything. A handful of other people were out in the park, and I was surprised at how few of them stared at us. I think it was because Klaue was so immediately recognizable. People tend to stare at faces they're sure they've seen somewhere before, in some film or magazine, but can't quite place, but to stare at someone as unmistakable as Klaue could only have been interpreted as gawking, and everyone seemed to want to feel above that.

We walked toward the far south end of the park, where there were almost no people. Klaue stopped at the low iron fence that ran along the edge of the river and stood looking out across the water.

"It is so beautiful," he said, "this time of year when everything is just beginning. I feel I must be outside—see it as much as possible . . ."

He fell silent. Then he asked, "Have you seen Ludwig recently?"

"He's been hard to get in touch with."

Klaue turned to me with his mouth closed, and seemed to be waiting for me to say more.

"No, I haven't seen him," I said.

He looked back toward the water.

"I am concerned about him," he said.

"Well, me too," I said. "Lydia sees him sometimes."

"Does she? And what does she say about him?"

"She said that he was upset about our fight."

"Naturally. But how *is* he?"

"I don't know, Klaue. Why are you so curious?"

"It's simply that I haven't heard from him in so long," he said.

"He's not sending you any more of his manuscript?"

"Well, I am not interested in his notes about Mops Hacker. I knew Mops, I fought by his side in the revolution, so there is no reason for me to read about him. But still I expected Ludwig to keep in touch with me. Perhaps you could write to him and find out whether you could see him. You see, his— illness is rather advanced. And I would like to know . . ."

"What's going to happen," I finished.

"Yes, and how quickly it progresses."

"Well, I did just write to him recently," I said. "Lydia asked me to."

"She would like the two of you to see each other again, I suppose."

"Yes, I think so."

"That's very good. Perhaps I will leave it in her hands, then."

"Is it true that the other dogs are all starting to become sick? Is that why you're so curious about Ludwig?"

"Why would you ask that?"

"Well, I hear things, you know . . ."

"From whom?"

I didn't answer. I was sure he must know my source was Lydia, and I was afraid he'd be angry with her. But instead he asked, "It wasn't a human, was it?"

I shook my head. He seemed relieved, but he took a step closer to me so that he stood looking down into my eyes, and said softly, "The general public is not to know, do you understand, Cleo? They must not suspect. You and I will help see to that. Do you understand?"

"So it is true?"

"Answer the question."

"Yes," I said. "I understand. But what will you do about it? What's going to happen?"

"We have our own scientists, dogs, working on the problem. Most of the others are not worried yet."

"But you are."

"No," Klaue said.

"But I am . . . What if they don't find a cure?"

"I have plans," Klaue said softly. "There is nothing to be afraid of. But it's best if you don't know them, Cleo. You won't be tempted to reveal anything this way. Let's end our discussion now." He turned and began to walk back toward the north end of the park, where we had come from. His bodyguards, beeping and crackling, strolled behind him, glancing from side to side as they went.

When he saw that I was not following, Klaue stopped. "Come," he said. "Come on." I still didn't move.

"I will walk you back to your apartment."

I sighed and started toward him. I supposed there was nothing I could do to make him say more now, and I wasn't sure that I wanted to know, anyway. If the dogs were all going to go insane, maybe it was better not to think about it for as long as possible. There wasn't anything I could do to stop it.

"Good girl," he said as I came up alongside him. He held out his arm, but I didn't feel like taking it and pretended not to notice.

LUDWIG DIDN'T answer my second letter, either, but Lydia invited me to dinner again two weeks later and told me that he was in better spirits, and it might be best to leave him alone for a little while now because he was absorbed in his work and hard for even her to reach.

Lydia and I got into the habit of dining together every week or two at her apartment. She seemed to enjoy my company, and sometimes I would sit for an hour or more in the big armchair listening to her play the piano after we ate, or if it was warm she would bring a piece of embroidery out to the terrace and sew while I worked on articles for Klaue, pausing occasionally to read them aloud and ask her advice. When my *Vanity Fair* article came out in mid-May, she was the first one I showed it to. In fact, immediately after I found the June issue at the newsstand I called her from a pay phone on the corner, got into a taxi, and took it to her. She said it was marvelous, called to her servant for Campari and sodas, and asked me to stay for dinner, although it was only two o'clock when I arrived. After that I would often phone her in the middle of the day or in the late afternoon if I was bored or stuck on something I was writing and go up to visit her.

There seemed no question of my ever inviting her to my tiny apartment, and besides, although she knew I owned a dog, I felt a little awkward about having her actually meet Rufus. She didn't like to leave home much, anyway, unless there was a very good reason, because she hated going out in public. Sometimes she would invite others to dine with us.

"I've got the most wonderful dog for you to meet," she told me one day. "His name is Burkhardt Weil, and he wrote the libretto for the opera that's going to be performed in Neu-hundstein's concert hall."

"Great," I said. "Can I interview him?"

"Let's just have a nice evening first, then maybe you can ask him," Lydia said. "You shouldn't work all the time. It's too stressful for you."

"You're right," I said.

Burkhardt Weil was a short, round-headed Bull Terrier who wore a monocle and a lopsided cravat, which gradually worked its way loose over the course of the evening until by the end it was almost completely untied. Part of the reason for this was that he had a habit of scratching his neck while he thought, which would sometimes bring the knot all the way around to one side, and then he would absently pull it forward without bothering to tighten it. He also liked to punctuate the conversation with waves of his fork, and sometimes there was food on it, so that by the time we had coffee he was covered with greasy spots and looked very disheveled.

"I wasn't *in* the battle in Rankstadt, you see," he told me. "I had two broken legs, if you can believe that. Two broken legs. I would have perished in the fire if someone hadn't re-membered to come and get me out of the attic. I could hardly drag myself. Some friends brought me out into the woods so I wouldn't get hurt. So I couldn't even see it. But by God, I wish I could have been there. What a fight," he said, flinging a piece of quail into the air.

"It was awful," Lydia said.

"You are so tenderhearted, Lydia," he said. "She is so tenderhearted. Although she has nerve when it's needed. We know that. But you've got to have real guts to be a soldier. It's different. You've got to be a dog, really, that's the thing. Be a dog," he said.

"What do you mean?" I asked.

"I mean dogs are different. There is a reason that we make perfect soldiers, if you don't mind my saying so. We feel about fighting and killing that it's a part of life. Sometimes the end of life, to be sure, if you're the one who's killed, but it's all very natural. That's the way we feel, and that's the way we were brought up, too. And we enjoy it. No matter what they have done to our brains we're still dogs, and the smell of blood does something to us, it's the most fantastic thing in the world, better than anything. Tell me, Lydia, haven't you ever felt that way?"

"Yes, of course, how could I help it?" she said.

"Then why, if you don't mind my asking this very personal question, but I'm curious, why didn't you join in the battle?"

"Because I felt it was wrong," she said. "That's all."

"How very, very interesting," Burkhardt said. "But I would have fought, you can be sure of that. I suppose that's why I was so interested in writing the libretto to tell the story. It's a small compensation, there's no smell of blood, but it's better than nothing. And that's something I miss in your culture, by the way," he said to me. "No blood. Everything is so sanitized. There are hardly any butchers' shops. And yet the slaughterhouses that supply your meat, I've seen them on television, they're really appalling, hellish. It's not natural at all. You don't have the chase or the fight or the smells that make everything worthwhile, and yet the most abominable suffering is created. And what do you do all day, you sit in little offices and think. It's a very bad way to live."

"Burkhardt," Lydia said, "that is exactly what you do all day, too, you sit and write your librettos. Isn't that true?"

"Well, I wouldn't if there was anything else to do. But there's not much opportunity for hunting in Manhattan. And of course there's nowhere else to go now. I don't mean that we ought to live in the wilderness like wolves. That isn't what I'm talking about."

"Certainly not, that wouldn't work at all. Oh, look, you're all out of wine," Lydia said.

"Yes, I am, thank you," Burkhardt said as the servant filled his glass. "Well," he continued, scratching his neck, "but you see, Cleo, that's why we've been reluctant to talk about the whole business of the battle, really."

"What do you mean?"

"Well, it's, it's prickly because, you know, we killed quite a few people. Nobody knew them, it's true, so there aren't any friends or relatives to come looking for us. You and a few other people, well, quite a few other people, but not the general public, know that we really did away with everyone in Rankstadt, but we weren't sure how the masses would feel about that. But now I think we're secure enough in our places in society that we can tell the story. People know us. I personally think it's ridiculous that in a place where dogs are killed by the millions for no reason whatsoever and humans are allowed to kill each other *en masse* in wars, though not for perfectly legitimate personal reasons on the street, it's ridiculous that anyone would feel we ought to be brought to justice for settling our own quarrel in Rankstadt, but that's what the worry was. Because we're not human, you see. If we were humans who had rebelled against an oppressive government in some tiny country, no one would blame us for it, or even care, most likely, but as we are dogs who have killed humans, the feeling was that people might, because they didn't know us very well, they might think—but I don't think it will happen now."

"It won't," Lydia said.

BURKHARDT LEFT at eleven o'clock, but I stayed to talk to Lydia. It was a warm June night and we sat out on her terrace. In the summer she set out two long planters full of bamboo that rustled in the breeze, and hung garden lanterns in between the stalks.

"Isn't he funny, with his cravat?" She laughed.

"But why didn't you tell him what you thought about the battle?" I asked. "I would have liked to hear that."

"Well, I don't like to talk about it," Lydia said. "It isn't that I'm trying to be secretive, but I just don't know how. It seems so complicated, and it's over now, and our lives are different. Burkhardt likes to talk about it because he wasn't in it."

"But you weren't, either, were you?"

Lydia bowed her head and closed her eyes. We were both a little bit drunk. A warm wind blew from behind her and lifted her mane slightly, and the lanterns cast long, swaying bamboo shadows across the table. "Oh yes," she said. "I was in it. I didn't fight against the humans."

"What did you do?" I asked.

"When it was almost over, when all the humans were dead, I killed two dogs. I had once cared for one of them very much. But it wasn't difficult. Perhaps if you, as a human, had been in my situation, it would have been. It's very hard to explain these things. I think we are different, humans and dogs."

"What was his name?" I asked.

"It was Mops Hacker. I thought that someone had already told you the story," she said, glancing at me. "But I guess not."

She dabbed her nose with a handkerchief and then yawned into it, her ears flattening against her head.

"Won't you tell me the story?"

"How can I tell you?" Lydia said softly, as if to herself. "We had known each other all our lives; I watched him grow up."

"What was he like?" I asked.

"Oh, he was bad, very bad, always missing school . . ." She smiled to herself, and then shook her head. "He was very rebellious and annoying when we were young. I remember he spilled ink on me one day. I was perhaps eight or nine years old. We—whatever they'd done to us, you know, made us mature at about the same rate as human children, although we seem to begin aging faster after about twenty. I don't know why. But at any rate we had the same sort of school as the human children did, with a human schoolmaster, only we had a separate schoolhouse, of course. So on that day Mops was sitting in the corner by himself, at his desk, because he had done something wrong. All the rest of us were sent home for lunch, and he had to sit there and write something, to make up for what he had done.

"I was the last one to leave the classroom, because I had a new coat, which I didn't like at all—it was very tight, and complicated to button up, and of course I didn't need it because I have very thick fur. So I wasn't able to get my coat on for some time, and when I did, the schoolhouse was empty except for Mops. When I walked past him, he—he simply took up the inkwell, like this, as if he were showing it to me, and then he threw it at me. I remember he was laughing very hard, and I lunged at him, and we had a fight. The schoolmaster heard the fight and came back in and broke us up. That was the only time I was ever really in trouble. I bit him, you see. My fur is so thick that he hardly scratched me at all, but he was bleeding terribly, because I'd been holding on to him when the school-master pulled me off, so there was a great big gash. He wasn't hurt. It was the scruff of his neck.

"I often wondered afterward why he had done that. I think it was because my fur was so white, and my coat was white, too, and he had a bottle of black ink, and it—just seemed irresistible to him. It makes sense, after all. And nobody was looking. But, my God, it took me forever to get it all out. I had to cut a big patch of fur off, and I looked very strange for a month afterward. I was so angry! I growled at him every time we passed on an empty lane or ran into each other at the edge of a field. He was terrified of me." Lydia laughed. "But after a while we forgot all about it."

"Was he in love with you?" I asked.

"I suppose so," she said. Her eyes gleamed as she looked from my face to the rustling stand of bamboo behind me.

"Of course, most of us were forbidden to talk to him. He always wore ragged clothes, you know, and his master was a drunk."

"But you cared for him."

"It was hard not to like him. Well, a lot of the dogs didn't, when we were younger. But he was so clever. He never seemed to give up. I used to speak with him in private sometimes, in the year before the revolution. He had such ideas . . ."

"About what?"

"Oh, about everything. He wanted us to go off and live in the hills together, or he wanted all the dogs to found a new city somewhere. It was always one thing and another. But then he had his last great idea."

"The revolution?" I asked. Lydia nodded. "And then what happened in the battle?"

She shook her head. "Things got out of hand then—with all of us. And so many innocent people were killed . . .

"But now it's behind us. That sort of battle has its time, and feelings that go along with it, like a love affair, and there really isn't any way to describe it afterward. It will be interesting to see Burkhardt's opera. But I can't tell you . . . he had shed so much blood, so very much, and then we had a fight, and I just—I just killed him. And I am a dog, after all. Not only a dog but one bred to do certain things, although I may choose not to sometimes. I don't know whether that is a kind of freedom . . ."

We sat in the gently swaying light of the lanterns. Beyond the french windows, I could see one of her servants turning out the lamps in the living room.

"Oh, look how late it is now," Lydia said, "and you look so tired, too. Should I ask Yusif to carry you down to the limousine?"

"No, I'm not that tired," I said. "Besides, he's probably already in bed. Don't wake him up."

"Well, at least have the doorman get you a taxi. He's awake."

As I lay in bed later that night, I tried to imagine Lydia killing someone. Would her face have taken on the blank, consumed look of a dog in a fight, her peaceful eyes have gone hard and shallow? It was not a side of her I had ever seen, but I could picture it. It didn't surprise me.

11

(CLEO)

I met Luitpold in the middle of summer. It was a stifling day when brick and concrete baked in the dull sun, and even the shade provided no more relief from the heat than the darkness of an oven would. There was some respite in the immediate auras of a few green trees along the street, but these were sparse as I walked up First Avenue toward the bus stop.

I was planning to visit Lydia, who I'd discovered had the biggest marble bathtub in the world and who didn't mind my coming over to lie in it on days like this. We were in the middle of a terrible heat wave, with temperatures going up to 107, and I had no air conditioner. I might have been able to afford one, but money from the articles was coming in slowly and disappearing quickly, and what little was left over I was determined to save so that I would never have to be as afraid of poverty as I had been in the past, before I'd worked for Klaue. Besides that, there was a wonderfully luxurious feeling about going

from my apartment to Lydia's. I would write in the morning
next to the fan, holding glasses of iced Spanish coffee against
my neck and throwing ice cubes into Rufus's water bowl, and
when it became unbearable I would take Rufus down to my
neighbor Sam's apartment to lie in front of his air conditioner
with the two miniature poodles who, along with the ex-
girlfriend they belonged to, had become more or less permanent
fixtures in Sam's life. Having decided that we wouldn't date,
Sam and I had become friends, and in fact during the occasional
months when Nancy and the dogs disappeared, Rufus and I
would sometimes spend the night in the comparative coolness
or warmth of Sam's apartment—he had a big down comforter,
too—an arrangement that suited us both much better than trying to date.

   After dropping Rufus off I would walk three and a half
long blocks to the bus stop and wait, sweltering, remembering
all the times I had stood there during college summers on my
way to temp jobs in midtown, even last summer, wearing sticky
nylons, calculating over and over the amount of money I would
make that week, that month, that summer, and how I would
spend it, and knowing that I would never be able to budget it
the way I ought to. And now, instead, it was eleven o'clock in
the morning, and I was on my way to Lydia's to throw myself
into a marble bathtub the size of a swimming pool and eat
slices of chilled melon that her servant would bring to me on
a big pale yellow platter.

   I was sort of enjoying myself, trying to imagine that I was
going to a temp job and then surprising myself with the fact
that I wasn't, and so I was a little disappointed when a large
black limousine pulled up in front of the bus stop. There was
nobody there but me, and I knew it had to be a dog. I supposed

it was probably Klaue. But when the driver's tinted window slid down, I saw the face of a chauffeur I didn't recognize.

It was a middle-aged man with pleasant, horsey features and large ears. He smiled politely and asked whether I was Cleo Pira, and I told him I was. He invited me to get in, and I heard the click of a lock and opened one of the back doors.

"Please close it quickly," said a deep voice from the air-conditioned darkness inside. It was only at that moment that I thought to wonder if I should just be getting in a strange limousine whose owner I didn't know.

"Who are you?" I asked, holding the door open.

"My name is Luitpold Helmholz," the voice said. It was soft and grave. Even as I heard it, my eyes adjusted to the lack of light and I saw an enormous fawn-colored Great Dane, wearing a white shirt, a black jacket, and a loose cravat. I got in and closed the door.

"I am the president of the Society of Dogs," he said to me as I settled into the cool seat. "Where were you going, Miss Pira?"

"To Lydia's," I told him. "Do you know where that is?"

"Of course." He tapped on the back of the front seat with a large silver-headed cane. "Please, Mr. Bucks, to Lydia Petze's apartment," he said.

"Sure, Mr. Helmholz," the driver answered.

I thought their formality was charming and silly, and I liked Luitpold right away.

"Well, Miss Pira," Luitpold said, putting out his large gloved hand, "I am glad to make your acquaintance."

"Thanks. It's very nice to meet you," I told him. "Please call me Cleo—if you want," I added, feeling that perhaps I was being too familiar for his taste.

"Very well." He nodded his huge head. "You may call me Luitpold. I am never certain," he said as he took his hand away, "how to act here. I believe some people cater to us because of our wealth, and adopt our manners, which are more formal than yours. So I reciprocate, to indulge them." He smiled to himself. Actually, what he did was lower his head, ears forward, and open his mouth very slightly into his cravat for a split second. Then he looked at me again.

"I have invited you into my car," he said, "because I have very much wanted to meet you. I was not able to obtain your telephone number."

"No one would give it to you?"

"Well," he said slowly, "I did not know that you were a friend of Lydia's. Ludwig said he had lost the number."

"And Klaue . . . ?"

"He was reluctant to give it to me."

"I wonder why?"

"Cleo," Luitpold said, "there are some things I would like to discuss with you. Perhaps we could meet in private to talk. Would you mind that?"

"Not at all," I told him.

"I don't mean to be secretive," he said, gesturing toward Mr. Bucks, "but it is a matter of business and I would like to discuss it at length, in a more comfortable place."

"Okay," I said.

"Now"—Luitpold settled back into the seat—"I believe I will call on Lydia also. I have not seen her in a long time."

"Are you friends?" I asked.

"Yes," he said.

He folded his hands over the top of his cane, which rested on the floor between his legs.

"It's hot out," I commented.

"It is. I am so seldom out in the open air," Luitpold said. "The weather hardly affects me. I miss it, sometimes."

I nodded. "Do you miss Canada? The wilderness and everything?" I asked.

"Yes. Of course."

"You know, I was just wondering, if you don't mind my asking—why don't all the dogs have estates out in the country? You could, couldn't you?"

"I suppose we could," Luitpold said. "But the city suits our tastes in other ways. It is so fascinating. And here, too, we have a sense of community. I think we fear to be away from one another's company for too long."

"I can understand that."

We rode for a while in silence.

When we arrived at Lydia's, we found her sitting by the french windows in her living room and looking out onto the terrace, wearing a pale green-and-yellow kimono. A bowl of green grapes sat on a little table next to her chair.

"Luitpold is also here, ma'am," Yusif, her servant, announced as we came into the room.

"Luitpold!" she said, getting up.

"I'm sorry," he said, "I should have had my driver call as we were coming up, but I didn't think of it."

"And here I am in my kimono—but never mind. How are you?"

"Very well," he answered, standing with his hands folded over his cane. "And how are you?"

"I'm very well, too," she replied. "Cleo," she said, turning to me, "I had Yusif get a bath all ready for you, but if you came up in Luitpold's car I suppose you're not hot anymore."

"I'm not."

"Oh well. Cleo comes up here to swim in my bathtub sometimes," she said to Luitpold. "She doesn't have an air conditioner."

"No air conditioner! That is inexcusable," said Luitpold. "We can't expect you to write articles without an air conditioner. We must allocate some funds."

"Oh no, it's all right," I said. "I like it this way. It's sort of like taking a sauna and then jumping into an icy lake."

"Well, if you enjoy it, I suppose it's all right," Luitpold said. "But do tell us if you would like one."

"Cleo spends quite a lot of time here working on her articles," Lydia said.

"Really."

"Sometimes she reads them out to me and I give her advice. Of course, I don't know the first thing about writing. But it works out well."

"Oh yes, that's very good," Luitpold said. "But I suppose that Klaue changes everything later?" he asked me.

"He doesn't really," I said. "So far he seems to like most of the things I write."

"I see."

"I don't think," Lydia said slowly, rolling a grape between her fingers, "that Cleo knows anything she isn't supposed to, yet."

"Aha," Luitpold said. The two of them stood there contemplating each other, their nostrils flared, as if they were each trying to catch the scent of what the other was thinking.

"*What* don't I know?"

They both looked at me, surprised, as if they'd forgotten I was there.

"Let's have a drink," Lydia said. "Yusif! Luitpold would like scotch."

"Oh no, thank you, Lydia, it's rather early for me," he said.

"All right, a glass of water, then. And Cleo and I will have the usual."

"It's a little early for me, too, Lydia," I said. "It's not even noon yet."

"So, bring us three glasses of water. I suppose we will just have to drink later. Now," she said to me and Luitpold, "I am going to put some clothes on while you make yourselves comfortable."

I settled onto the sofa with a sigh, while Luitpold took one of the armchairs.

"We don't mean to be secretive, Cleo," he said to me. "The situation is complicated, you understand. It's a matter of trying to decide what the best course is."

"Sure," I said.

We sat there without speaking until Lydia came back, wearing a long, straight-skirted dress of aquamarine and pale green with a deep V neck. She sat down on the end of the sofa nearest to Luitpold.

"A lovely dress," he said softly.

"Oh, thank you. Now, what shall we talk about?"

Luitpold glanced at me. "I feel that we should tell Cleo what we know."

"Yes, I think so, too," Lydia said. She looked at me, sadly, I thought. "Well?" she said to Luitpold. He lowered his head, either nodding to her or indicating that he didn't want to speak. Lydia turned to face me.

"Things have gotten rather bad with the dogs," Lydia told me. "Almost all of the others are ill. We still have no idea what the cause is. It's the same disorder that Ludwig has."

I nodded.

"No one is as badly off as Ludwig, yet, from what I can gather, although I talk to Ludwig so seldom. But Klaue is not doing well at all."

"I didn't realize that," said Luitpold.

"It's true," Lydia said. "He has rather frequent periods of illness now. You realize, Cleo, that the general public is not supposed to know about this. But the real problem is that Klaue now seems to be making some plans that he is reluctant to tell even us dogs about."

"He has bought some weapons," Luitpold said.

"Oh," said Lydia. "I knew about the armory he built into the castle—"

"He is stocking it. He seems to have forgotten that I, as president of the Society, have a key to the files in which he keeps the records of his expenditures, and so I look at them every so often, without telling him, of course. Until now he has done nothing very much out of the ordinary."

"He shouldn't have done that without asking your permission," Lydia said.

"Of course not. But if I should confront him, he will move his files to a place where I can't look at them."

"He shouldn't be allowed to do that," Lydia said.

"He is not allowed. However, I think that he would move them, and it would be difficult for me to stop him. He has a certain number of friends among the dogs, as you know."

"Yes." Lydia sighed. "So we do really need Cleo's help."

"I am afraid we do. That is, if she would agree to help us."

"What do you want me to do?"

"Just to find out what you can, that's all," Lydia said.

Luitpold looked at her thoughtfully, and then gave a low sigh. "What can he possibly want with an arsenal in the castle? It can't be a good thing . . ."

". . . not a good thing," Lydia murmured. She looked at me.

"I'll do my best," I said. "He doesn't always want to tell me things, but I'll see what I can find out."

I THOUGHT of many subtle ways to probe Klaue for the information, but somehow when I next talked to him I was struck with stage fright and they all disappeared. He had called to discuss my writing about the premiere of the opera, which was to be in September. I answered his questions distractedly.

"What is the matter, Cleo? You seem not to be paying attention," he said.

"I'm sorry, I was just . . ."

He waited.

"Actually, I've heard a rumor, that's what it is," I said. "And it's been bothering me."

"I see. About what?"

"About an arsenal in the castle," I said. That at least wouldn't get Luitpold in trouble.

"Who told you this?"

I hesitated. "Everyone. It's all over the place. Not humans, but all the dogs know it, and they're all wondering what it's for. Did you know that they were talking about it?"

"No, I didn't know that," Klaue said.

"I didn't think so. That's why I thought I'd better tell you."

"That is very interesting," Klaue said.

"What *is* it for?"

"How do you know that *all* the dogs know about it?"

"Because—different dogs that Lydia has had over to dinner have said that. Those were the words they used."

"I see. Cleo, I have some business to attend to. But you will hear from me shortly." He hung up the phone without bothering to say goodbye.

An hour later one of his secretaries called and asked me to come to a meeting at the Dogs' Club that evening. When I'd first agreed to write for Klaue I'd thought that I would be allowed to attend all of the general conferences there, but in fact this was the first one I'd been invited to.

My cab got stuck in a traffic jam, somehow, and I was late when I arrived at the Dogs' Club. There the door was opened by a man who looked more like a security guard than a butler, who led me up the same narrow, carpeted stairs I'd taken when I had first come to visit Klaue, and then up a second flight and into a parquet-floored anteroom to the conference chamber.

"The meeting's already going on," the man said. "You'll have to wait until I leave this room to go in; the big doors over there can only be unlocked from outside when the anteroom door is closed." He left me in the eerie, shining silence for a moment, and then I heard a bolt click. I gently pushed open one of the wide double doors and let myself into the big room.

Here the dogs, all one hundred and fifty of them, sat around a long mahogany table. Klaue stood at the head, wearing a new uniform, similar to the old Prussian one in which he'd first arrived in New York but a little more modern-looking, simplified and boxier, with larger buttons, as if it were a stage-costume version of the original. All eyes were fixed on him, and nobody seemed to notice my arrival except Klaue himself, who glanced up briefly from the table when I entered. All the other dogs were dressed formally for the meeting, too; and although some of the males had given up their military coats in favor of tuxedos, enough of them still looked like soldiers to give the impression of a small army. Ludwig was there, in a dark navy suit, and Lydia, in a pale lavender gown, sat next to him. Neither of them seemed to notice my arrival.

The only empty chair I could see was far away from the door, so instead of walking all the way around the room I leaned against the wall.

"And yet if our scientists do not find a cure," Klaue had been asking as I came in, "then what will happen?"

His question was followed by a general silence.

"It is a terrible future to imagine, and yet I ask you, now, not to turn away from it but to face it bravely, as soldiers. What will happen?

"The disease will progress and spread, as it has been doing. Gradually, all of us will lose our minds. We may try to hide it from the world, but our servants are already beginning to talk. Once we are helpless, insane, then what will happen? We will no longer be able to refuse the human doctors and scientists who are so eager to examine us. If some of us are sane, we can perhaps protect the others, but if there are none left—then what? We will be confined in their laboratories and hospitals, and we will live on there, helpless, alone, humiliated. We may long for death, but they will not allow it. Should we refuse to eat, lose the ability to move, even to breathe, they will attach us to their abominable machines and keep us alive, prisoners. We do not fear death, but this—we cannot allow it to happen.

"If we all move into the castle, we can be stronger, unified, and yet, if we are all mad, who will, in the end, prevent them from coming and taking us out?"

Klaue paused and looked around the room.

"So I have built an armory in the castle," he said. "The rumor is true. I did not announce it because it seemed, perhaps, too early to force all of us to consider this terrible eventuality.

But this was an error in judgment. We are not afraid to face unpleasantness. We do not need to be protected from it. We must join together to plan our future course. I have no more power than any of you, but as it has fallen to me to lay out and build the castle, I was, of necessity, the one who put the armory in it.

"There will be no unnecessary use of force," he went on more quietly. "The castle is a fortress. It will not be easy for people to enter it against our wishes should we decide to barricade ourselves inside. If the time comes, we will make our desire quite clear: that we wish to be left alone. Only those who go to great trouble to disregard our wishes will suffer. There is no question of our taking an offensive stand against any humans. There are millions of them in this city alone, and if they united against us we would, of course, be helpless, so we will give them no cause to do so. And in particular we will not allow them to know about our armory or our weapons."

There was a general murmur of assent.

"If anyone opposes this plan, let him speak freely." Klaue paused, but no answer came.

"So," he said. "Let us call this meeting to an end and go back to our homes. There will be time enough to think about these difficult things in the future. For now, we must live, and enjoy our lives, while we can."

Slowly the dogs began rising from their chairs. Klaue picked up a little device that looked like a TV remote control from the table and pressed a button on it, the room's big double doors slid open, and the dogs filed out into the hall, silent except for the rustle of skirts and the taps of their canes against the floor.

I wanted to find Ludwig and Lydia in the crowd, but Klaue came up behind me and took my arm.

"Cleo," he said, leading me to a far corner of the room. He

held my upper arm tightly and looked down into my eyes. "Do you understand what I have said tonight?"

I returned his stare, thinking. Before I could answer, he said, "The armory will contain weapons to be used only for self-defense, in the most dire emergency. Yet perhaps this seems, to you, excessive. You think we should not arm ourselves. Is that so? After all, you yourself have never been in a situation where it was necessary to be armed."

"That's not exactly true," I said, thinking of the little laser gun I still carried occasionally in my boot. "I do live in—"

"But," Klaue continued, ignoring me, "I must ask you to put yourself in our position, although I realize that is difficult . . ."

"But I do understand," I said.

"Do you? I mean specifically," he asked, "do you understand the importance of keeping it a secret?"

"Yes."

"All the dogs know you were here tonight. We usually hold our meetings in German; I spoke in English only for your benefit. Some of them felt that you should not be allowed at the meeting, but I explained that as certain dogs had already let you into their confidence by telling you about the armory, it was necessary. Obviously several of the dogs already trust you, since they told you this."

He paused. It wasn't true; only Luitpold and Lydia had told me, and I wasn't supposed to let on that I knew, only probe Klaue for information.

"I guess some of them do trust me," I said cautiously.

"Those who meet you sense that you will not betray us," Klaue went on softly. "That you will not divulge this information even to your closest friends. I chose well when I assigned you to write about the castle project. Didn't I?"

He loomed over me, filling my field of vision and blocking out any possible answer except one.

"You did," I replied.

"Of course, many of the dogs have not met you. That is why they expressed reluctance to have you at the meeting. If any humans should find out about our plans, these dogs will blame you. It's a difficult position for you. But if you should hear of the rumor spreading, somehow, you will tell me immediately, so we may be able to stop it. We will not give the dogs any reason to mistrust you."

BY THE time I left the room, all the dogs were gone. I took a taxi home, hoping to find a message from Lydia on my answering machine, thinking she might want to talk about the meeting, but there was none.

She didn't call me for three days, and when she did, no mention was made of the meeting, the armory, or the weapons. We had lunch with Luitpold later in the week, and nothing was said about it then, either.

I didn't ask any questions. If they didn't want to think about it now, that was all right with me. And what would there have been to discuss, anyway? It seemed dangerous to put the arsenal, potentially, into the hands of a group of dogs who were losing their minds, and yet I could believe that the weapons might become necessary for their self-defense, and in any case the dogs clearly wanted them, so to prevent them from having guns would have necessitated betraying them, and it did not even occur to me to do that. Really, I was glad not to have to discuss the guns or anything at all having to do with the future; I did my best to ignore it all.

Lydia and I went back to our regular pattern of visiting. If

I had allowed myself, I would have realized that there would never be another summer like the one that was then drawing to a close. I did know, really, both of us knew, but we spent longer and longer evenings out on the terrace talking about everything else in the world, in the forest of shadows thrown by the garden lanterns. In the last days of August, fireflies appeared among the bamboo, more of them than I'd ever seen in New York, and they settled everywhere, on our table, our hands, in the folds of our clothes, so that we'd be throwing off little swarms of them even after we came inside.

In spite of my best efforts to get rid of them, two or three would often come home with me, and I'd fall asleep watching them circle in the darkness. I wondered what they were saying to each other as they blinked on and off and whether, now that they were so far away from the others on the terrace, their messages were being received. I left the windows open so they could escape to the sumac trees in the empty lot behind my building, but I was afraid that they didn't like it there, among the tough weeds and the garbage, any better than inside my apartment, and that they probably went out into the city looking for other fireflies and got lost among all the lights, the complicated signals not meant for them.

12

(CLEO)

The opera opened on an evening in September. Lydia had convinced Ludwig to attend, and we'd all agreed to meet half an hour early in one of the finished rooms adjoining the concert hall where hors d'oeuvres and drinks were being served before the performance.

Since the castle grounds were only a block and a half from my apartment I walked there, in my new purple dress, trying to catch glimpses of myself in the ground-floor windows between Avenues C and B. It was the year that strange wedding-dress style first became popular, a short full skirt with a kind of wide train hanging down behind to ankle length so that it looked like a cutaway version of the dogs' 1880s dresses, and I'd never worn one before that afternoon. Mine had a neat little tailored jacket on top with sleeves that stopped just above the elbow and a V neck, both trimmed with purple fur, and I had a matching pillbox hat of dyed fox, short gloves, and a small parasol. It was an outfit that might have come out looking terrible, but the designer who had made it was so neat and conservative that I looked overall like a slightly furry version of a 1940s airline stewardess, which I thought, as I watched my reflection in the windows, was a nice effect. I found that if I opened the parasol and twirled the skirt I had the appearance of a paper flower on a parade float, but I decided not to do this.

As I approached the castle's wide brick gatehouse on Avenue B, I saw that a crowd had already begun to gather outside the entrance, probably hoping to catch sight of the famous people who would show up for the performance. I passed by and went to a little side door on Second Street, which was guarded by two very polite men in matching red uniforms. Although I'd never seen them before, they seemed to know who I was and let me past the velvet ropes with generous smiles and no questions. I went up a few steps and then through an open door on the inside of the gatehouse and into the big central courtyard. A handful of dogs and a few important people were milling around on the flagstones, holding drinks and commenting on the building. Its exterior was almost finished, except for some of the towers and a large section of the roof on the west side, which wasn't visible from where we stood.

"Look, it's Klaue!" a woman in a bronze-colored, drapy dress said as I passed the little group she was standing in. I turned and saw that she was pointing to the highest peak of the roof across the courtyard from us. There, sure enough, a hundred feet above our heads, was a gold statue of a dog standing on its hind legs and holding a sword upright. Judging from the fullness of the fur it might have been Klaue, but then again it might just as well have been Lydia, except for the long military jacket, or it could have been any number of other dogs.

"Hmm," I said to myself. The woman glanced at me, frowned, and turned back to her companions. I wondered if she was frowning at me, the nobody who'd been given permission to write about the castle, or at my outfit. I didn't know who she was, so I guessed that she didn't know me either. I wished I'd shown the dress to Lydia before I'd worn it out. What could I have been thinking? Or maybe it was the hat.

"Cleo, look at you!" said a voice from off to my right.

"Oh, Lydia," I said.

"It's perfectly adorable. Stop worrying," she said.

"How did you know I was worried?"

"Well, I don't know . . . Anyway, it's charming." She put her hand on my arm and stepped back to look at me.

"Thanks. And you look really beautiful," I said. Like most of the dogs at formal events, she was dressed in the style of Rankstadt, in a long, elegant, bustled dress of moss green, and she carried a large parasol, as she always did when she went out, which she never opened but used as a cane.

"Thank you. Ludwig is here, but he's inside. I came out because I saw you through the window. Shall we go find him?"

"How is he?" I asked as we walked across the flagstones.

"As well as he can be," Lydia said. "I'm glad he agreed to come."

"Me too. I haven't seen him in a long time."

We went into the main building by way of a flight of stone steps that ran up the side of the long gallery flanking the courtyard on the right. Past the heavy wooden door at the top of the steps was a little hallway, and to the left was the room in which the food and drinks were being served. It had a small chandelier and a table crowded with silver platters of hors d'oeuvres, and a bar at the side. The wallpaper had been hand-painted with scenes of nymphs playing among grapevines.

"Isn't this nice?" Lydia said. "I can't wait until the whole castle is finished."

"Are you really going to give up your apartment and live here, like Klaue said all the dogs will?"

"Oh, I don't think so," said Lydia. "I'd prefer just to visit. But I suppose a lot of the dogs will."

"You can have dinner parties here."

"What? Oh yes, that will be fun. Here's Ludwig," she said.

He was standing at the tall, narrow window with a glass in his hand, looking out into the courtyard. As we approached, one of his ears turned toward us, and then his head followed.

"Hello," I said.

"How nice to see you again." I heard the whisper of clock-work gears distinctly when he spoke, either because his voice was softer than usual or because the faint mechanical whir behind it was more pronounced. I took his hand, and his stiff fingers closed briefly on mine before he dropped it.

"How are you?" I asked.

"Oh, very well," he replied. One of his ears turned sideways as if he was annoyed at the question.

"I'm doing well, too," I said quickly. "Look at the outfit I bought. Do you like it?"

"It's lovely," Ludwig said. "You always look lovely, Cleo."

"Thank you," I said, touched. I didn't think he'd said anything like that before. "How's Rob? I haven't seen him in a long time, either."

Ludwig's ear turned even farther back. "I have let him go."

"Oh. That's too bad, I liked him."

"Well," Ludwig said. His eyes flickered vaguely, and then, as if dismissing something, he lifted his drink and finished it in one swallow.

"I am really so glad you came, Ludwig," Lydia said. "I'm glad that the three of us can be together for a time."

"Yes," he said.

We talked for a while about the castle, and when it would be finished—late winter was what Klaue had told me—and what it would be like for the dogs to be living together in it. Ludwig had no intention of leaving his apartment either, although Klaue was trying hard to convince them both to move in.

A little while before the performance was to begin, Lydia suggested that we take a stroll in the courtyard, to see it in the twilight, and so we went down the long stairs and out into the evening.

Although most of the rooms in the building weren't finished and many of the windows still had no glass, Klaue had managed to put a light in every one of them. There were floodlights along the walls, too, and strings of white bulbs outlined some of the details, so the whole structure had the look that buildings sometimes get in thick New York night air of being made of luminous stone and surrounded by a haze of light. We walked slowly around the edges of the courtyard, saying nothing at all to one another. When we were at the far end I caught sight of the golden statue on the roof again, floodlit from underneath now so that it seemed as if it meant to leap upward into the pink sky, but I didn't mention it.

THE OPERA that was performed that night, and every night for the rest of that week in September 2010, has never been shown since, and given everything that happened afterward I doubt it will be seen again. It was not videotaped and the libretto has never been published because Klaue, who had put himself in charge of everything that went on in the castle, decided that it should be experienced only in the concert hall at Neuhundstein. I heard that the librettist, Burkhardt Weil, and the composer (a Rottweiler named Heinrich Kohlhaus whom I never met), and a lot of the performers argued with Klaue about this. They would have made money if the opera had become more widely available. But Klaue won.

Now Klaue, Burkhardt, and the composer are gone. Since the artists themselves didn't oppose publication of the libretto, I feel that there's no reason to keep it secret anymore. There's so little left to remind us of the dogs, anyway. I know that in spite of the libretto's being made available, in spite of all that Ludwig has written and anything I write about them, they'll be forgotten eventually, as everything is. And yet I can't help wanting to raise any dam, however small, against the flood of time, to hold it back for just a little longer. So here is the libretto that tells the story of the dogs' last days in Rankstadt.

13

MOPS HACKER: THE OPERA
Heinrich Kohlhaus
Libretto by Burkhardt Weil

(TRANSLATED BY CLEO PIRA)

CHARACTERS

MOPS HACKER, *a mutt*—Tenor
OTTO, *a Bull Terrier, friend of Mops*—Bass
MAX, *a Belgian Shepherd, friend of Mops*—Baritone
FRIEDRICH, *a German Shepherd, the Mayor's dog*—Bass
LYDIA, *a Samoyed*—Mezzosoprano
THE MAYOR, *a man*—Bass
HANS, *a young man*—Tenor
WILHELM, *a young man*—Baritone
MOPS'S MASTER, *a man*—Baritone
AUGUSTUS RANK, *a man*—Bass
TWO FRIENDS OF LYDIA, *dogs*—Alto and Soprano
THREE MEN—Tenor, Baritone, and Bass
A BOY—Soprano
Other residents of Rankstadt, DOGS *and* HUMANS

Place: *Rankstadt, an isolated town in the Canadian wilderness*
Time: *September 1999, but the culture resembles that of Prussia about 1882*

ACT ONE

SCENE ONE

The town green in Rankstadt, surrounded by quaint houses, a church with a clock in its steeple, and, in the background to the left, the great laboratory, a dark barnlike building. The MAYOR *addresses the* HUMANS *and* DOGS.

MAYOR. Tomorrow marks one hundred years
    Since our town was founded here
    In the wilderness of Canada
    By the great Augustus Rank.

HUMANS. Tomorrow marks one hundred years
    Since our town was founded here,
    Our Rankstadt.

MAYOR. He laid plans for a mighty race of soldiers
    To be created by his loyal men.
    Then, seeing age and feebleness approaching,
    Rank took his life. He promised to return again
    To lead his army.
    For years his followers labored in our town,
    Then their children, and their children's sons,
    In secret, undiscovered, undistracted by the world,
    Striving always to complete the noble task.
    Then thirty years ago we finished it at last!

HUMANS. All our lives we've labored, labored
    In the service of his noble cause.
    Now his army is completed,
    Dogs with nimble hands in place of paws,
    Voices to call across the battlefields,
    And no mercy in their hearts at all!
    Vicious soldiers, loyal and fearless!

Among all armies that have ever been they're peerless!
Dogs!

DOGS. Dogs!

Dogs with hands to grasp a sword and aim a gun
And minds to understand how wars are won.
If only Rank will come and tell us who to fight,
We'll leave no living, breathing enemy in sight.

MAYOR. He left us, but he promised to return in spirit
When the soldiers were completed.
And here they are!

HUMANS. Here they are! Soon Rank will return!

ALL. They/We are brave and mighty soldiers,
Fearless noble dogs are they/we.
Hail Rank, who gave these things to us!
Soon he will return.

MAYOR. And now we must prepare
For tomorrow's centennial feast.
To honor Rank, his soldiers,
Our labors, and our town.

HUMANS *and* DOGS. Tomorrow marks one hundred years
Since our town was founded here
By the great Augustus Rank.
From dawn to dusk we'll celebrate and then
We'll dance all night till morning comes again.

SCENE TWO

MAX *and* OTTO *stand at the edge of the deserted town green.*

MAX. Why do you loiter, Otto? We must get to work.

OTTO. My heart is strangely heavy, Max.
There are no soldiers to celebrate at tomorrow's feast,
For we are only slaves, nothing more.

MAX. We serve the humans who created us
    While we wait for Rank's spirit to call all of us forth to war.
OTTO. But we sleep on the floor like dogs,
    And wear these collars. We must serve at the tables
    And swim in icy rivers after game we may not eat.
    It is disgraceful. I'm sure Rank never intended this.
MAX. Don't speak so loud—I hear young Hans and Wilhelm
    approaching.

WILHELM *and* HANS *approach.*

OTTO. I only want to be treated with respect
    As one of Rank's noble soldiers.
WILHELM *(to* HANS*).* What kind of talk is this?
HANS *(to* WILHELM*).* Perhaps Herr Freund has beaten him again.
    I've seen him whip brave Otto with a stick
    For failing to outrun a hare.
WILHELM *(to* HANS*).* A man may do whatever he likes with his
    own dog, Hans.
    That's no business of ours. But we should see to it
    That they get to work.
                (to MAX *und* OTTO*)*
    Why do you linger here? Go and prepare for the feast.
MAX. We were just going, but Otto had a stone in his paw
    And I stopped to help him.
HANS. Let me see.
OTTO. It's all right now! Let's go, Max.

MAX *and* OTTO *exit.*

SCENE THREE
MOPS HACKER *is asleep by a large rock in the woods. His* MASTER
can be heard calling from offstage.

MOPS'S MASTER. Mops Hacker! Mops Hacker! Where are you?
>   Cursed dog, you'll make me a laughingstock
>   If you don't show up to help prepare for the feast.
>   You've hidden too many times before. Mops! Mops!

MOPS *(Stirring but not waking).* Cursed master, this morning I
>   won't answer you.
>   But if only once I could answer you properly, with a sword!
>   Oh, what joy!
>   What joy to split his ugly head
>   And leave him lying there for dead,
>   To burn his house and all that's in it,
>   To stand up finally to fight, and win it!
>   Oh, how I long to kill him.

MOPS *curls up again. A golden cloud of smoke appears.* MOPS *yawns,
and the smoke flies into his mouth.*

MOPS *(Waking).* What's this! I am filled with strength
>   As if another's spirit had entered me.
>   I feel as if I could easily crush
>   My master's head between my jaws.
>   Oh, blissful dream of strength, how often it has come to me.
>   Yet when I wake it's gone.

MOPS'S MASTER *enters carrying a large stick.*

MOPS'S MASTER. Damned dog! There you are! You'll pay for
>   this.

Beats MOPS *and chases him offstage.*

SCENE FOUR

MALE DOGS *are setting a long table on the town green.* MOPS *is carrying a stack of plates.* FEMALE DOGS *walk by carrying garlands and flowers, led by* LYDIA.

MALE DOGS. Look! How beautiful they are!
FEMALE DOGS. How pretty the streets of our town will be
    Decked with ivy and flowers.

FEMALE DOGS *exit.*

MOPS. Lydia! Snow-white Lydia! How beautiful she is!

While watching LYDIA *go,* MOPS *bumps into* FRIEDRICH *and drops the stack of plates.*

FRIEDRICH. Stupid Mops, look what you've done.
    Why do you bother to stare at Lydia?
    She'd never look twice at an ugly mutt like you.
MALE DOGS. Staring at Lydia, ha ha ha!
    She'd never look twice at an ugly mutt like him!
MOPS *(to* FRIEDRICH*).* You call me stupid?
    I've seen her resist your advances, too.
FRIEDRICH. She won't resist forever.
    She says she doesn't love me, but
    She's not so pure as you think.
    No bitch is. I'll win her.
    She may act chaste around you,
    But that's only because you smell bad.
MOPS. Cur!
MALE DOGS led by FRIEDRICH. Staring at Lydia, ha ha ha!
    She'd never look twice at an ugly, smelly,
    Lop-eared, ragged, matted, scruffy bastard mutt like you!

MAX, OTTO, *and a few other* DOGS *enter, carrying provisions, just in time to see* MOPS *overturn the banquet table in a rage. There is silence.*

MOPS. You call me bastard who should be my brothers.
    You scorn me, when we all are sons of Rank.
    Well then, I have no brothers. I denounce you all.

MOPS *begins to leave.*

MAX. Where are you going?
MOPS. To kill myself.

MOPS *exits.*

MAX. Wait.
OTTO. Don't be so rash.

MAX *and* OTTO *exit, following* MOPS.

FRIEDRICH. Better he should kill himself than receive
    The beating that awaits him now.
    The Mayor, my master, shall hear of this.

SCENE FIVE
MOPS *stands next to the large rock in the woods.*

MOPS. Brotherless, fatherless, loved by no one,
    I will kill myself with this knife.
    It is hard, but I must be as brave as my master
    Augustus Rank was when he took his life.
    I must die.

A golden cloud of smoke appears. In the center of it is AUGUSTUS RANK.

RANK. My son, stop.

MOPS *falls to the ground in amazement.*

MOPS. Augustus Rank! You have returned.
RANK. You call me master,
    You alone among the dogs
    Reject the feeble man who owns you
    And long to serve me.
MOPS. It is true, it is true.
RANK. Do you remember your dreams of the cloud of gold,
    How it filled you with fire,
    How it filled your soul and made you strong?
MOPS. I do.
RANK. In the center of that cloud was this:
    My heart.

RANK's *heart begins to glow in his breast. He removes it and gives
it to* MOPS.

MOPS. Master, I am only a dog.
RANK. A dog with the soul of a man.
MOPS *(Taking the heart).* A dog with the soul of a man.

ACT TWO

SCENE ONE

MAX *and* OTTO *are alone in the clearing by the rock.* LYDIA *and her*
TWO FRIENDS *enter.*

LYDIA. Where is Mops?
OTTO. We found his dagger here,
    With no blood on it.
MAX. We know he isn't dead.
LYDIA. But where is he?

OTTO. We don't know. Why do you ask?

MAX. Do you care for him?

LYDIA. Oh no, no. I was only wondering.

LYDIA *and her* FRIENDS *walk away and talk among themselves, but* MAX *and* OTTO *eavesdrop.*

FIRST FRIEND. Not at all?

SECOND FRIEND. Not just a little bit?

LYDIA. Be quiet! My master plans to marry me
    To Friedrich, the Mayor's dog, tomorrow.

FIRST FRIEND. Oh, so you've had to endure his awful
    Sloppy kisses!

SECOND FRIEND. Ugh.

LYDIA. No, *I* haven't.
    Friedrich doesn't know about it yet.
    It is to be announced at the feast.
    But if anyone heard me say I wanted something
    That my master wouldn't approve of,
    Especially Mops—
    The humans say the dogs seem restless lately,
    They're worried, they don't like their servants disobeying.
    One man said he'd go to any lengths
    To stop rebelliousness from rising.
    Even killing—do you understand what I am saying?

BOTH FRIENDS. We must be very, very careful when we speak.

LYDIA. We must seem nothing but obedient and meek.

FIRST FRIEND. But poor Mops, what will become of him?

LYDIA. I only hope . . .

SECOND FRIEND. What?

LYDIA. I don't know. Let's go.

LYDIA *and her* TWO FRIENDS *exit.*

MAX. We must warn Mops!

OTTO. He must not go back to town.

MAX. At least until he knows, so he can be careful.
　　We'll wait for him here,
　　Where we've met with him so many times before
　　To talk and pass the summer afternoons.

OTTO. He's sure to return here soon.

SCENE TWO

At the large rock in the woods, MAX *is reading silently and* OTTO *is impatiently throwing stones at birds. Suddenly* OTTO *stops, sniffing the air. He directs* MAX's *attention offstage.*

　　MOPS *appears, walking slowly toward them. He has exchanged his ragged clothes for the uniform of a nineteenth-century Prussian general.* MAX *and* OTTO *watch, amazed, as he mounts the rock and addresses them.*

MOPS. My only friends, my brothers, hear what has befallen me:
　　Our father's ghost has come to me, here in these dark woods.
　　He gave his spirit to me. Augustus and Mops are one.
　　Our victory is nearly won. The dogs will soon be free!

MAX. The spirit of our great creator
　　Is no subject for jokes, Mops Hacker.

MOPS. I am no more that ugly bastard mutt.
　　The glowing heart of Rank consumed my own.
　　Poor stinking Hacker's kicked the bucket, but
　　Now Rank's burning heart is mine alone.

OTTO. Come down from that rock! You've lost your mind.

MOPS. Only a dog with the soul of a man
　　Can lead you all to freedom; only I
　　Have the soul of Rank.

MAX. How can you say this?

MOPS. A dog needs a master, but a man does not.

OTTO. What nonsense, Mops! Come down from there.

MAX. You betray your race! No dog can say such things.

MOPS *(Drawing his sword)*. I'll kill you both!
  No dog's a friend of mine who will not follow me—
  Or are you really slaves, and wish to stay so?

MAX *and* OTTO. No!

MOPS. Or do you mean you long for freedom
  But lack the nerve to stand and fight?

MAX *and* OTTO (OTTO *brandishing his sword*). No!

MOPS. But you mistrust your good friend Mops,
  You dare not follow him?

MAX *and* OTTO. No . . .

MOPS. Then you will follow me and wage
  The glorious war for freedom? Or—

MAX *and* OTTO. We will! We will!

ALL. The dogs are free!
  The men shall die!

MAX. The humans say they fear the dogs
  Grow restless in their slavery.

OTTO. So no delay! We must act now.

ALL. The dogs are free!
  The men shall die!
  We'll rise to our destiny,
  Wage the great war.
  Augustus's children
  Are slaves no more.

SCENE THREE

*Nighttime. The clearing by the rock is illuminated by torches, and
a crowd of* DOGS *is gathered.* MAX *and* OTTO *are seated on the rock,
directing other* DOGS *who are distributing weapons.* MOPS *mounts*

*the rock from behind and appears standing on top of it. He gestures
to his friends to get off.* MAX *lingers for a moment and* MOPS *kicks
him, perhaps accidentally.* OTTO *stands proudly beside the rock, his
hand on his sword hilt, like a soldier.* MAX *stands in a similar
attitude on the other side, but shifts his feet impatiently.*

CROWD. Proud dogs, slaves no more,
   The sons of Augustus are going to war!
   Hand me a sword, pass me a gun,
   Limb from limb we'll tear them—every one!
MOPS. Silence!
CROWD *(Quieting down).* Limb from limb we'll tear them—
   every one.
MOPS. It gives me joy to see you all before me
   Gathered to advance our noble cause.
   Even worthy Friedrich here has joined us,
   He whose longtime, bitter foe I was.
FRIEDRICH. All's forgotten, Hacker, take me on.
   I'll be your soldier till the battle's won.
   Let's shed our petty rivalries and be
   Allied against our common enemy.
                    (Aside to MAX*)*
   I only hope your brave friend there
   Is the best dog to lead us in this important fight,
   Because if he's not—
MAX *(Stiffly).* I have given Mops my word
   And sworn allegiance to him.
FRIEDRICH. I meant no offense,
   Honorable Max.
   I know you would never break your word.
                    (To MOPS*)*
   Listen, Hacker, here's my solemn vow:

Friedrich is your humble servant now.

MOPS. Excellent, excellent.
  All you dogs, take heed!
  Leave your little differences behind.
  One and all, unite against the men.
  Tomorrow, at the feast, we will attack.
  We'll join the celebration, with our swords drawn!
  Are you with me?

CROWD. Yes!

MOPS. One thing we must not do is tell the bitches—
  They'd beg us to be merciful and weak.
  If you tell them anything, just speak
  Of how we'll take control and seize the riches,
  Houses, money, laboratories, farms,
  And when we've made our point, lay down our arms—

OTTO. Don't tell them that we'll tear the bastards all to shreds!

MAX. Don't tell them that we'll cut their throats and crush their
  heads!

MOPS. Yes, tell them we'll be gentle, firm but fair.
  Say exactly what they want to hear.
  We do not wish to burden them with care,
  But between each other, let's be plain and clear—
  All the men must die! No mercy!

OTTO *and* MAX. No mercy!

MOPS, *then* ALL. Kill them all! No mercy!

SCENE FOUR
Night. At the edge of town.

HANS. The town is strangely empty, Wilhelm, have you noticed?

WILHELM. I think the dogs are meeting somewhere secretly.

HANS. Perhaps we've gone too far with threats of punishment.
   They are offended.
   They wish to be treated with dignity,
   And they deserve to be.

WILHELM. A slave has no dignity to speak of; a dog has even
   less.

HANS. Yes, it's true. Let's seek them out and tell them
   We'll plead their cause tomorrow, before the town.
   Rank's noble soldiers merit more respect
   Than they have been shown.

WILHELM. You may be right after all, Hans.
   Let's go and find them.

HANS. They must be in the woods—I'll bring a lamp.

HANS *exits*.

WILHELM. Yes, Hans, bring a lamp
   So we can see their villainous faces.
   Bring a lamp, my friend,
   So I can aim my pistol truly
   At the traitors' hearts.
   It's a simple problem, really:
   Rank's intent is clear to me.
   He'll return when we are ready,
   Dogs and men, united side by side,
   Disciplined and orderly, awaiting his command.
   Therefore all dissenters must be killed.

HANS *returns with a lantern, and they exit*.

SCENE FIVE
At the dogs' meeting, the crowd is divided into REVELERS *and*
PLOTTERS.

REVELERS. We are brave and mighty soldiers,
    Noble fearless dogs are we.
    All the men shall die!
PLOTTERS. Hand me a sword, pass me a gun.
    You shoot the Müllers, I'll stab their son,
    I'll cover you when you go for the Mayor,
    You grab Frau Mann from behind by the hair.
    All the men shall die!

HANS *and* WILHELM *enter. There is a commotion.*

REVELERS. Men!
PLOTTERS. Kill them!
OTTO *and* MAX. Wait! Bring them before our leader!
    What does he say?
MOPS *(to* HANS *and* WILHELM*).* Who are you?
    Why have you come here?
HANS. It is you, Mops Hacker!
MOPS. It is I. What is your business?
HANS. We came expecting just a few
    Disgruntled dogs.
    This is more serious than I thought.
MOPS. Indeed.
HANS. We came to tell you we will be your advocates
    And plead your cause before the town tomorrow.
    You deserve—
MOPS. What?
WILHELM. To be treated with dignity.
MOPS. Dignity!
    A softer cushion on the floor, you mean?
    A dainty collar made of bridle leather?
    No more rubbing our noses in shit?

HANS. No, more than that.

    It isn't right that you are slaves.

    You should be given wages.

MOPS. Wages!

    A penny for every time I fetch

    My master's slippers in my mouth?

WILHELM. A little more than that.

ALL DOGS. Ha ha ha!

MOPS *(Drawing his sword and pointing it at* WILHELM*).* You already owe us more than you can pay.

OTTO. Kill them now! We have no time for this.

ALL DOGS. Kill them, kill them!

MAX. Otto, you forget

    Hans has shown us sympathy.

    Perhaps these men can serve us somehow, Mops,

    If we will spare them.

ALL DOGS. No one will be left alive tomorrow!

    Why spare them now?

WILHELM *(Drawing his pistol).* You're planning a massacre!

    (He fires a shot, but is quickly brought down by the dogs.)

    Help, help! Murderers!

                  (Dying)

    Murderers!

HANS. Oh, God! I beg you all to reconsider.

    We can reason with the townsmen.

    There are other ways!

MAX *(to* MOPS*).* He may be right—

OTTO *(to* MOPS*).* What is this?

    Where is our resolve?

    Will we spare anyone who pleads with us?

    If you do not slay him now, there will be no revolution.

MOPS *(At first conflicted, then showing resolve).* Make your peace
    with God, Hans.

(to DOGS*)*

  Kill him.

The DOGS *cheer and fall on* HANS.

MAX. Wait!

MOPS *(to* MAX*).* Shut up, Max. I have spoken.

FRIEDRICH *(Aside to* MAX*).* Max, you were right,
    We're going too far.
    Mops is growing drunk with power.
    You would make a better leader.

MAX. I saw you bare your teeth
    And shout that Hans should die.
    You hypocrite—
    You're trying to create dissent,
    You hold a petty grudge because
    Mops stared at Lydia, your fiancée,
    On the day before your wedding.

FRIEDRICH. My wedding?

MAX. You didn't know!

FRIEDRICH *(Loudly).* The Mayor plans to marry Lydia to me!
    Tomorrow!
    Is that what you're saying, Max?

MAX. Yes.

MOPS. No!

FRIEDRICH. Noble Mops, you must delay
    The fight till the end of my wedding day!
    She'll never marry me of her own accord,
    But once it's done and she's given her word—

OTTO *(to* FRIEDRICH*).* Quiet, you fool!
    Don't you know Mops loves her, too?

FRIEDRICH *(Oblivious)*. Generous leader, help your friend
   Put off the attack until the end—
MOPS *(Draws his sword)*. Cur! Traitor!
MAX. Mops, hear me this time!
   Don't slay him,
   It will divide us.
MOPS. Have at you!

Kills FRIEDRICH.

FRIEDRICH *(Dying)*. So close to happiness! O Lydia! How sad
   for me.
   I never even drew my sword . . . The bastard . . .
   Avenge me, brothers.
FRIEDRICH'S FRIENDS *(Drawing their swords)*. We will avenge
   you!
MAX, OTTO, *and* OTHERS *(Drawing their swords)*. You will not!
MAX *and* OTTO. Come, shed your petty rivalries and be
   Allied against your common enemy,
   As your friend Friedrich said.
   Too late for him; he's dead—
   But we still have a war to wage
   To usher in the golden age
   When dogs, not men, shall rule,
   And then you'll have your duels,
   As many as you want—but not tonight.
   We'll have no honor to defend with duels if we lose this
      fight.

All but TWO *of* FRIEDRICH'S FRIENDS *put away their weapons.*

TWO FRIENDS *(Lunging)*. For Friedrich—we gave our word!

MAX, OTTO, *and* OTHERS *fight against the* TWO *until the* TWO *are subdued. They are brought before* MOPS. *He kills them. All* DOGS *murmur disapproval.*

MAX *(Aside).* First humans, then his canine rival, now these
    two—
  They were only standing up for honor.
  He should have spared them.
  This grows worse and worse.
MOPS. This is but a little price to pay, my friends.
  Revolution leaves no time for weeping;
  Everything must serve her single end.
  She won't hesitate to trample those who're sleeping
  Or who turn away in dull defiance,
  Weakening the bonds of her alliance.

  Raise your noses high and tell me, dogs:
  What is that high, thin note upon the midnight breeze?
MAX. Winter.
OTTO. The smell comes from the north; it's far away, though.
MAX. It's not so far away.
MOPS. How I long to see the coming snows
  Fall through the gaping roofs
  And blow through the broken walls
  Of our masters' houses.
  How many times have we stood at the windows
  And looked to the woods, longing to run through the hills
  In the cold, in the cleansing snow,
  Wild and strong, as our ancestors did.
MAX. Mops, we are not wolves.
MOPS. We are not dogs, we are not men.
  Many voices call to us.

We try to be one thing and another,
Sometimes we feel we are nothing.
My mother—

MAX. And what would we do without their houses
In the winter?

MOPS. —died when I was barely weaned,
My father before I was born.
I grew up in a shack, unattended, torn
By the voices of many spirits seeking to guide me.
But one call rose above the rest,
One word each voice in its different tone repeated:
Freedom.
Battling, clamoring, each voice was defeated by the rest.
But when they spoke together, shrill or low, frenzied or
    slow,
Together, they joined in a moving harmony, and they said:
Freedom.
They said:

MOPS *and* DOGS. Freedom.

MOPS. Rank has given me his heart,
The strength to start the war,
To show his soldiers what they were intended for.
But the word has been in my blood since I was born.
I hear it echoing in yours.
Hot-blooded or clever and cold,
Large or small, slow or quick, young or old,
I hear it echoing in yours.

MOPS *and* DOGS. Freedom.

DOGS. Freedom.

MOPS. With every pulse, one word:

DOGS. Freedom.

MOPS. What if the cozy fires were loosed from the grate?

What if the tables where our masters ate were split in two?
What if the wild, cold winter snow blew through
The ruined parlors where we served and swept away the
 traces,
The traces of our slavery?
The bodies of our masters will be silent
Underneath the freezing ice. The snow erases everything,
Everything, and we are left with—what?

DOGS. Freedom.

MOPS. And now it is time to prepare for war.

ACT THREE

SCENE ONE

The HUMANS *of Rankstadt are gathered for the centennial feast.*
The DOGS *move quietly among them, serving food and obeying*
orders.

FIRST MAN. Everyone is here but Hans and Wilhelm.

SECOND MAN. Where are they?

FIRST MAN. No one knows.

THIRD MAN. My dog is missing, too.

FIRST MAN. And mine.

THIRD MAN. And worst of all, the Mayor's dog
 Didn't answer his call this morning.
 He was to be married today to a white Samoyed.

SECOND MAN. Apparently he would rather share
 Some other bitch's bed.

THIRD MAN. Quiet!
 The Mayor is trying to pretend that nothing's wrong.

FIRST MAN. But I'm afraid something is. Listen.
 Last night I overheard Hans and Wilhelm talking.
 They said the dogs should have more rights,
 And went off into the woods to meet some of them.

SECOND *and* THIRD MEN. What?

MOPS *(Setting a platter on the table near the men)*. I heard something, too, masters.

FIRST, SECOND, *and* THIRD MEN. What did you hear?

MOPS. That certain dogs, the missing ones among them,
Are planning to stage a protest at the feast.
I don't know what they're going to do, but I think
We should all be on the lookout for mischief.

FIRST MAN. I'll go and warn the Mayor.

MOPS. No, his dog was among them.

OTTO *(Bringing a platter to the table)*. It would greatly upset him.

MAX *(Bringing a platter)*. Let him make his important speech
first.

OTTO. I heard they're not planning to come until after dessert.

MAX. We're trying to dissuade them.
Perhaps we can stave it off and save him—

MOPS. From embarrassment.

MAX *and* OTTO. Save him from embarrassment.

SECOND *and* THIRD MEN. Quiet! The Mayor is going to speak.

The MALE DOGS *range themselves behind the seated people. The* MAYOR *of the town addresses the crowd.*

MAYOR. Townsmen, raise your glasses high.
Today we honor great Augustus
And the hundred years gone by
Since he founded our fine town.

We honor, too, his proud creation,
Canine soldiers fierce and loyal.
This wine begins our celebration—
Raise your glass and drink it down!

HUMANS. This wine begins our celebration—
  Raise your glass and drink it down!
MOPS. Wait!
  Though I'm only a dog, and not allowed to speak,
  I've poured myself a glass of wine, and humbly request
  That I may make my own toast to Augustus Rank.

  I long to honor him; who will deny me?
  He gave us hands; why not then raise a glass?
  He gave us voices; why should we not use them?
  Praise him, drink to him, at last?

  Too long have we been silent; who'll deny this?
  We are but dogs, yet pity us, O men.
  Mere monsters, yet we long to sing his praises . . .
                    (Pauses suddenly)
  . . . We long to open our throats and let our songs of praise
    pour forth like wine! Like wine!

MOPS *signals to the* DOGS, *and each one cuts the throat of the* MAN
*seated in front of him. Large amounts of blood flow. In the ensuing
confusion,* MOPS *continues to sing.*

MOPS. Too long have we been silent; who'll deny this?
  We are but dogs, yet pity us, O men.
  Mere monsters, yet we long to sing his praises.
  Raise joyful cries: Rank has returned again!
ALL DOGS. Rank has returned again!

Since there are more HUMANS *than* DOGS, *many are still alive, and
a vicious battle ensues.*

MOPS'S MASTER. Cursed dog! Be merciful to me!
  I raised you!
MOPS *exultantly kills his* MASTER.

A young BOY *fights bravely with* MAX, *but* MAX *backs him against a wall with his sword at his throat.*

BOY. Powerful dog, be merciful to me!
  Spare my life! I never harmed you.
MAX. You never harmed me, it's true.
MOPS. Go on, kill him!
MAX. He's only a child.
OTTO. Max, silence, the others will hear you.
  It's much too late to be weak.
  We must fight now.
MAX. Against children! I won't do it.
  Their fathers, not they, enslaved us.
OTTO. Weren't their fathers children once, too?
  Be quiet, I tell you, the others will hear you.
MAX (*Raising his sword against* OTTO). And be persuaded not to
  murder the innocent?
OTTO (*Raising his sword*). The time for this talk is past!

MAX *and* OTTO *fight and* MAX *is wounded, but* OTTO *will not kill his friend and leaves him lying on the ground. Many of the* FEMALES *gather on one side, and some try to hold back the* MALES. *Other* FEMALES *have joined in the battle and are ruthlessly killing humans.*

A WOMAN *with a* CHILD *in her arms is running from* TWO DOGS, *and* LYDIA *rushes to her aid and fights with the pursuers, who turn on her.* MOPS *sees this and kills one of the attacking dogs, while* LYDIA *subdues the other. As* LYDIA *begins to walk away, her op-*

ponent makes a slight movement and she leaps at him again and kills him, perhaps accidentally.

The battle begins to die down.

MOPS. Lydia, snow-white Lydia, how beautiful you are!
     For years I've desired you.
     Lydia, how I long to make you mine.
     The time has come. We've won.
     Together we can rule, we two, as one,
     The victorious, free Nation of Dogs.
LYDIA. Never, Mops.
MOPS. But we can. The town is ours, it's ours.
     We will live in the Mayor's mansion together.
LYDIA. Once I cared for you,
     But now in my eyes you
     Are nothing but a murderer.
     I despise you.
MOPS. Like the wild winter snows that come from the hills
     You will cool my burning heart.
     The flames that scorch me, the troubles that torture me
     Will die in your arms, in the driven snow of your love
         forever.
LYDIA. No, Mops, never.
DOGS. Victory is ours!
MOPS. Rankstadt is mine, and you must be mine, too.

MOPS *tries to take* LYDIA *by force into the ruins of the Mayor's mansion.*

OTTO. Mops, stop! What are you doing?
     You've grown drunk on your power.
MOPS. Stand back! She's mine.

OTTO. Even the great Mops Hacker
  Is not above the law of honor.

MOPS *and* OTTO *fight.* MOPS *kills* OTTO. *As* MOPS *pauses over the body of his friend,* LYDIA *stabs him in the back.*

LYDIA. Too many have died at your hand.
  This will end it.
MOPS. Lydia!

MOPS *dies.*

The battle has ended. Several DOGS *carry the body of their leader to the center of the green, and a howl of mourning rises from the soldiers.*

MAX, *weak from his wounds, stands up by* MOPS'S *body.*

MAX. Don't howl for Mops!
  He's dead, his debt is paid.
  Hundreds are murdered, our town is in flames.
  Howl for yourselves and the carnage you have caused,
  For you are still guilty. And I
  Am the guiltiest of all, for I knew, I knew,
  And yet I did not stop it.
  There is only one way for me to pay for it now.

MAX *kills himself.*

LYDIA. So many dead!
DOGS. So many dead!
LYDIA. We must leave this place.
DOGS. No! Where will we go?
LYDIA. We'll go where the madness of Rank cannot follow us.
  Where we can live in peace, renounce bloodshed and war.

FIRST GROUP OF DOGS. But that's what we're for!

    We're soldiers, children of Rank,

    And nothing more.

LYDIA *and* SECOND GROUP OF DOGS. We can be our own masters.

    Rank is long dead.

    We've never seen the world before.

    Let's go explore it.

FIRST GROUP OF DOGS. It will take us ten years to get out of the forest.

    Winter is coming, and who knows what we'll find

    Out in the world among humankind.

LYDIA *and* SECOND GROUP OF DOGS. Adventure and freedom and peace, perhaps.

    Do you fear freedom?

    Nothing's left here.

    All of the houses are burning.

    Always we were yearning for freedom.

    We have it. Will we waste it here?

    Let's go.

FIRST GROUP OF DOGS. No.

SECOND GROUP OF DOGS. Let's go.

FIRST GROUP OF DOGS. Let's go.

    Our leader, Mops, and Rankstadt are no more,

    And if we aren't soldiers, who knows what we're for?

    But we're free, we're free, and we'll go.

SECOND GROUP OF DOGS. We're free, we're free, and we'll go.

    We don't fear the cold and the snow.

    We'll take to the hills and find peace, peace.

FIRST GROUP OF DOGS. Freedom, adventure.

ALL DOGS. Freedom and peace.

14

(CLEO)

"And was that how it happened?" I asked Lydia, one evening after the opera. We were sitting in her apartment, as we did sometimes now, instead of out on the terrace. The weather was warm, but we both had the feeling that summer was ending. That afternoon I'd had the first premonition of winter, not a chill or a sense of increasing darkness but a certain change of pace, like flat yellow panes dividing one hour from the next.

"Yes, more or less," Lydia said. She was searching through her sewing basket for some embroidery thread, but she seemed to be thinking of something else.

People have asked me whether I was shocked to learn that most of the dogs, and especially Lydia, had killed. I wasn't. I had suspected it ever since my first lunch with Ludwig, when, after all, he had referred to the battle as a massacre. What weighed on me this evening was the sense that the life the dogs had led in Rankstadt was so utterly gone. They had left behind what had been, until then, their entire world—and for what?

The light of a grainy sunset came in through the french windows near where we sat, and it felt slow and magnified, as if you might be able to see the individual particles entering in pulses.

"Did you really love Mops?" I asked.

"Yes," Lydia said.

"Have you ever loved anyone since then?"

"Certainly. I always love. Taking a life doesn't make you incapable."

"But I mean, like that."

"There is no such thing. No love is like any other."

"Okay," I murmured. She didn't seem to be answering my question, but maybe no answer existed.

The sunlight thrummed at the windows. "And have you found what you were looking for since you left Rankstadt?"

Lydia gave up her search and laid her hands in her lap, or actually between her haunches, which were folded under her wide skirt. "What *were* we looking for?" she asked. "We didn't all feel as hopeful when we left, I think, as Burkhardt made it seem in the opera. Perhaps some were. I just wanted peace, really . . ."

I closed my eyes, but the particles of light went on swarming, so slowly, like pebbles tumbling underwater.

"But what are you all going to do now?" I asked. "So much was lost, wasn't it? I mean, what gets you through every day now?"

"Why, just the things that need to be done. Cleo, what's the matter?"

"I'm just . . . I'm worried about you," I said.

"Don't be ridiculous. We can take care of ourselves."

My eyes were still closed, but I could feel her looking at me.

"But what about you, Cleo? What will you do after we're all gone? That might be sad for you."

"What?" I said, opening my eyes. "Where are you going?"

"I mean if . . . the sickness proves to be as much of a problem as some of us think."

"Well, that's what I'm worried about," I said. "What will happen to you?"

She didn't answer.

"Suppose you all lock yourselves up in the castle, like Klaue said, then eventually——"

"But let's not talk about it, Cleo, please. We must just face things as they come, and not waste time fearing them."

"Aren't you afraid?" I asked. "You must be."

"No," Lydia said. "I don't seem to be afflicted by the illness, but even if I am eventually . . . suppose we all die of it—well, so what? The end must come, there's no escaping it."

"I wish you wouldn't be so——"

"It's not fatalism, Cleo. You don't understand."

I looked into her eyes, and I didn't believe she wasn't afraid. I saw fear there, rippling like the surface of water. But beyond that was a wide, bright space, not empty but full, like a snowy sky.

"Just have courage," she said.

I supposed that wasn't exactly the same thing as lack of fear.

"But, Lydia . . ."

She rose from her chair and went to the kitchen as if she hadn't heard me. At first I watched her; then I leaned my chin in my hands and turned my face toward the other side of the room, the bookshelves, the fireplace, trying to find something else to think about.

LATER IN September, I began to visit Ludwig often. Although we'd actually spent very little time together before then, in that early autumn it came to seem that we'd been friends forever, and our conversations all seemed to be continuations of other conversations we had begun long before. When I think back on that time now I see images of Rankstadt as vivid and random as if they were my own memories: its narrow cobbled streets with their names painted on little white signs, Pfenniggasse and Hundlistrasse, a boy leading a pony down a back lane, the window of the bakery on a yellow morning, snow piled in drifts against the buildings with rectangles dug out where the doors and shutters had to be opened, or in the spring a backyard, first thing on a bright day, the chickens and the doorposts and the linen on the line so white you can hardly look at them, and Ludwig, very young, leaping out the door on all fours, without thinking, into the new world. These scenes must have come from stories he told me, and yet, though they're all so clear, the stories themselves are lost to me now.

Ludwig wasn't well. I never saw him during one of his episodes, as he called them, because he could feel when they were coming on and would ask me to leave, but I knew he was having them more and more often. He didn't keep a servant anymore, maybe for that reason, so sometimes I'd bring groceries and cook dinner for both of us. Occasionally I cleaned the apartment, too, if he'd let me. It was something to do.

He lived on the ground floor, and there never seemed to be enough light in his rooms even during the days. In the evenings, the bulbs in his lamps struggled to shine through the heavy antique shades. If we wanted to read, we would each huddle separately under table lamps and bend down close to our books. It's funny that I don't remember feeling sad at the time, because it must have been a very sad winter. Not at Lydia's apartment, which was always airy and warm, not on my tours of the castle, which was growing more elaborate and beautiful every week, but those afternoons in Ludwig's living room, listening to the whisper of gears that accompanied even his breathing—it seemed something had come loose in his voice box, but he wouldn't allow any doctor to examine it. He was trying to improve my German and teach me to read that old typeface called *Fraktur*, and now whenever I see those complicated letters with their little flags and spikes they make me think of broken machinery, as tiny as the works in a music box or a watch, and the words always seem to be accompanied by that sound.

"ARE YOU afraid of the future?" I asked him once. We were sitting in his kitchen, at a low butcher-block table, drinking tea. An assortment of huge pots that hung from the ceiling, little used now, gave a gentle coppery tint to the dim afternoon.

"I don't think so," he said. "I expect it will be a welcome release."

"What will?"

"Whatever comes next. There are still so many things to do . . . I should like to write extensively about Rank's years with his followers, for instance; how he obtained and kept their loyalty. There are papers I have hardly looked at, which might shed some light on that question, and I think that would be quite interesting. But at some point one wants to be taken away, to feel a hand on the shoulder and hear, 'Come, you have done enough.' Don't you agree?"

"But you don't have to wait for somebody to say it," I said. "You can always stop working on one thing and do something else, can't you?"

"No, I must keep working on my project. But you are young."

"Not so incredibly much younger than you."

Ludwig's mouth opened in a slight smile and he shook his head. "But the scientists in all their wisdom were not able to slow down our aging process quite enough to match yours. After a certain point it begins to go very quickly with us. Even if it were not for the illness . . . You know this already, you can see it."

"But you don't seem old enough to give everything up, Ludwig."

He gave me a look of intense, blurred sadness and then picked up the remains of a lemon slice from his saucer and held it absentmindedly in his hand. "One would not willingly give everything up," he said. "But the time comes."

"Also," he said, "there would be no point in living if I were entirely mad."

"But you wouldn't ever kill yourself, would you?"

"What difference does it make? Of course, I would have to do it before I lost my mind completely. Afterward I would not be able to, perhaps I would not remember that I had meant to. So in that sense I suppose some time would be lost."

"You can't do that," I said.

Ludwig smiled again, in a secret, bitter way that I didn't like. "You wouldn't be able to prevent me. But Cleo, why must we talk about this? Even if it were to happen, it would be far in the future."

"I didn't bring it up."

The hardness of the smile remained on his face. "We can argue about it some other time," he said.

We did, two or three times, but it was always the same: we didn't agree. He would not concede anything, and behind the obstinate expression his face would take on there lurked a distant, unmistakable wolfiness against which I knew I couldn't fight and which would creep closer, like a creature coming toward the edge of a dark wood, if we stayed on the topic. Once we'd talked about it just before I left for the evening, and the next morning when I woke up I felt that animal presence near me, a hunched and bristling shape like a drawing made with a charred stick, maybe a warning scratched onto a rock. After that the subject didn't come up again for a long time.

Often when I was in Ludwig's library, or the dining room which adjoined it and had a view into it, my eyes would linger on the portraits of Maria Rank that hung along the walls. There were six of them, not counting the ones that were kept in storage, all made by the man Ludwig said had been her lover. In the left-hand corner of the library she stood like a column in white silk, arranging flowers in a tall vase, kind and amused. In the center of the far wall she sat leaning forward, trying not to move, and in another painting lay back on a couch with her eyes half-closed—these were the two I had looked at so intently on my first visit to Ludwig's apartment. On either side of those, in smaller pictures, she sat on a horse and lay under a lilac bush; and in the right-hand corner she stood leaning against a tree as though she needed its support, looking a little apprehensive, waiting for someone, maybe, who wasn't visible.

It seemed if you could be that person and walk up to her you could surely think of something to do to make the worried expression go away, and she might take your arm and smile at you, and be glad you were there. But I wasn't. The moment when she'd had that expression had passed long ago, and I hadn't been there.

I thought her spirit, forced to be present in the room because of the portraits, must be aware now of what her son Augustus had done and what the results had been, and I wondered if she was sorry for it, or if she had something to say that might help us. But although she watched always, with her many eyes, it was impossible to tell what she thought; she seemed mainly to be straining to see through the haze of years, shining hazily like a light through frosted glass.

I wondered what Ludwig thought of her, too. I was never able to see the resemblance between her and myself that he said had led him to stop me on the street a year ago.

"What is it about Maria?" I asked Ludwig one day, as we were going into his library to look up some historical point I needed for an article I was writing.

"I think her portraits are very beautiful. And I own them. It would be a shame not to keep them on the wall, don't you think so?"

"But she means something to you."

Ludwig took off his spectacles, rubbed his eyes, and glanced at me, and there was a flicker of that sadness I had seen when he'd been sitting at the kitchen table, that other afternoon, holding the slice of lemon. He put his glasses back on and considered the portraits. "She is the mother of Augustus Rank, and of course I am interested in him. There are no paintings of him, but even if there were, I don't think they would be so pleasant to look at. I suppose I feel that I can learn something from these, they add another dimension . . . but perhaps, also, it's simply that I find her very beautiful. These paintings keep me company.

"I very much wonder," he added after a pause, "what it would be like to be human."

"Do you?" I asked. "Can't you imagine what it's like?"

"I spend a great deal of time trying to imagine it. We all do, because we want to be like you, of course."

"I try to imagine what it would be like to be you, too," I said.

"Why?" Ludwig was very surprised.

"Well, because . . . I just wonder."

He shook his head. "Being a dog is nothing," he said. "Literally. It is nothing but an absence, a negative. If we had been soldiers, perhaps . . . but that is finished. The canine instincts, the soldier instincts, are worse than useless now; they are destructive, ridiculous. But nothing can be done about it." He folded his hands over the top of his cane and looked at me again. "Perhaps if I were human I would be a painter, like Dominique Clément," he said, nodding toward the pictures.

"Why don't you ever paint, then?" I asked. "Do you?"

"Oh no. It is much too late for that."

ONE EVENING in February, the last evening I ever spent with Ludwig, we were sitting in the library reading. I had an old German copy of *Wilhelm Tell* and I was just about to ask him the meaning of a word when he leaned back in his armchair, pushed his spectacles up above his eyes, and said, "No more now."

"What's the matter?" I asked.

"I am very, very tired, Cleo," he said. "I think you should leave."

It wasn't unusual for him to ask me to go if he felt an episode of the illness coming on, but I had never seen it come so suddenly, or make him change the way he had now. He looked all wrong, as if someone had put their hand on his face and slightly disarranged his features. His eyes were too small and they were half-covered by his milky inner lids, while the upper halves were sunk in darkness so you couldn't see into them. A trace of whitish foam lightened one corner of his mouth.

"Why don't you go to bed and I'll bring you something," I said, frightened.

"No, I want you to leave." His breathing was labored. With great effort he tried to raise himself from the chair, and I thought he wouldn't be able to and would fall over.

"Don't, Ludwig."

"No more, now—no more. Get out."

AS SOON as I got back to my apartment, I called Lydia and told her what had happened.

"Do you think he's going to try to kill himself?" she asked.

"I think so."

There was a long silence. I could hear a slight sniffling at her end of the line, as if she were trying to get more information by smelling me through the phone.

"Oh no," she said finally. "What do you think ought to be done?"

"I've been thinking about it a lot," I said. "I think we should lock him up, actually. Just in his apartment. He doesn't go out anymore. I have keys and I go there every day, so I can look after him. I can sort of get things out of the way that he might use to hurt himself. I mean, there are really only three things, knives and medicines and his guns, and I know where all of them are.

"Do you think I should get rid of them?"

There was another pause.

"Have you discussed the matter with him?" she asked.

"He's not going to agree to it—"

"No, of course."

"You think it's wrong, don't you?"

"I can't tell you," Lydia said stiffly.

"Do you think he should be allowed to kill himself if that's what he wants?"

"I don't know," Lydia said.

"You're not being much help."

"Cleo," she said, "Ludwig and I belong to a different race of creatures from yours. We are dying out, and you know that. Even if we all live to old age, there will never be any more of us. Perhaps you cannot understand his despair, but I can. For that same reason, I cannot tell you what to do. You are his friend, and you may do what you think best. I won't stop you."

"Well, what I actually was hoping for—"

"I will not help you. No."

"Why not?" I asked. She didn't answer.

"Ludwig means a lot to me," I said. "Maybe you—"

"I know," she said.

"Thanks a lot," I said. "I can't do it by myself; he's bigger than I am. Thanks a lot." And I hung up on her.

I FELT terrible after I did that. It was like hearing a phrase that echoes a nightmare you had forgotten, and brings it back to you. The abrupt ending of our discussion felt exactly the way I knew Ludwig's suicide would. The dead line suddenly, in the middle of a conversation; the little click that brings everything to a halt, and ends all speech and motion. The awful feeling, after that instant, that it was a mistake, that if you could only go back three seconds—a stupid accident. But it was done.

I picked up the phone again and dialed Klaue's number.

"Hallo," said a thick voice with a German accent.

"Klaue?"

"*Ja,* Klaue."

"Did I wake you up or something?"

"No, Cleo, no, no," he said, recognizing my voice. "What is the matter?"

"I—I have something to ask you. It's about Ludwig."

"Ah. What is the matter with Ludwig?" I could hear Klaue sitting up in bed as he said it.

"He's, ah—I think he wants to commit suicide. I was just talking to him tonight. I'm really worried about him—"

"Ah, I will dispatch someone to go and get him immediately," he said.

"No, no. I was thinking of something."

"What is that, Cleo?"

"I was thinking that I would take care of him—" I rushed, knowing that Klaue would object. "But what I would do is, if I could get some help, I want to change the locks in his apartment and keep the key, and then I could go over there every day, and that way he'd feel more comfortable, if he could be in his own place and everything."

"Ah-ah. I understand. Yes, well."

"I really have been thinking about it a lot, and I am his best friend."

"Yes, Cleo. Well."

"If you approve of the plan . . ."

"Yes," Klaue said. "All right, then. All right, you will need some help, then, I suppose."

"Yeah. What do you think?"

"Very well. I will dispatch a committee in the morning. Some dogs who will help you. They will bring the equipment. You will meet them there at . . . ten o'clock?"

"Oh, okay," I said, a little surprised at how quickly it was all happening.

"Good, well. Is that all?"

"Yes, uh-huh, I guess so."

"Very well, then, Cleo. Good night."

"Good night," I answered, but he was already reaching the phone over to its cradle, and I heard him murmuring, "Now then," to someone else as he hung up.

"Okay," I said to myself. I opened my sock drawer and searched for some cigarettes, which I usually hid from myself in there, but I didn't have any.

"I'll go to the store," I said, getting my coat. "Want to go to the store, Rufus?"

Rufus lifted his head from his paws and slapped his tail against the bed.

"Come on, want to go out?"

He leaped up, and I put his leash on and took him out. But we didn't go anywhere—we just ended up walking. A tiny, gentle snow was beginning to fall, and the city was beautiful in that hour, quiet and damp. Voices seemed to rise from a cushion of still air: a man selling drugs, a couple having an argument, someone in the shadow of a doorway saying that he liked the way I walked, he loved me, didn't I hear him?

I walked past everything, through the steady, silent flurry, under the streetlamps' speckled yellow light, over the wet, dark sidewalk. It was all over now. Tomorrow I'd lock Ludwig up, and he would never talk to me in the same way again.

I was about to do this thing, and there wasn't any stopping it. Klaue wouldn't let him alone now, even if I changed my mind. Klaue, who seemed to have to be in the middle of everybody's business. And I'd put him there, like an idiot; but there wasn't any point in dwelling on it now.

Maybe Ludwig would find a way to end his life anyway, maybe he'd die hating me, or maybe he'd kill himself tonight, and never know what I had done.

What had he thought was going to happen? He let me make sure that he ate well and that his apartment was clean and that he wasn't lonely. Did he think I would let him die? He must know that I wouldn't, I thought. He must know.

MORNING. NOISE. I hit at my alarm clock; it didn't stop. I squinted at the numbers and saw that it was 5:43 a.m. The noise came again—it was the phone. I picked it up.

"Hello?"

There was only breathing at the other end.

"Hello?"

More breathing, then a kind of snort, and then silence. It was a dog calling me, whoever it was.

"Ludwig?" I said.

I heard a deep mumble, disturbing and incoherent. Then another snuffle, closer to the phone, and louder unintelligible muttering.

"Please say something."

"Lydia," he said hoarsely.

"No, this is Cleo."

"I called the wrong number." Silence.

"This is Cleo," I repeated.

"Sorry." There was another silence, and then he hung up.

I dialed him back. The line was busy. I called Lydia, but her line was busy, too; she must have been on the phone with Ludwig.

I sat in bed and thought for a minute. I was so tired, woken from the wrong part of sleep, and a disjointed dream kept crackling on like interference from another station that I couldn't tune out. It was a dream about boats, and water, and ropes that were slipping, and disappearing. I lay back and slipped, down a slick angled deck, into the moving sea.

Here I was standing on a jetty, with some gluey mask on, meant to protect my skinless face, but stuff was getting into my nose, and I pulled at it. Ludwig was some way off, on a little boat, but I couldn't call to him because the sticky mask stuff was in my mouth, and there was a lot of hair in it, and it was choking me. I was wearing a dog's head, I realized with concern, and Ludwig wouldn't know who I was if I couldn't say anything. Then someone began licking it off me.

It was Rufus, wrapped around my head, his tail all over my face. He stuck his wet nose in my eye, and when he saw I was awake, he started wagging furiously.

"All right, I'm up," I said, pushing him out of the way.

I got out of bed and turned my alarm off so it wouldn't start buzzing in half an hour. Rufus barked at me, meaninglessly, as I walked toward the kitchen.

"Shut up."

"Wurrrr," he said.

"Shut up." I filled the kettle and turned the radio on, loud. Then I called Lydia.

"What did he say to you?" I asked her.

"I couldn't understand him."

"Not at all?"

"No. He called me 'Maria,' and that was all I understood."

"That was the name of Augustus's mother," I said.

"Yes, I know that."

"Has he ever done anything like that before?"

"No," Lydia said.

I knew I should apologize for hanging up on her last night, but I didn't feel like it. She was being too cold, and I was too worried about what I had to do in four hours.

"All right, I'm going to go," I said. "I'll call you and let you know what happened . . .

"Goodbye."

Lydia didn't say anything, so I hung up.

I ARRIVED in Ludwig's neighborhood early and walked around the streets of the West Village for a long time. It seemed as if Ludwig were gone already. I remembered then—and I remember now, as I'm writing this, though I haven't thought about it in a long time—how in the months after I first met him, I sometimes used to wander around after classes and find myself in the maze of narrow streets around his building, Bedford and Barrow and Commerce, where the little old houses leaned into each other, cracking and covered with vines. I would try to imagine what it felt like for Ludwig to live there. I thought about how that part of the city, like no other, had corners and ancient shrubs for ghosts to hide in, places where the residue of the past hadn't been swept away by thousands of moving bodies and buildings going up and down. The past had always seemed to be Ludwig's element, and every forgotten thing in those corners vibrated somehow in harmony with his spirit.

On that morning in February I walked out near the river,

where it was empty, and I could hear the wind moving in deserted garages and past the long, doorless walls of warehouses. Over the water a helicopter chopped its way through the ice-brown sky, pulsing light, sending indecipherable signals out into the empty air. It occurred to me that I loved Ludwig, and I had never said it to him. I wondered whether it would have been something worth saying or whether he knew.

When I turned the corner to his block at a minute to ten, the dog committee was there, standing in the frozen, slanting light, near the door of his building. They all wore long blue coats which had a military look to them, but which I didn't recognize. A new uniform. Three limousines waited at the curb, and a couple of gawkers stood across the street, speculating about what might be going on.

The leader of the group was a soft-spoken Husky whose face was both wolfy and gentle, with blue eyes.

"My name is Berthold," he said to me as I came up to them. "Klaue sent us to help you."

"Thanks, I'm Cleo," I said, though he obviously knew that.

"This is a delicate matter, so there will be no humans involved, other than you. We have locks and tools, and also restraints. I suggest we go in," he said, already opening the outer door. "You have the keys, I assume?"

"I have them—somewhere," I said. "Here."

I opened the door, and we went in. Outside Ludwig's ground-floor apartment, my heart pounded and my arms felt numb. I could smell everything—the tile, the wood, the steam heat.

"Here it is," I said. I knocked, didn't get any answer, and then unlocked it.

"Ludwig?" I called, leaning in, and to my surprise he was sitting right there, in the living room beyond the foyer, working at his computer. He turned around, and I felt everything inside me collapse. If I had thought of what I was going to say to him, I forgot it.

"Cleo."

I motioned for the dogs to stand back, but it was pointless, because he had smelled them.

"What is this?" he asked.

"I, ah—"

Ludwig rose from his chair, taking the cane that was leaning against the desk. He stepped toward me, his nose quivering.

"No. No. This is absolutely unacceptable. Whom have you brought here?"

I didn't get a chance to answer, because the dog committee came in, passed me, and grouped themselves around him. Ludwig looked at them, and said nothing. He looked at me.

"I was—" I began, but I stopped, because there wasn't any way to explain this. It was wrong; I realized that. It had been a mistake, and there was no way to fix it.

I looked at the dogs, and then something took hold of me, and led me, and I gave myself up to it.

"I am going to change the locks on your doors, and take the keys. I'll come in every day to check on you, and bring whatever you need. But I will not allow you to kill yourself," I said.

Ludwig was silent, eyes wide, muzzle narrowed with fear, whiskers straining forward. I knew he was thinking of fighting, that the others could see that, and that they were going to tie him up.

I turned around and looked at the floor, knowing they would take over. It hadn't even been necessary for me to come, and I could leave now if I wanted to.

I was not going to cry.

"Ah, Berthold," I said, staring at my feet like an idiot, "do you need me anymore?"

"You must take the new keys, Cleo," he said. I could hear motion behind me, but no struggle. Then the Husky's furry legs came into my field of vision.

"These are the keys," he told me as I looked up. "Thank you. Klaue will remain in contact with you."

"Thanks," I said.

I took them and stood there, staring at the window. I couldn't see outside. One of the dogs had drawn the shade. I had the impulse to say something, but no words came to mind, and so I left.

Once I was again in the hallway, my senses were sharp. There was a kind of tension in the air, as if everything around me had been arrested in frantic motion and stood balanced in an awkward position. It was like the atmosphere around an accident the moment after it happens, when everything is frozen just where it was, and all the observers are paralyzed for a split second with stopped hearts and open eyes, unable to keep the diagram of disaster from imprinting itself on their minds.

This, I was to understand later, was a premonition

Part Three

Neuhundstein

15

(CLEO)

My God, it was lonely the night after Ludwig was locked up.
I kept wanting to call somebody, but then I would remember
that there wasn't anyone left, really. I didn't want to talk to
Klaue, or Lydia, and I was pretty sure Ludwig wouldn't want
to talk to me, even if he was capable of holding a conversation.
I hadn't spoken to Monica in over a month, although it didn't
occur to me at all until that night that I'd fallen out of touch
with her. There was no very good reason not to try her, except
that I didn't feel I could work up the energy, right then, to go
through the whole process of catching up and explaining why
I hadn't called for so long when I didn't know myself. And I
realized then that everyone else I knew was, or had become
over the course of the past two years, what I would consider
an acquaintance rather than a friend. I was surprised when I
thought this, though less surprised at the obvious truth of it
than at the fact that I hadn't noticed it before.

I lay down on top of my covers, but after a few minutes I
was shivering, so I got under the blankets. That was strange. I
never used to get cold at all; I liked to keep my bedroom window open a little even in winter, for the fresh air. But now it
felt as if some protective layer of myself had been removed,
leaving me exposed to the elements. Or to put it another way,
I thought, I was just sad, and that makes you feel cold more
easily. I pulled the covers up around my shoulders.

I *was* sad. I closed my eyes, and scraps of memories began
to detach themselves from a hidden place and drift up past me,
like ashes rising above a fire. They concerned love, mostly;
John—not John, but the wastebasket underneath our kitchen
sink, the dish drainer with our mismatched cups on it, the
living room with his enormous TV and evening fading in the
windows behind it, a pattern of shadows from the leaves of
sumac trees across our bedspread, little piles of soot collected in
the corners of the windowsills. Those were exactly the things
you lost when you lost someone, I thought. The larger things,
like camping trips and fights and anniversary dinners, stayed
with you, or at least showed up every now and then to upset
or comfort you or make you glad the person wasn't around
anymore. Even the small details that you could remember
weren't gone, really; it was all the uncountable other tiny things
that had strung them together that were missing.

I FELL asleep thinking these things, and I had a terrible dream.
Or rather, the dream itself was beautiful, but when I woke up
from it, I knew immediately that something awful had happened while I'd been sleeping.

I was in Maria Rank's parlor in Frankfurt, the room that

was so familiar to me from the paintings. We were sitting on
the couch together, and she was reading aloud to me from a
little green book that she held in her lap. I wanted to look at
the book myself, because I knew it concerned a lot of things
that I'd always been curious about, and I was so distracted by
my desire to hold it in my own hands that it was hard for me
to pay attention to what she was saying. Maybe it explained
how I had come to be where I was; I know that half of it made
sense to me and half of it didn't. But I couldn't remember it
afterward.

As she read, Maria kept glancing up to see whether I was
following her words, and she could see I wasn't. Finally, in
frustration, she put the book down. Then all at once she took
me by the arm and pulled me close to her. "Listen," she
said.

There was something in her black eyes that was as insub-
stantial as light but at the same time slower and darker than
water, slower than anything I had ever seen. It reminded me
of one of those moments of sadness that sometimes come when
you're waiting for an inconsequential thing, like an elevator or
a stop on the subway, and feel a pause that is so still that it
seals itself up around you, lifts away from the stream of time,
and hangs suspended there. I felt drawn toward her, the way
molecules in motion are drawn toward empty spaces.

"Listen."

I held my breath and I heard a soft, muffled sound like
pebbles tumbling over one another in a riverbed, and then the
rustle of her skirt as she dropped my arm and leaned away
from me. She settled down against the back of the couch, but
an afterimage of her face lingered where it had been, inches
away from mine.

"You had better go," she said, and I could tell by the tone of her voice that there was something I was supposed to do.

I WOKE up about a minute before the phone rang. It was early morning.

"It seems he escaped through an air vent," Klaue said, "and jumped from the roof. He is in St. Vincent's Hospital."

"Is he badly hurt?" I asked.

"Yes. There are no visitors permitted now."

"But they must allow family members. He doesn't have any family, does he?"

"He has no living family, that's right," Klaue said. But when I asked if he thought I might be allowed to go, he said that it would probably be better for me to wait.

LYDIA CALLED later in the morning.

"I hope you don't feel responsible," she said. "Because I don't think you are."

"Of course I do. Who else could be responsible?"

"Don't, Cleo," she said. "He wanted to die. That isn't your fault."

"Was he really trying to kill himself when he went over the edge of the roof," I asked, "or was he just trying to escape?"

There was a pause.

"There isn't any point in thinking that way, Cleo. You couldn't have known what would happen."

"But I knew it was wrong. I did know," I said.

For several days I stopped working and spoke to almost no one. When I finally heard more news of Ludwig, it was only that he was expected to be in the hospital for a month and that it would still be better for me not to visit him.

The castle was nearing completion, in fact was finished except for some interior decorating, and was due to open in less than two weeks, in early March. I had articles due about the plans for the opening gala and somehow I managed to get back to them, and then I discovered that I was able to do nothing but work all day, except for taking Rufus out and occasional trips to the deli, and that there wasn't time to do anything but work, there never had been, but I'd somehow managed to ignore that fact for most of my life. I spent most of the rest of February at my desk, next to cups of coffee that were glued to its surface by the residue of countless other coffee cups.

The picture of Ludwig lying in a hospital bed was too vague in my imagination and too sad to hold in my mind for long, and my own actions before the morning of his accident now seemed like chess pieces that had been knocked onto the floor. Their arrangement suggested no future and rendered meaningless the intentions and plans that had existed before; they were inert, only damning. If I ever did stop working I would find myself sitting motionless or lying on my bed, not exactly thinking about these things, but enclosed by them in a hanging, swarming emptiness while hours slipped by unnoticed, and the day would be lost. I tried not to let that happen.

16

(CLEO)

The castle opened on March 9, 2011, one year and three days after I had flown with Klaue in the helicopter and watched the buildings collapse to make way for it. Every single dog except Ludwig turned out for the pre-opening party, along with four hundred people all dressed, in honor of the dogs, in enormous skirts or top hats and tails and looking for the most part exactly as if they were going to a party in 1882, except for a few variations like dresses made of vinyl or fur and one very nice one made of Rhodophane, which looked like flexible glass, and, for some reason I couldn't figure out, a couple of those dangerous hats that were around that year that had aerodynamic metal constructions on them. A few women had the fronts of their long skirts cut out, like the one I'd worn to the opera, and showed off narrow trousers or metallic silk stockings with delicate pumps. I'd decided that was a risky style that too often looked terrible, so I'd chosen a simple bustled dress in gray-blue silk, with short gloves and a small hat.

We sat down to dinner at long tables set up in the throne room, which was so full of gilding and mosaics and bright-colored murals that the effect was dizzying and didn't really make you want to eat. If I had designed the party I would have kept the lights on the walls and ceilings dim, at least until dancing time, but of course Klaue wanted to show it off and so the whole place was lit up like a stage. I sat next to Lydia, but, either in spite or because of the fact that we hadn't talked much recently, we said little to each other.

After dinner the tables were cleared away and a small orchestra came in to play waltzes, and as the crowd began to mill around I unexpectedly found Rob, who had been Ludwig's servant. It had been nearly a year since I had seen him, and he was noticeably taller and had cut his hair very short. There was a little blue lightning bolt tattooed under his left ear. He tried to say something to me but the music had just started, amplified too much by speakers hung all around the room, and I couldn't hear him. After trying a couple of times he shook his head and smiled, then leaned toward me and shouted in my ear, "Dance?"

I nodded and we went out on the floor, and stayed together until Burkhardt, the Bull Terrier who had written the opera libretto, tapped Rob on the shoulder and took over.

"Nice to see you again!" I shouted.

"This music is much too loud!" Burkhardt replied. "Somebody ought to do something about it!"

"Yes!" I agreed.

He was a clumsy but enthusiastic dancer, and I was enjoying myself until somebody I had never seen before cut in. "I'll see

Klaue about those damned speakers!" Burkhardt said as I was
spun away from him by a very tall man in olive-colored tails.

"Hello," I said, straining to see up into the man's face.
"Who are you?"

"Casanova," he said. Far away as I was, I could smell scotch
on his breath.

"Okay," I said. He was a good waltzer, anyway. Before too
long the music was turned down to a reasonable level. The
man in olive hung on to me for a little while, but then someone
else I'd never met took me away. He was tall, too, but had a
pleasant round face with kind gray eyes.

"Jim," he said, smiling.

"I'm Cleo," I said, but we had barely started dancing before
I was in someone else's arms. Everybody seemed to become
fascinated by the idea that they could cut in and dance with
anyone they wanted to, and all the girls began to get whirled
back and forth every few minutes, until people could hardly
keep track of who their partners were and started to clump up
and separate into parties of more or less than two. Then the
orchestra took a break and everyone staggered off the floor
toward the bar.

I found Lydia, who had been dancing but had left before
things got frantic. She was sitting in a chair in her dress of
lavender voile, holding a little ivory fan in one hand and a glass
in the other. One of her ears was turned sideways and she was
staring vaguely at people's shoes as they walked in front of her.
Her whiskers, pointing forward a little, seemed to be following
them more closely than her eyes.

"Wonderful," she said as I sat down next to her.

"Lend me your fan for a second," I said, but she handed
me her drink instead, which was something mixed with a lot
of cold soda water, and I finished it.

"I'm going to die if I have to do that again," I said, rolling the empty glass back and forth against my neck. "How long before they open up the big gates?"

"It's going to be soon, I think," Lydia said. "But we'll keep dancing up here anyway. They'll have a separate event for the general public downstairs. Klaue says that there's an absolutely enormous crowd waiting, and they're going to have to keep some people out, or perhaps rotate the crowd inside. He's trying to figure it out now."

"They're opening the gates!" someone called from across the room, and we all trooped out into the hallway and headed for the windows that faced across the courtyard toward the gatehouse at the other end. There wasn't nearly enough space for everyone to see out, but Lydia and I found a spot with a view and held it as the crowd heaved around us. Some people climbed the curtains, which were suspended from rods so massive that if they had fallen down, each would have knocked over a dozen of us; but they seemed to be holding.

There was a little display of green and blue fireworks outside, and then, as we watched, people began to surge from the street into the courtyard, which was floodlit and lined with men in red-and-black uniforms.

At first everything was all right, but then scuffles began to break out as the dark crowd pressed some people too hard against the courtyard walls. Some of the uniformed men fanned out into the middle to try to form a barrier, it seemed, across the yard to hold some of the people back, but were unsuccessful. They were caught in the press and couldn't keep their places but were pushed forward until some of them were carried almost into the wall of the main building, directly underneath our windows. Voices began to shout through loudspeakers for people to turn back, but no one did, or even could anymore. It had become a stampede. Policemen in blue started to leak in through the edges of the gate to help, but it was too late and they were separated from one another and tossed around like shells inside breaking waves.

Up in the windows we held our breath. Then someone, one of the policemen, we thought, fired a shot into the air. It had no effect on the crowd. Then another shot followed it. And then many more shots followed, and they didn't all seem to be coming from the courtyard. Some of them, apparently, were coming from the windows in the stories above us.

At the noise of gunfire a commotion rose in our hallway and people began to back away and push one another toward the throne room. Lydia stayed by the window and I stayed with her. Her ears and whiskers pointed straight forward as she watched the scene below us, and her fur rose at the back of her neck into a great big mane, but she stayed absolutely still.

"Who's shooting at them, Lydia?" I asked.

"We are. The dogs are. There aren't any humans with weapons inside the castle, you can be sure of that. But look," she said, glancing at my face, "they're not shooting *into* the crowd. They're just trying to turn it back. It's not a war, Cleo, don't faint." She took my arm and pulled me back a little from the window.

"I'm not fainting," I said. "Look, they're going back. They're stampeding the other way." I got free of her and went back to the window.

We watched as the crowd poured out the gate. Before they could all leave, though, the entrance was barred, and a few hundred, a tiny fraction of the mob, were left stranded in the courtyard. Some were gathered around people who had fallen on the ground, but there was barely time to notice that before paramedics with stretchers began to come in a line through one of the side doors and carry them away. Some people followed them out, while others stayed milling in the yard, looking up at the castle, or headed up the long flight of steps that led to the main door, which seemed to be open.

"There must be people inside, downstairs," Lydia said as she watched them go in. "I wonder what's going on there."

"Do you think they're going ahead with their party? Let's go look," I said. "Everyone else is." The few people who had stayed at the windows were heading for the staircase now, along with larger groups who were coming out of the throne room.

As we began to descend we could hear music playing, big-band jazz, and when we got farther down we saw that a lot of people were dancing to it, although some hung around the edges of the room, with drinks, looking concerned or angry. There were hardly any dogs anywhere. As we reached the bottom of the steps, a Husky in a blue uniform came up and bowed politely to Lydia, barring our way. He was the same one I'd met on the morning Ludwig had been locked up.

"Berthold," Lydia said. "What is it?"

"It's very serious. The castle is closed," he said.

"Closed?"

"Yes. A meeting has been called just now. Please come with me, if you will."

He led Lydia off toward a door in the side of the big room into which we'd descended, and I started to follow, but he stopped me.

"I'm sorry that you are not allowed to attend the meeting, Cleo," Berthold said.

Lydia exchanged glances with me, but she didn't say anything as she went away with the Husky.

I didn't feel like dancing, or doing anything, so I went to the staircase and sat down on the bottom steps. I tried to lean

my head back against the banister, but it had so many carved
leaves and knobs and animals' heads sticking out of it that I
couldn't find a comfortable place to rest, and gave up. I was
suddenly very tired. Finally I picked my skirts up and dragged
myself back upstairs, where I found an unoccupied couch in a
dim hallway, lay down on it, and fell asleep.

"THERE YOU are," Lydia said, waking me.

"What happened?" I asked.

"It's not all that serious," she replied. "Everything's been
worked out with the police and the mayor. He's just left. It
clearly wasn't anyone's fault."

"Weren't people hurt?"

"Not very many."

"What did Berthold mean about the castle being closed?" I
asked.

"Well, no one else is allowed to come in, but everyone can
leave. Except the dogs. We're going to stay for a while."

"You mean move in and stay here?"

"I suppose so. It seems best that way. By the way, Cleo, you
have a room. Wasn't that thoughtful of Klaue? We both have
very nice ones up in the south tower. I suppose you might as
well spend the night there."

"I can't," I said, "I've got to go home and walk my dog.
It's only a couple of blocks away."

"You may have trouble getting back in again if you leave,"
Lydia said.

"That's ridiculous. I'll talk to Klaue about it; he can make
it so I can get back in again," I said.

"Well, talk to him in the morning. Everyone is very tired
now," she said.

So I called my neighbor Sam and asked him if he could take care of Rufus for a little while, until I was able to figure out what was going on. "I'm sort of stuck in the castle," I told him. "I'll call as soon as I know what's going on."

It turned out to be a week before I called him, and then it was only to tell him that I still didn't know when I'd be coming home. Things had begun to get very strange there. Many of the people who had gotten in on the first night, feeling privileged now to be in the closed-off castle, decided to stay, and they were allowed to. The reporters among them, who phoned in stories to their editors constantly, were especially reluctant to leave, since once they did, they would not be allowed back in again. Klaue claimed the closure of the building was only temporary, and that the museum, restaurant, and hotel would be opened as soon as some things were put in order, but he seemed to be making no attempt to end the strange party, which had spread out to all the public rooms, consisted of about six hundred people and all the dogs, and went on around the clock, day after day. The humans, who didn't have bedrooms in the building, set up temporary camps in hallways and sitting rooms and in the corners of the palatial bathrooms. Everyone was kept supplied with meals and drinks and music from the remnants of the jazz band and orchestra. Apparently there had been a plan to perform some Wagner opera in the concert hall soon after the castle opened, and although the public couldn't be invited now, according to Klaue's orders, some of the performers had come to the opening party and stayed on and could be heard practicing in empty dining rooms at all hours.

One day Lydia and I were sitting in a parlor, having a lunch that we'd brought in from the dining room on a tray, when we heard the muffled sound of a gunshot. Lydia stopped eating.

"It's started," she said.

"What?"

"Someone has gone mad."

"What are you talking about?"

"I didn't see the need to mention it before I had to," Lydia said. "But there it is. It's a way to end the sickness with dignity. It makes sense to us. Since we're all in the castle, no one out-side needs to know. I know it seems strange to you, Cleo, but it is a private matter among the dogs. I hope you will try to understand."

"You mean you're all going to kill yourselves?" I asked.

"Oh no, that would be too difficult—who knows what one would do with a gun in that state of mind. Klaue has appointed a small committee."

"Of murderers?"

"It isn't murder if the victim has agreed to it," Lydia said.

"But what if the dogs on the committee go mad?" I asked.

"Then they will be replaced."

"But what if the dogs in charge of replacing them go mad?"

Lydia stood up, and her plate crashed to the floor. I don't know whether it was an accident or whether she threw it down. She looked at it, and then at me.

"Everything has to end sometime," she said, stepping away from the shards on the floor. "You're perfectly safe, anyway. No one wants any difficulties with the humans." We watched each other's faces for a moment, and then she turned and left the room.

I called Sam and told him I didn't know when I'd be com-ing back. On the one hand Klaue had given me permission to come and go as I wanted, but on the other hand I had some idea that I could convince Lydia to escape, if only I could talk to her enough; I didn't see why she would want to stay if she still wasn't going mad herself. And so I stayed.

17

A few days later, a servant knocked on the door of my room and delivered a note in a small envelope. It said: "Ludwig requests that you visit him." There was no signature or other indication of where it had come from. I supposed someone at the hospital, maybe a nurse, had phoned the receptionist at the castle switchboard, but it didn't matter, anyway. I didn't even care if it was true. I was just glad of an excuse to see him.

I went to the gatehouse to make sure the captain of the guards knew who I was and that I was to be allowed back in again as Klaue had promised, and he did. Then, wearing the long ermine-lined coat in which I'd arrived at the party over my silk dress, I ran the block and a half east to my apartment, waving to one neighbor I passed on the sidewalk but pretending not to notice his expression of surprise at my appearance as I jogged by. At home I changed into regular clothes and put the dress and coat into a bag, which I took with me, and then I went across town to St. Vincent's.

When I came into the hospital room, I saw Ludwig lying on his side, facing away from me. The sunlight coming in at the window in the far wall seemed unnaturally bright and stale. But although everything was absolutely still and quiet, there was a feeling of frenzy just around the edges of the room, as though something were darting around by the walls, and I kept glimpsing it out of the corner of my eye. The odors of dog and antiseptic were strong, but even worse than that was a fainter, terrible metallic smell that somehow spoke to me of spilled blood, and knives.

"Ludwig?" I said, cautiously. I couldn't tell whether he was asleep, but his ears moved slightly when I spoke.

"Are you awake?" I asked as I came toward him. He still didn't answer, so I went around to the other side of the bed. His eyes were open, but he was staring at nothing. I had seen dogs sleep that way sometimes, though, so I wasn't sure what to make of it. I sat down in an uncomfortable upholstered chair and reached for his hand, which was stretched out in front of him. Then his eyes turned toward me.

"Ah hah," he said softly, almost in a whisper. He mumbled something that I couldn't understand at first. It sounded like "This is goodbye"; but then I realized that he was speaking German.

"Es ist vorbei," he was saying.

"What's over?" I asked him. "Was ist vorbei?"

"Oh, Maria," he began, and then he launched into more complicated muttered German that I couldn't make any sense of at all.

"I'm not Maria, you know," I told him quietly, when he

was finished. He didn't answer. "Well, never mind," I said. "It's all right, you know. Nothing is over . . . I mean—"

"Ah, *Cleo,*" he said suddenly. His voice was still foggy around the consonants, but it sounded a little clearer now. "Oh, *God.*" He moved his head so that he wasn't looking at me anymore, and then closed his eyes. "Go away," he said.

"Oh, Ludwig, please—"

"Go away right now," he said. "I am falling asleep. You may come back tomorrow," he added kindly, but he was mumbling again, so I could barely understand him.

"Tomorrow?"

"*Yes.* Go *away,* Cleo."

"All right. I'll come back, then," I told him. I let go of his hand and stood up, and that smell hit me again, that awful metallic odor.

WHEN I came back the next day at the beginning of visiting hours, I was told Ludwig had requested that no one be allowed to see him. For a moment I wanted to argue, but when I looked into the face of the tired, preoccupied receptionist behind the desk, and thought of the last, pointless conversation I had had in Ludwig's room, my anger found nothing to catch hold of, and it died down as quickly as it had flared up. I shut my mouth and turned away.

At the front of the lobby I paused with my hand against the window and looked out into the street. Rain lashed against the glass, the infuriating kind of rain that turns umbrellas inside out and finds its way under your collar and down to the roots of your hair. I was still cold and wet from having been out in it. There was a heater just inside the door, blowing warm air downward, and standing directly underneath it, I suddenly felt dizzy and exhausted. It occurred to me that my head was ringing with hatred, or rage, something that had been echoing around inside me for a long time. There was nowhere for it to go; I had no one but myself to blame for everything.

I tightened my scarf around my neck, pulled the zipper of my jacket as high as it would go, and walked out into the rain. I knew it would be impossible to get a cab in the downpour, so I didn't bother to look for one. It had been that warmth inside the door, I thought, like a memory of comfort, that had made me feel so dizzy. I would walk it off. There was no way I could be forgiven for what I had done to Ludwig, but it wouldn't do anyone any good for me to collapse now because of it. There would be something I could do, sometime; for now I just had to get on with things.

As I got to the middle of the block, I noticed a car slowing down beside me, a limousine. It drew over to the curb, and I saw Klaue, sitting a little distance away from the open window to avoid getting wet.

"Cleo," he said. "You're drenched. Get in."

"Oh, no, Klaue," I said. "I'd ruin the seats. Thanks anyway."

"Don't be ridiculous. Have you been to see Ludwig?"

"No."

We looked at each other for a moment, measuring something.

"Get in," he said again.

"I really don't want to."

He shrugged. "All right, then."

I caught the expression in his eyes as he glanced away, a flicker of sadness followed by something grim and hard. I think, now, that this might have been the moment he realized

I had become unfriendly to him. I should never have let him
see it, but I was too wrapped up in worrying about the mistakes
I had made in the past to see the new ones I was making at
that moment.

I walked until my bones ached, until I was so wet and cold
that it didn't matter anymore. Water seeped under my leather
jacket, my scarf got soaked and began to siphon the rain down
the front of my shirt, my jeans clung to me, and my boots were
wet through. I couldn't go into any place to get out of the rain
looking like that, or even get on a bus, really. I could have
called to Neuhundstein for a car, but then I'd have had to stand
around and wait for it to come, so all in all it seemed I might
as well just go on walking until I got to the castle.

When I got there, I went straight up to my room, not looking at anyone I passed in the halls, leaving a trail of water along
the floor and up the tower stairs. I shut my door and leaned
against the inside of it, dripping. In the stillness and the warmth
of the room, my fatigue and everything else caught up with me
again. I'd known they would, but I was surprised at the sud-
denness and force with which they came rushing into the empty
space. I stood there for several minutes feeling stunned, with
no thought in my mind at all, surrounded by a cloud of un-
directed hatred, until it threatened to dissipate and leave behind
a kind of sadness that I could feel would be much worse. I
unzipped my jacket, unwound the scarf from my neck, and
then slowly took off everything else I was wearing and left it
in a sodden pile on the floor.

I went into the bathroom and took the biggest towel I could
find off the long brass rail along the wall. It was bright red, an
inch thick, and it had been hanging near a heating grate, so it
was warm. It must have been the size of a small sheet, because
I draped it over my head and wrapped it around my body, and

there was still enough of it left to drag on the floor. I walked over to my bed and sat down on the edge of it, looking into the fireplace. There was no fire in it. The castle had central heating, so it didn't really matter, but I thought it would have been nice if somebody had kept it going for me. Usually someone did, some servant, so it had never gone completely out before, but now there was definitely nothing there but ashes and little chunks of charred wood. I sighed and lay down on my back, stretching my arms above my head to straighten my spine, and stared at the ceiling.

"THE SMELLS are maddening, Cleo. I can't stand it anymore."

I stood by the velvet divan in Lydia's tower room, in the evening, and she lay on it, stretched out full length, her heavy bustled dress unlaced and looking somehow as if it didn't belong on her, although it was perfectly tailored to her body.

"Then let's leave," I said.

"No."

"Why not? What do you want to stay here for?"

"I have nowhere else to go," she said. "There simply is no other place."

I started to say something, but she stopped me.

"Cleo," she said. "Listen. I know you can't understand it, but at least admit to that, and leave it be. I am a member of a dying race. There is no place for me in this world. I have no past, and no possibility of a future. If a human were to say that, you would want to talk them out of it—of course. But I'm not human. Do you understand what I'm saying?"

"You're saying, don't think of you the way I'd think of a friend. Is that what you're saying?" I asked.

"No, of course not."

"Look," I said, "I don't pretend to understand what it feels like to be you. All I know is that I want you to live, and you're not going to live if you stay here."

At that very moment, the sound of a gunshot echoed through the stairwell. Another dog down.

"My God," Lydia said quietly.

"I'm going downstairs," I said. I wanted to get Lydia out of her room and throw her into the middle of everything, so she'd see how horrible it had become, but I couldn't do that, so I decided to go down myself. At least I could tell her what I'd seen.

OH, BUT it was magnificent down there. It was the kind of thing I'd only see once in my life, and I relished it. I think half of my anger at Lydia then was annoyance at myself; it was me trying to pull away from my own desire to be buried in the mad, ridiculous world of the dogs' last party.

The middle of the fourth floor, onto which the door of the stairwell opened, was a vast, empty space. All around the edges, dogs and humans were packed close, staring toward the center and toward a point to the left of me, where I couldn't see anything but the crowd. As I stood by the door, trying to figure out what was happening, a cheer went up, and then some voices yelled, *"Eins!"*

A second later, twice as many voices yelled, *"Zwei!"* and then *"DREI! YarrRRR!"* and, to my complete surprise, a huge chandelier—at least thirty feet in diameter—came crashing into the middle of the marble floor. The left edge of it hit first, and then the whole pyramid of metal and swinging crystal collapsed sideways and shattered, causing a breathtaking explosion of sparks and splintered prisms. The crowd yelped and cheered.

"My God," I said, inadvertently. I was answered by a loud, mechanical laugh just to the right of me, and I recognized it.

"Klaue," I said, turning toward him.

"Ya-HOWW!" he answered, his mouth aimed directly at my ear, though he was staring at the ruin in the center of the floor.

I tried to work through the crowd, away from him, but I felt my upper arm clenched in his gloved hand. I turned around.

"Hello, Cleo!" He grinned. He was drunk, and his voice was far too loud, even granting that he was trying to be heard over the racket.

"Hi, Klaue," I said, figuring I wouldn't get anywhere by fighting. He didn't let go of my arm.

"How are you, Cleo?" he yelled. The liquor had given him a more pronounced German accent than usual.

"You're hurting my arm there."

"Oh, I'm so sorry! Oh, so sorry!" He let go and brushed at it.

"Yeah, well, I have to go and find a—"

"What? Cleo, you are MUMBLING! You must SPEAK UP!"

"I, ah—I've got to go and find Lydia."

"Lydi-*ah!* How *is* she? I am so glad she *joined* us! So much work to *convince* her! How is she enjoying herself?"

"You know, Klaue," I said, turning back to face him, although I'd been in the process of leaving, "you really . . ." But I looked at his face and knew I wasn't going to get anywhere. "You really are proud of yourself, aren't you?" I finished.

He stared at me, and I thought his eyes went blank and flat. Maybe it was just the liquor.

"It is love-*lyy*." He smiled, his tongue out. Then he closed his mouth and stared again, dumbly, for a split second.

"Don't you think it is lovely, Cleo? My Neuhundstein?" His tongue protruded again, and remained stuck between his front teeth, its tip showing, when he shut his jaws.

"I think you're drunk, Klaue," I said.

His eyes opened wider, but he didn't say anything.

"I'm leaving now, okay?"

"Okay, Cleo," he said, his tone mocking.

"I don't believe my name is Klaue," he murmured, sotto voce, as I walked away through the thinning crowd. He seemed to have gained control over his voice, and his accent was no longer so pronounced. "No . . . Rank-Mops-Augustus-Hacker, something like that. *Doktor,* to you," he added more loudly, as I went out of hearing range.

I WANTED to leave the room, but I didn't feel like talking to Lydia again just yet, or like being alone. Since the crowd was dispersing, I decided to go down to the third floor and see if anything was happening there. First, though, I stopped at the bar, feeling that a drink would help somehow, although the entire atmosphere was disorienting enough without one.

I carried my whiskey and soda down the broad staircase, which was clogged with seated groups of dogs and people talking with varying degrees of coherence. The jazz band was playing on the third floor, and a lot of dogs were trying to waltz to the music, not knowing any other kind of dance. A few of them were wearing garish, complicated costumes out of whatever Wagner opera they were planning to perform, or had been performing. On closer inspection, some of the creatures dressed

up this way turned out to be humans wearing disturbingly realistic canine heads, with ears and mouths that moved awk-
wardly and in a nonsensical way, operated by hidden strings
and pulleys. There was a suffocating odor of burnt food and
also of incense, probably meant to cover it up, and the whole
thing was starting to make me feel rather sick.

I wanted to find someone I knew, someone I could talk to.
From the third stair, I could see a Great Dane sitting far down
by the right wall, his head bowed, holding his top hat and
looking at it.

"Luitpold!" I yelled, though I really didn't know whether
it was he, or whether the dog over there was mad or drunk. I
just said it to hear my own voice, and it didn't seem to matter
much either way.

"Luitpold!" I made my way toward the wall, pushing
through a clot of people who were standing in front of the dog,
and praying that it was he, and he was all right. When I pushed
my way through the last bodies, I found myself a foot away
from him.

When I saw him up close I reeled backward, half falling
against the people behind me, who looked at me as if I were
crazy.

What I'd seen was a dog with his neck broken, head hanging at a terrible angle, skin detached from his chest. Throat
cut? I saw pink flesh, then—a death rattle! —No— No, it was
one of those stupid idiots wearing a dog mask, asleep and
snoring.

"Oops," I said, and forced my way back from the wall, head
bowed.

"Luitpold," said a deep, quiet voice behind me, and someone touched my back.

"What?" I spun around, braced for the next horror.

"Here," he finished, "at your service."

"Oh, Luitpold. It's you. How are you holding up?"

He shrugged, an unnatural gesture for a dog, but somehow graceful on him. Not affected, the way it would have been on Klaue. He looked at his hands, which were folded over the top of a large silver-headed cane.

"Are you—all right?" I asked, trying to look into his eyes.

"I am. All right," he said, raising his head, but not directing his gaze at me.

"Do you want to go somewhere and talk, maybe? This place is making me sick." (And, I thought, I didn't know if I'd ever get the chance to talk to him again.)

"Yes." He offered me his arm.

I think I've forgotten to mention that before going downstairs I had changed back into my gray-blue silk gown, the dog-style one I had worn at the opening night. I was still the only human allowed free access to the castle; the others could only go out once and never come back, and a couple hundred of them still hadn't left. Most of them remained in their formal clothes, washing their outfits in bathtubs sometimes and hanging them by fires overnight, because they didn't have anything besides what they'd been wearing when they'd come in. And so to fit in with the atmosphere, or maybe just because I wanted to wear it, I spent a lot of time in the bustled skirt, which was slightly crushed and deflated now but still, I thought, a pretty dress. My escort wore long black tails and a top hat. I think those few moments on his arm, as we walked down the edge of the ballroom floor, were some of the most beautiful of my life. Luitpold, so slow and enormous, seemed to create an atmosphere of stillness in the middle of the noisy crowd.

After we'd taken about five steps, it was so lovely that I thought I was going to cry, so to prevent that, I ruined the moment.

"I saw Klaue upstairs," I said. "I think he's going insane."

"What the hell kind of a name is that anyway—Klaue?" I asked when Luitpold didn't reply. "That's not a name, is it?"

"It is a nickname," Luitpold said. "It means 'claw.' "

"Oh," I said. I wondered how I had known Klaue for so long without ever finding that out.

We walked on, over the marble floor, past the dancers; past some human with a wooden sword making a speech from *Julius Caesar*; past a weeping, swooning Belgian Shepherd being supported by her friends, who were offering her smelling salts and fanning her.

"Where can we go that's quiet?" I asked.

"There is a small room that I like, with a window seat," said Luitpold. "It's in one of the stairwells."

"Good, I'd like to sit by a window. I'd like to be reminded that I'm in New York."

"You are," he told me, as if I'd asked him to.

I sat on blue cushions embroidered with gold while Luitpold stood beside me.

"How is Lydia?" he asked. "I have not seen her in several days. Partly because I was indisposed. I care for her a great deal, you know."

"She's sort of been locking herself up in her room lately," I said. "I think it would be good for her to see you."

"Yes, perhaps I should go and find her," he said. "I am afraid . . . there is very little time left, now."

We lapsed into silence and looked together out the window

at the red evening sky and the trees across Houston Street, still bare, as they were lashed by the March rain.

LATE THAT night I woke up with fur in my mouth, crying. My face was buried in Lydia's deep mane, and it was dark. I had come to her room to talk a few hours ago, but she hadn't been there—maybe Luitpold had found her—and I'd fallen asleep waiting for her. She must have just curled up beside me when she'd come in. Now we lay together on the big velvet couch, and though it was warm and quiet and my cheek was pressed against Lydia's comforting fur, I felt terrible. I couldn't tell what I was crying about. It wasn't Ludwig, who was gone forever, or the dogs whose bodies had been thrown into the incinerator last night and now floated as dissipated invisible smoke above the city, though they must have been part of it. It wasn't the hopelessness of all of the dogs' situations, or the lost spirit of Rank, whose last living advocate was never going to write another word about him, and never going to bring him back to life, though that was part of it, too. I felt that I had wandered out beyond the edge of a circle of light where I'd always lived, onto an endless plain.

I went back to my own room and lay there, in the darkness, staring out of my window at the pale red sky. I'd picked up one of Lydia's nightgowns from the floor before I'd left her, thinking it might make me feel better somehow. It was much too big for me, but I liked the feeling of being wrapped in all that linen with ruffles and lace hanging off it everywhere, just being buried in it.

Maybe all I was thinking that night while I looked up at the red cloudy sky, wrapped up in Lydia's nightgown and crying, was that I wanted to be with the dogs, wherever they were going, even though I knew it was impossible. They weren't even gone and I already missed them so much that my whole body ached. The raw pain of having joints and muscles and organs, the uncushioned feeling of living, without hope or love, my throbbing heart, it all hurt so much. I just didn't want to be in the world without them.

It was while I was lying there, thinking these things, that I heard the doorknob turn. At the moment when I heard it, I didn't really care who it was. Maybe I was hoping it was someone who would see me crying and sit down on my bed and comfort me, lick my tears away and let me bury my face in their fur. Maybe I was half hoping it was Klaue, mad, with a gun, coming to kill me.

Well, that's what it was. He opened the door and came softly over to the window. I didn't turn my head to see who was there, so I didn't see him until he stood directly in front of me. He was wearing a tailored blue jacket with big brass buttons, and he looked down at me silently for a moment before he spoke. When he did, he lifted his arm and I saw that he was holding a long, antique-looking pistol that had a dull oily gleam to it in the faint light from the window.

"Cleo," he said softly, as if he wasn't sure whether I was awake and didn't want to disturb me.

"What?" I asked, looking up at him with blurry eyes. I saw everything; but it was as if it was preordained, and I wasn't surprised. At least my mind wasn't, but I felt my heart speeding up and the word sounded like a gasp when I spoke it.

Klaue sat down on the edge of my bed, and moved the gun closer to my body. He pointed it at the mound of ruffles covering my chest, and leaned toward me.

"I know you want to die," he whispered. His muzzle was

so close to my ear and his voice was so dense and intimate that I felt as though his wet tongue were touching me, and I shuddered.

"No, Klaue," I said. It was true. If I was going to die, I wanted to do it on my own terms, not his.

"But you said that you did," he whispered. Had I? I couldn't remember having told him that, but I might have.

Now he moved his mouth even closer to my face. He licked his nose, and his tongue actually did graze my cheek for an instant. My muscles went rigid, but my insides were liquid with terror.

"Come on, Cleo," he said, cocking his head and speaking directly into my ear. The gun moved closer, nosing in among the ruffles over my heart, lifting the lace-edged linen slightly so that it draped delicately around the shaft of the pistol.

"Don't!" I said as the muzzle pushed in closer to my body.

Suddenly, I heard a resounding crash. Klaue, startled, turned to face the door. In the same split second, I grabbed the gun in both my hands and wrenched it to the left. I had gotten it only inches away from my body when it went off, sending a bullet into the wall behind me. At that moment I caught sight of Lydia, just passing the high point of an enormous leap that must have begun at the door and would take her all the way over to the bed. She was dressed in a red silk kimono, which streamed out behind her like a banner. Her face was terrifying and distorted, black lips drawn back from her teeth, ears plastered against her head, the fur of her mane standing up so stiffly that even the force of the air as she leaped could not flatten it completely. Her face was so shortened and twisted with rage that she didn't look like herself at all but like a caricature of herself, a gargoyle, a monster.

As she descended from the leap, her extended hands reached Klaue's chest, and she knocked him over backward and landed

on top of him, gripping his forelegs behind the elbows, her
hind feet digging into his belly. Her teeth closed on his throat
and he let out an animal yelp, a kind of noise I had never heard
from him before. Even in his madness he had not let down his
façade of humanness. But now, fighting for his life, he was pure
dog. He gave two fast half-barks as he twisted under Lydia
and tore himself away from her jaws, then another short,
deeper bark, which turned into a snarl as he lunged back at
her. He caught her on the side of the snout and she squealed
for a moment in surprise, but the sound was barely out of her
throat before she pulled free and opened her jaws. She caught
Klaue's muzzle straight on. He made a terrible sound as he
tried to catch his breath with his nose inside Lydia's mouth.
His head whipped to the side, but Lydia held on. She was
slipping off Klaue's chest now, and he managed to right himself
so he was standing on all fours. Still Lydia did not let go of
his muzzle. He pulled backward, making wet, ragged, choking
noises as he tried desperately to breathe.

They took a few stiff steps along the side of the bed, Klaue
backing up and Lydia following him. Finally she simply let go
of him. Klaue took another step and then sat down facing her.
He looked absolutely doggy and ashamed. His mouth was
slightly open and he kept perfectly still, breathing, too stunned
even to lick his nose. After a moment he lay down. Lydia sat,
heavily, licking her lips and curling them into little almost-
accidental snarls as she did so, keeping her eyes on Klaue. He
didn't move. Then she put her hand on the edge of the bed
and slowly drew herself up onto her hind legs. She took an
awkward step, trying to catch her balance, and then fell down
on all fours again.

She threw a quick glance in my direction. I was sitting
on the bed, exactly where I had been before Lydia came into

the room. She snorted, turned around, and headed for the door.

"Lydia, wait," I said, but she ignored me. I watched her leave, and then turned back to Klaue. He was still lying near the wall, looking at nothing, his eyes glazed. The gun was halfway across the room, on the floor. I got out of the bed, went over to it, and picked it up. Klaue's ears and eyebrows seemed to move slightly as I passed in front of him, but he didn't turn his head or shift his gaze. I went back and sat down on the bed again and looked at him.

"Klaue?" I said. His ears pricked a little, but that was all. He didn't even look like Klaue. He just looked like an ordinary dog. He was still wearing the blue jacket, and he was lying on its tails so that it was stretched tight at an angle over his shoulders and back. He was panting.

I went out the door to look for Lydia.

I FOUND her lying on the couch in her room, still wearing the torn-up kimono, and there were flecks of blood on the side of her muzzle. Her eyes had a flatness about them that reminded me of Ludwig's, the last time I saw him. I didn't like it.

"Lydia?" I said cautiously.

"It's all over now, Cleo," she said softly, but distinctly.

"You're not going mad, are you?" I asked. "Just tell me you're not."

"I'm afraid I *am,* Cleo," she answered, drawing her hand over her eyes. Her gloves were very delicate brownish pink kid, and they were speckled with dark stains from the fight. She didn't look tired. In spite of the cast of her eyes, there was a kind of slow brightness about her, like the gently pulsing glow of an ember.

"I can hear you," she said. "I heard you calling for help, and that's why I came."

"Well . . . I believe you," I said. "That isn't madness."

"It isn't right," she said.

She settled her head back among the cushions and smiled slightly at the ceiling.

"It was lucky for me," I said.

"Yes," she said. "It was."

18

(CLEO)

It's difficult to describe what happened in the week after Klaue and Lydia's fight. Every day, groups of people gave up at last and left the party. Although the servants were being paid for their time, many of them deserted the castle, too. The few people who had stayed on would turn up in unexpected places. I'd find a little drunken pile of them in the corner of a dining room or a man in the ruins of a tuxedo sitting on a windowsill, scribbling things on scraps of paper, or hear someone picking out tunes on a harpsichord late at night. There was a cellist who serenaded us every morning at dawn from the dais of the empty throne room, and sometimes people would gather there to listen to him. But it was often possible to wander through the halls for long periods without meeting anyone at all.

Neither Lydia nor I saw Klaue again, and we assumed the worst. We didn't know who was in the band of executioners, how many were remaining or whether any of them were sane, but we heard their gunshots echo through the corridors, and saw fewer dogs every day. Most of the time we kept to our rooms, with the doors locked.

Ludwig began to send me strange handwritten letters from the hospital. When the mail stopped being delivered to my room, I searched the ground floors and found the mail slot so that I could get them myself.

LUDWIG'S LETTER POSTMARKED MARCH 21, 2011

I have discovered the cause of my insanity.

Cleo, I am already insane. You have said that I am not, to comfort me, and to comfort you I have agreed, at times, but I cannot pretend anymore. It is all over with me.

I now find myself in the difficult position of having acquired a certain very valuable piece of knowledge through my insanity, and being unable to convey it to you, because I am mad. What I now know could, I believe, save all the dogs, if I could explain it to them. You are also in danger, Cleo. The dogs can all go to hell, but I wish I could speak to you. I want to save you.

It is so clear to me. Cleo, please try to understand.

We move forward through time in only one direction. It as if we were one-dimensional creatures moving along a straight line. We cannot see anything to the left or right, above or below; we cannot even comprehend the meaning of the words "left" or "down." The whole breadth and height of the world are veiled to us.

If we were to stop moving forward, the cover would be pulled away and the entire static universe would be revealed to us.

*Hope is motion. Curiosity, desire, and hope alone can
keep the surface from being drawn back to reveal the
terrifying mechanism of the world. I would give my life,
Cleo, to keep you from having to hear the noise it makes.
It is a dead hum.*

*My desire for you is the last thing. You are my spark.
Where there is no communication, there is insanity, and if
I can convey this one last thought to you, perhaps I can
live, but that doesn't matter; what matters is that you
should live.*

*In order to live, Cleo, you must feel desire. It is so
simple! If only you could see it. Do not turn backward
and cling to us after we are gone, for it is not possible to
go backward, and you will only succeed in halting your
forward motion. Do you see how simple it is?*

*And yet it is not simple, for desire is so often fixed
upon earthly things, and hope is so often bound together
with the unfolding of events over the course of time in this
life, and curiosity also must be aroused by earthly things. I
say* must be, *all of this must be, if you are to live; and
yet these things are temporary, so you will fix yourself
upon something and then its time will come to an end.
You must fix yourself to it firmly, and bravely, and never
want to release it, for your very life depends upon holding
on to it. This is difficult, and complicated. It is a paradox.
If you cling to us, you will die with us; if you do not
cling to us, you will die of despair, for you will not feel
desire. And yet—and this is the paradox—you can, if you
do neither one nor the other, still live. In the space
between desire and despair . . . In the space between
desire and despair, between holding and letting go,
between clinging and release, and between my desire for*

you and my desire for your happiness, which things cannot
exist together, and yet which could not exist separately . . .
Can you see this? In this space is the unspoken thing, the
thing that lives.

What lives in you lies at the center of a network of
veins and arteries; this is the net of blood. Light, or
electrical energy, runs through the nerves of your body;
this is the net of gold. You exist always caught in this net,
under this net of blood and gold.

You are caught on something; you are resting on
something, under the net of blood and gold.

This is all I can tell you.

LUDWIG'S LETTER POSTMARKED MARCH 22

The Clinging, Fire
That which is bright rises twice:
The image of FIRE.
Thus the great man, by perpetuating this brightness,
Illumines the four quarters of the world.

Cleo, Cleo,
That which is bright rises twice:
You are the little flame inside the lamp,
The image of fire.
The dust in the bowl of the flower, the light.
Thus the great man, *the lamp and the flower,*
        by perpetuating this brightness,
Cleo, I am in agony—
Illumines the four quarters of the world.
Oh, Cleo, I love you! I love you! Cleo—

Why do you not love me?
Is it because I'm a dog?

LUDWIG'S LETTER POSTMARKED MARCH 24

Cleo,

I am consumed by my desire for you, and yet I feel I am losing the ability to communicate anything to you, like the soul of someone who has died, cut loose from the anchor of his body, being pulled by currents of air farther and farther away from the living world. I am being drawn up toward the passionate flames of heaven, I can see them, a canopy of stars, but they are so far away, and I must spend such a long time traveling through blackness, in these winds, before I reach them.

Having been consumed, I am ashes, and it is in the form of ashes that I must travel through the great distance of empty space before I reach even the sphere of the moving stars; and how many miles beyond that to the sphere of the fixed stars, and how far beyond that must I travel before I come even to the lowest circle of heaven?

Having been consumed, I am ashes, and as each part of my being separates from every other part and is taken away by the currents of the moving air, you may ask, how is it that I can still feel desire? Where is that desire located? But there is still one burning ember here, a little thing, diminishing, exhausting itself, casting off one layer, and then another, and another, until there will be nothing left of it. Nothing!

But for now it is still here! It still burns, and in that burning, in the process *of burning, is my desire. So in saying I am consumed by desire, I am like one of those*

characters in Shakespeare who shouts that he is murdered
before he is quite dead, you see. But we are all burning,
we are all murdered, anyone who lives is consuming
himself, rushing avidly toward the sword, the disease, the
accident, toward the day on which his life will end. One is
not murdered just at the moment when the blade pierces
him, and he knows he will die. For we always know that
we are going to die; it is only a question of time, and
however long it will take, it is always a certainty, as
certain as if we had already received the fatal wound.

So we burn, Cleo, but we must burn joyfully, and
give off light. Our little glowing hearts grow smaller every
minute, and with them, the length of time that we have
left upon this earth, and yet we must go on, for there is
nothing else to do.

But I am ashes! In agony I watch myself dissolving,
disappearing, not just from my life—I could almost bear
that by itself—but I couldn't! for how could I die
knowing I had not loved anyone?—but from your life,
also. Did you ever love me?

Not my soul, Cleo, not just my spirit, but the smell of
my fur, the look in my eyes, and other things, things you
could not describe, and will not remember, the things that
will not stay with you after I am gone. For all the rest is
nothing to me; you can go on thinking about me, and
loving me in spirit, just as well whether I am dead or
alive, near to you or far away. I mean, perhaps, a moment
when you put a cup down on the counter in my kitchen
without thinking about it, or had a brief idea while we
were talking that escaped you when the conversation took
another turn—will you miss those things?

But how could you, since you can't remember them?

*Perhaps what I mean is, did you ever touch my arm
unconsciously, and feel comforted by it, or look into my
eyes and see an unexpected expression, which was so
fleeting that you did not bother to try to figure out what
it was, but which pleased you somehow, for an instant,
before it was gone?*

*You can't know, of course, because you have forgotten.
But it is just those things that I long for, those little lost
details that make up the entire difference between thought
and experience.*

*I mean did you ever love me as a living creature? I
mean was there anything, ever, about standing next to me
that you could not put into words, or keep in your heart?
Those are the things that remain unsaid, the little sparks.
They cannot exist on their own; they must cling to
something else, for they are nothing in themselves; they
only make up the spaces in between those things that can
be perceived.*

*You, inside your nets of blood and nerves, are always
surrounded by these empty spaces. They are sparks of light.
The earth is full of them, and so is heaven, full of little
sparks.*

Ludwig

Something strange had begun to happen to me. When I lay
in bed at night, just before falling asleep, or in the morning
just before I woke up, the thoughts that came to me would
have a kind of solidity and unexpectedness about them. I mean
for instance, somewhere in the middle of the usual flow of
images, I would suddenly see the inside of a plane, with a
snowy airport outside its windows, and I would think, Oh,
somebody is getting on a plane. They're going home from

school, and they're sad; they're leaving someone behind. And then the image would be gone, and I'd go back into the stream of my own thoughts. Or I'd suddenly have the idea that someone was sitting by a second-story window in a small town, looking at an icy field, and they were cold, and there was something cooking on the stove behind them, or that someone was crying on a bus that was driving through Chicago, or that someone was walking by the edge of a lake, remembering the house where they grew up. I didn't know who these people were. Usually I felt glad to see them, as if they'd needed someone to visit them for a moment, and I had. I didn't particularly think that any of them noticed my presence. It was more like maybe they'd transferred something to me, some small part of a burden, and that might have helped them.

This could obviously have just been my imagination—I mean, especially the way everything was then—but over the course of the week these things, whatever they were, got much more frequent. It was as if I was getting better at receiving them, those little, faint signals that people were sending out from all over the world, all the time.

I know they really are there. I mean, I know that people really are having feelings, everywhere, at every moment. Whether the idea that they reached me is wishful thinking on my part or not, I don't know. But I think that it doesn't matter. I had the feeling then that I was practicing for something, either way, or rather that I was being made to practice something that I couldn't comprehend at all, like a very young child taking ballet lessons.

I told Lydia about it one day, and she said that she had been experiencing exactly the same thing. She said that usually it was dogs that she would see, regular dogs, jogging along the side of a highway, or barking incessantly in a little cage at the far end of someone's backyard, or lying on a metal table. I asked her if she thought it was madness.

"Probably," she said.

"But I've never heard of any of the other dogs going through it," I said, "and besides, why would it happen to me, a human, if it was?"

She didn't answer.

"I think it's something else," I said, "something similar to the madness, but not quite the same. I feel that we're seeing clues, like pieces of thread that lead somewhere. Does that make any sense to you?"

"Clues, yes, but to what?" she said. "Maybe they don't lead somewhere, but it's more like they're part of a fabric, and when we see all these images, what we're doing is stepping back and seeing how they're woven together."

"Or maybe," I said, "it's like all of these threads, these strands of other people's lives, are coming together in us . . ."

"Yes. The madness is a kind of unraveling, or dispersion, whereas this thing that we're going through could be a kind of gathering."

After she said that, we both kind of looked at each other and realized that we knew precisely what the other one was talking about, and that for that exact reason we didn't want to talk about it anymore. For one thing it was unnecessary, and for another thing I think we were both slightly unnerved by it. She said she was going to take a nap, and I left.

FOR TWO days it was absolutely quiet, and I had none of those visions. A deep loneliness overcame me.

On the night of the second day they came back. I lay down to sleep, but I couldn't, and I saw strange things—a bird crashing into a wire, a piece of something rolling down a hill. I didn't like it. I stayed in bed, in the dark, with my eyes closed, but instead of sleep came more of those visions, and they made no sense now—glassy puddles edged with fire, a charcoal-colored cloud being pulled apart by the air, a seam of pearls in the earth.

Finally, at about four-thirty, I fell asleep, and I dreamed about Maria. But it wasn't exactly her—she was so complicated she was more like a building, or a city, than a person. Something was burning in the distance, and she leaned forward to kiss me, and I could see everything moving inside her. It was like looking down at a sprawl of highways at night from an airplane.

I woke up craving food; endive, oysters, chard, chocolate, and some dark, bitter, smoky thing I couldn't identify. I felt like I hadn't eaten in a hundred years. I thought of going down to see if there was anything left in the big kitchen, but it had looked pretty bad the last time I was there. Lydia and I had stocked up on things when they'd shot the cook, who was a dog, a couple of days before, but most of it was locked up in the armoire in her bedroom, and I didn't want to wake her. At last I closed my eyes again and fell into a black, dreamless sleep.

LETTER FROM LUDWIG POSTMARKED MARCH 28

I have seen the souls of the dead, traveling in a branching river; they look very much like white blood cells, a pale doughnut-like shape, I cannot tell whether there is anything in the centers, or whether the centers are empty. When one of them comes to a fork in the river, it need not go either one way or the other; it may go both ways.

It is able to do this because souls are not bound by time in the same way that living bodies are, so that it is able to exist in what we would understand as two places at once. Also it can move either backward or forward in time, in addition to what we might call this sideways motion, this ability to exist simultaneously in different spaces. Some souls are interested in our world and try to speak to us, but it is really very difficult for them to have much effect, not having bodies of their own, and some of them go around looking for people to talk to, but there are so few of us who can hear them. The recently dead are remembered by the living and so they can speak to them for a while, these people are receptive, but those who are long dead have a much smaller chance of finding anyone and they become fuzzy, their particular features are worn away as they go tumbling along in the great river. They glow, they wait for us, but we cannot find them. Sometimes you will hear one calling from very far away, very faint waves or pulses like a radio broadcast from a planet in another galaxy, scattered signals that are almost impossible to distinguish from the static, which is made up of meaningless bits and pieces of other voices that have broken down over the great distance into a kind of dust. But in the midst of this static you will think you can identify one voice, sentences that you can almost piece together, as an archaeologist can construct an entire body from a few splinters of bone; but of course sometimes you will get it wrong, and this is a great tragedy, both for you and for the soul who is trying to communicate with you. I am talking to you, Cleo. Be careful. Can you understand what I'm saying?

I did understand. I tried to write back to him, but I couldn't. Drafts of letters lay unfinished around my room. At night I dreamed that he called me on the telephone. Among the dark tangled cables under the streets of the city I could see our particular wires, shiny gray and thin as hairs, with electrical pulses sliding along them like drops of oil. Something went wrong, only a crackly greeting came through, and then there was a break in the circuit somewhere and he was cut off.

LETTER FROM LUDWIG POSTMARKED MARCH 29

At the end it is very painful, like being forced through a sieve. The heavy remains behind, while the light is pushed outward through tiny holes. The body that knew the world

The body that knew the world

Cleo, you said you had come to visit me, but I do not remember seeing you. When were you here?

In the land beyond the sieve there is only light, and we will miss our bodies. We will be restless for them. Above the clouds, beyond the shadow of the earth, it is always day. but to see the world of the living so far away, going on without us, like a toy, so complicated, so small

"door of the morning"

19

(CLEO)

A fire broke out in the castle on the night of March 31. I had gone down to the pantries to look for food, and as I came to the top of the stairway leading to the third floor, I saw flames through the door of one of the big halls. A burning tapestry had fallen across the table in the middle of the room and ignited the stained tablecloth, and veins of fire were reaching out toward its edges. I ran the rest of the way up to the tower and told Lydia.

The phones in the castle had been out for the past five days, so there wasn't any way to call the fire department.

"There's a firehouse half a block away from us," I said. "We can go get them."

She gave me a regretful, distant look, and I understood that she didn't mean to leave the castle, even now.

"You can't stay in the tower while there's a fire downstairs,"

I said. "But if we stand here and talk about it we won't be able to get through there anymore. Let's go."

"You go, Cleo. You have to. You don't have time to argue with me."

"I'm not going to leave without you."

We stood there staring at each other.

"It's spreading quickly," Lydia said. "I can tell by the scent. But this building is made of stone. I don't think it will reach us here."

"Maybe not, but—but, Lydia, where is the armory, anyway?"

"Oh—it's somewhere near the base of our tower, I think."

"And what will happen if the fire gets to it? What if there are a lot of explosives in it?"

"I imagine a bad explosion could cause part of the building to collapse."

"Part of the building like our tower?"

"Cleo, if you're not going to leave—and I think you had better not, now—then sit down. You look as if you're going to pass out. That won't help things."

I sat down and took a deep breath, staring up at the ceiling. When I looked at Lydia again, I saw panic in her eyes.

"Everything's going to be all right," she said gently. "Do you remember whether you closed the door at the bottom of the tower steps as you came up?"

"I closed it," I said.

"That's good."

"I can't sit here while things are burning downstairs," I said. "I can't. I'm going to go out to get the firemen."

"Don't do it now, Cleo, it's too dangerous," Lydia said. "I really think it's best to stay here. I imagine there are still a few other people in the castle, and maybe one of them will be able to go out without passing through the third floor."

"I know, you're probably right, but I can't do it," I said. I got my jacket and headed down the spiral stairs. As I got close to the bottom, I could feel heat. I opened the door into a smoky but not impassable hallway on the fourth floor, and heard a cello playing somewhere, in a distant room.

"Hello?" I called out, but there was no answer. I headed toward the staircase and went down a few steps, but then I could see that I would not get through the third floor. The air was dark with soot and the doorways that were visible on either side of the stairs looked like the mouths of furnaces. Rivulets of flame ran over the big carpet in the room below me, and were beginning to trickle up the runner that covered the center of the staircase.

I paused on the stairs, and then took my Swiss Army knife out of the pocket of my jacket and bent down to the runner. I sawed at it until I had made a cut straight across, and then with a lot of effort I pulled part of it loose from the steps so that there was a few feet of space between one ragged edge of the fabric and the other, a little firebreak, and then, coughing from the smoke, I went back to the tower. The cello was still playing as I shut the door behind me.

Lydia was lying on her bed, her forelegs crossed in front of her and her head resting on them. She was looking at the window, or actually a little to the left of it.

"I can't get through," I said.

"Look, we have a visitor," Lydia said quietly, as if there were a timid animal peering out from behind her bureau.

"And that cellist is still down there," I added as I turned to see what she was staring at. "He's playing somewhere, I couldn't see him—"

There was a smear of light where Lydia's gaze was directed, like a reflection cast on a wall by a mirror, but it was hanging in the air between the window and the dresser. It was about as tall as a person, and I could see motes of dust floating gently inside it.

"What is that?"

"I don't know," Lydia said. "It looks like someone's spirit."

"It does, doesn't it," I said, sitting down on the bed beside her. Then we heard, from somewhere deep in the building, the echoes of a small explosion. We didn't know then that it had come from a locked closet full of guns a few rooms away from the armory, but even so we understood that it was a warning.

"Well—" But before Lydia could even get the word out there was a second, slightly louder explosion that caused the floor of the room to tremble. With that, as if a wall had cracked and revealed another room, I remembered a dream I'd had—when? the night before?—of Maria, dressed in gray wool, a scarf wrapped up to her chin, stepping forward in a dim place and saying, "I left something," and "Don't you—"

Phrases that had been running through my head for several days crowded in all at once around the edges of this memory. "Door of the morning," which I had heard before Ludwig wrote it, and "under the net of blood," which was the beginning of something . . . I had a vision of the dome of the sky, pricked full of holes, and the sphere of the earth, dotted with lamps and fires, and everything was so familiar, it all pointed toward one thing, if only I could remember what it was. It's always so close—

Then more of the dream came back to me—but now Maria was very young, maybe twelve, her hair in braids, pinned in coils to her head, but they were coming loose, and she was standing by an open window in a hayloft. Above her in the eaves was a sparrow's nest, the window's latch was broken, and, outside, fields of stubble sloped down to a border of black trees far away. Near those trees were some boulders on which grew very bright yellow lichen. It was March, there was smoke in the air, nothing in the woods had begun to stir. At that moment in Lydia's room I was certain I had been there, in that hayloft, for the smallest fraction of a second, and I felt that although so much was impossible to know, this was absolutely solid: Maria had been there with me, just as much as I was here now, and would be somewhere else later—but it only dissolves when I try to think about it, or branches out like a frayed wire. All I know is that when I saw her there I felt that Maria had brought me something, the answer to a question. I thought Lydia and I might die, and maybe the feeling was partly the effect of fear, a flood of adrenaline, arteries widening to take the torrents of blood that were being pumped out by the heart—yes, but there was something else, too, like a white curtain filling up with wind, as obvious as the sun, that I had never seen before.

"We've got to get out," Lydia began. "My God—you know there's a—"

"I know," I said. "I know exactly where it is, the window on the fourth floor."

"In the northern corner, not the other one," she said.

"Yes, I know."

Lydia ran, not on two legs, which would have been much too slow, but on all four; she had to wait for me at the bottom of the tower stairs and at the top of the ones leading to the fourth floor, although I was going as fast as I could. The air was thick, but we made it, somehow, to the corner window below which, about ten feet down, was the roof of the gallery that ran along the courtyard. The window was not designed to open; I had to wrap my jacket around my fist and break it. I laid the jacket over the shards of glass still jutting from the lower sill and, by holding on to it, was able to hang down by my hands so that it was only a matter of dropping a few feet onto the slanting roof. Lydia told me to stand back and then leaped from the window herself; she slid on the roof but caught herself on the edge. Then, after pausing to measure the distance, she jumped down to the top of the courtyard stairs. I followed, lowering myself first as I had from the window, and once we were on the landing together we ran, as fast as we could, toward the gatehouse. As we neared its red brick façade suddenly our shadows were running before us because it was lit up, as if by a flash of lightning, by an explosion that brought down the eastern wall of Neuhundstein.

Epilogue

(CLEO)

As soon as Lydia and I got out of the courtyard onto Avenue B, we heard the sirens of the fire trucks. We headed for a sheltered doorway, hoping to get away from the people who were already beginning to gather in the streets. As we approached we saw that there was already someone leaning inside, a tall, balding young man whom I recognized as the cellist who used to play in the throne room. He looked exhausted and his gentle, rounded face was covered with sweat.

"I didn't know there was anyone else still in there." He took off his glasses, wiped them on his ruined shirt, and then put them back on to stare at us. "Hey, I know you," he said, pointing at me. "I danced with you on the first night. Remember?"

I shook my head, too out of breath to speak.

"Well, my name's Jim," he said, moving back to make room for us in the doorway.

"The news trucks will be coming soon," Lydia observed quietly, as we stood watching the flames rise from the castle. "We really shouldn't stay here."

"Oh God, no, let's leave," said the cellist, and so we did.

LUDWIG DISAPPEARED that night. He demanded to be released from the hospital, but he didn't return to his apartment. An orderly hailed a taxi for him but later could not describe its driver. The driver has not come forward, and no one has reported seeing Ludwig since.

Neuhundstein stood empty for a year, ravaged, until a real estate company managed to acquire it and turn it into a hotel, with some residential apartments on the top floors and shops and restaurants on the bottom, which was more or less what the dogs had intended it for. Now, six years later, it seems as if it had always been there.

There were rumors that other dogs had escaped from the castle, but I don't believe them. Even if it was true, I have never heard from them, and neither has Lydia.

Lydia has said that she was going mad before we left the castle but that, like me, she felt something at the moment of the second explosion that affected her strongly, and that since then the dogs' strange illness hasn't returned to her. She won't try to describe what she felt; she says she isn't good with words, English isn't her first language and there's no one left who speaks the dialect of Rankstadt, so she could never convey it. Not even to me. And I don't know what I felt either, after all; there was a memory of a dream, a rush of fear, maybe courage . . .

Jim and I often take our daughter, Eleanor, up to see Lydia on the estate north of the city where she now lives. It's a secluded, peaceful place; she likes to keep it filled with friends, but she makes a great effort to stay out of the public eye.

MARIA RANK visited me once, shortly after Eleanor was born. I saw her leaning against a bureau in my bedroom. She didn't move or say anything, but when she disappeared she left in her wake a panel of pebbled, moving air. I had the feeling she wouldn't return, but that she had meant something good by coming.

Why did I dream about Maria in the days when the dogs were here? Did she have a hold on my imagination because I had seen her portraits so often? Had it been because of Ludwig's fascination with her; was she a clue to something about him that I didn't understand?

But I think she was really there. That last dream, the one that came back to me just before we left the castle, had been as real as a flake of mortar, or a nail, or a charred stick— instantly recognizable—and yet what it meant, what it means now . . .

SOMETIMES I pray to dream about Ludwig. I pray that when I sleep the channels will open up and I'll get word of whether he is still alive and where he is. Even if I couldn't know that, I'd like to have a dream about him, just to see him again. But I never do. I miss him.